searching for someday

a novel

JENNIFER
PROBST

Pocket Books

New York   London   Toronto   Sydney   New Delhi

The sale of this book without its cover is unauthorized. If you purchased this book without a cover, you should be aware that it was reported to the publisher as "unsold and destroyed." Neither the author nor the publisher has received payment for the sale of this "stripped book."

Pocket Books
A Division of Simon & Schuster, Inc.
1230 Avenue of the Americas
New York, NY 10020

This book is a work of fiction. Any references to historical events, real people, or real places are used fictitiously. Other names, characters, places, and events are products of the author's imagination, and any resemblance to actual events or places or persons, living or dead, is entirely coincidental.

Copyright © 2013 by Jennifer Probst

All rights reserved, including the right to reproduce this book or portions thereof in any form whatsoever. For information, address Pocket Books Subsidiary Rights Department, 1230 Avenue of the Americas, New York, NY 10020.

First Pocket Books paperback edition December 2013

POCKET and colophon are registered trademarks of Simon & Schuster, Inc.

For information about special discounts for bulk purchases, please contact Simon & Schuster Special Sales at 1-866-506-1949 or business@simonandschuster.com.

The Simon & Schuster Speakers Bureau can bring authors to your live event. For more information or to book an event, contact the Simon & Schuster Speakers Bureau at 1-866-248-3049 or visit our website at www.simonspeakers.com.

Interior design by Davina Mock-Maniscalco
Cover design by Lisa Litwack
Cover photograph by Getty Images

Manufactured in the United States of America

10 9 8 7 6 5 4 3 2 1

ISBN 978-1-4767-4493-3
ISBN 978-1-4767-4497-1 (ebook)

"Each friend represents a world in us,
a world possibly not born until they arrive,
and it is only by this meeting
that a new world is born."
—Anaïs Nin

I write stories about love and romance, but within
my books you will always find true friendship.
Without my tight-knit group I've known since
high school, I would not be the same person.
We may not see each other as much or as often,
but once we do, time melts away
and there is no distance.
Jodi Prada, Lisa Hamel Soldano,
Marlaine Scotto, Colleen LaPierre,
Kimberly Cornman, Nancy Chaudhry,
thanks for always being there.
For the late-night poker nights, through good men
and bad, through family crises and heartaches, and
during some of the funniest laugh-out-loud moments
of my life—I adore you.

Women rock.

prologue

IT WAS OFFICIAL.

She was on the date from hell.

Kate Seymour reached for her wine, forced a bright smile, and tried very hard not to stare at the lump of cheese hanging from her companion's chin. Okay, so he was a bit socially awkward. Still didn't make it right not to notice chicken parm was stuck on his face.

She patted her chin in a silent plea for him to grab his napkin. Signals were the universal gesture women used when toilet paper was stuck to their shoe or a price tag was hanging from their skirt, but this guy hadn't gotten the memo.

He kept talking about his marketing business, which was kind of interesting, but how could she focus when she stared at a lump of mozzarella?

"Umm, Bradley? You've got something, umm, r-r-r-right there on your—"

He swiped at it bare-handed like a bear grabbing a fish, and the cheese fell onto the plate. "Thanks. So, I'm really glad we finally got to do this in person. I enjoyed talking with you over the phone."

Suddenly not hungry anymore, Kate pushed the last of her salmon around the plate and nodded. "Me, too. Being a business owner, I'm always fascinated by PR and the best ways to brand. What type of s-s-s-services do you offer at your company?"

Stupid stutter. It always slipped out when she was nervous about making a good impression. Not that her date seemed to care about her thoughtful question. In fact, he seemed more interested in the busboy, giving him a bright smile and respectful silence when he swooped in to clean up the mess at the table.

Bradley plowed through the spaghetti and sucked the loopy strands through his teeth with a hiss. When he finally managed to swallow, he looked up. An odd expression crossed his face. "Well, I'm not exactly employed in that department. I will be soon, though, and I know more than most of the employees."

Huh. He'd insinuated that he ran an entire department. Odd. "Your title is social relations, right? What department is that?"

"Doorman."

Kate blinked. "Oh. Wow, I bet you meet a lot of interesting people."

Sauce stained his lips. She kept her gaze focused slightly to the left.

"Yes, I figured I'd start off with an entry-level position and make my way up the ladder."

This could still work. She admired ambition in a man. Sure, he had kind of stretched the truth about his job, but maybe he was embarrassed to tell her over the phone. Not that she judged: Kate couldn't care less what title a man bore as long as he liked his work. Even his looks weren't bad, more the average Joe, which she courted. Short dark hair, brown eyes, round face. A bit overweight but nothing out of the ordinary in a world filled with fast food and instant gratification. Kate despised the charming, good-looking types who looked at women only as a way to serve their egos.

"Smart. You went to NYU, right?" she asked. "I graduated from there, too, in business management. What did you study?"

"I took a class there once. Didn't get to finish, since I had to go take care of my mom."

Instant sympathy and hope flickered. A man who respected family was key to a good match. "I'm sorry, is she ill?"

Crumbs of Italian bread clung to the edge of his mouth. Yes, eating with him would be a chore, but a man who helped his mother must have a heart of gold. "She's got arthritis. Told her I'd move in and help her out."

Why did there seem to be more to the story? "Does she have trouble moving around? I've heard of severe conditions that can be very painful."

Bradley paused to slurp his water, which added to the entire meal he now wore on his face. "Her fingers hurt sometimes, so I can help her open jars and stuff. I keep her company, and she cooks and cleans for me. It works out pretty well."

The *Titanic* had nothing on this date, but she fought off the iceberg like a woman clinging to survival. Kate desperately needed Bradley to be *the one*. One hundred was a lucky number, wasn't it? One hundred dates spoke of patience. She'd waited, invested her time wisely, and believed in the process. As the successful owner of Kinnections matchmaking agency, she lived and breathed her business. She believed, dammit. And it was getting a little weird for the owner to still be single with no prospect in sight.

She flexed her fingers and fought the impulse to touch him. If there was even a slight tingle of connection, she'd deal with the job and his mother. Her gift of sensing strong energy between two people meant to be together was also a curse. How many times had she gotten an electrical shock from a couple who were soul mates? How many men had she surrendered to other women because she realized her date belonged with the waitress or customer service representative or store clerk? It served her well as a matchmaker but was pure hell on her personal life. The *touch* ran through the generations of women in her family, but none had decided to use it for business. Still, she preferred using science and skill to make her matches in Kinnections, and tried hard not to let the touch interfere with her main business plan. It was more of a way to confirm they had made the right match once a couple got serious. Not that she was ready to tell Bradley or anyone else about her secret weapon.

She studied him from across the table and refused to lose hope. Bradley was meant to be hers, but she wasn't ready to put her hands on him to confirm.

The waitress glided over and placed the check discreetly in the middle of the table. Kate held her breath, knowing this was the ultimate test. A man who paid for dinner on the first date had values. It was a make-or-break moment. Anticipation cut through her, and she held her breath.

Bradley reached over and grabbed the bill.

Giddiness spilled through her. Finally. She hadn't been wrong. Sure, rough patches needed to be worked out, but Kate believed.

Bradley scanned the bill and whipped out a pocket calculator. Heart sinking, she watched his fingers fly across the keys. "Okay, since it's not even, I'll take the higher portion. You owe $43.00 even and I'll pay $44.63. That's with a fifteen percent tip. Is that acceptable?"

Kate stared as her dream of a soul mate withered as fast as the Wicked Witch's body, but she didn't get any cool ruby shoes left in the process. "Sure."

"Great. Cash or credit?"

She reached into her Coach purse and pulled out her VISA. "Here you go."

"Thanks."

The busboy stopped at their table. "Are you done, sir? Miss?"

Bradley nodded, his gaze fixated on the young man's broad chest and muscled shoulders filling out his smart red and black uniform. Panic fluttered in her belly as the air charged around her. *No. Not possible.*

But she had to know.

The busboy reached for the plate, giving her date a sidelong seductive glance. Kate dragged in a breath and brushed his hand with her arm at the same time her fingers touched her date's.

A tiny shock shivered across her flesh and vibrated through her body. Bradley smiled at the busboy, his face carved out with pure want.

Ah, crap.

It was over.

She fought a sigh and surrendered number one hundred. "Bradley, I'll be right back. I need to go to the ladies' room."

"Of course."

She grabbed her purse and ducked down the hallway. After a few minutes, the busboy walked past and she reached out to touch his arm. "Excuse me?"

"Yes, ma'am?"

She glanced at his name tag. "Gabe, I'm sorry, but I wonder if you can relay a message to my date? I'm not feeling well and need to leave. I'm sure he'd love to stay if possible. Would you be willing to buy him a drink on your break?"

Gabe's face reddened. "Aren't you together?"

Kate smiled. "No, I'm not his type. I'm sure if you offered, he'd be interested."

Recognition sparked in his dark eyes, and he nodded. "I'd be interested."

"Thank you. Good luck. I'm going to slip out the side door."

She vacated the restaurant, caught between despair for her plight and happiness she had made a match. Damn, her gaydar completely sucked.

The March night was brisk and cold in Verily, and she breathed in, not wanting to go home yet. The shops stayed open on Saturday night, and it was only eight thirty. Her high-heeled boots clicked on the pavement as she walked, enjoying the artsy Hudson River town that boasted a variety of stores and cafés with an edgy, funky feel. White lights glittered around the trees that lined the sidewalk, and music spilled from Mugs, the popular bar that also served as a nightclub. A full moon hung suspended over the river line, illuminating the Tappan Zee Bridge, which glittered in the distance. She weaved her way through pedestrians with dogs on leashes and giggling groups of college students, and dropped a buck in the pail of the young man playing a guitar and singing about broken hearts.

Loneliness hit. She was so tired. When was it her turn? When would she finally find the connection for herself? Unless . . .

She never found it. Bruised from the consistent disappointments, she wondered if maybe giving up on the dream of finding her match would serve her better. Maybe, just maybe, there wasn't a man or woman meant for everyone. Maybe, just maybe, she was meant to be alone.

She fought the sudden urge to cry and wallow in a self-pity party. She was done. If she went on one more disappointing date, she didn't think she'd recover. The hell with love. She'd buy a new book, go home to Robert, and snuggle under a blanket.

Kate paused in front of the used-book store. Time for a change. No more dating. No more chasing love. She'd concentrate on her business, her friends, and doing things that made her happy.

With her head up and her new resolution firm, she stepped inside, and the bell tinkled. Scents swarmed around her in wonderful familiarity. Leather. Paper. Mothballs. Perfection.

She crossed the worn carpet and stopped in front of the marked and battered front desk. "Got anything for me, Hector?"

The boy behind the counter was reed thin, with a smattering of pimples and spiked purple hair. Hector shook his head with a grin. "Been waiting for you, Kate. I'm holding a new box of used books in the back. I had no time to sort them yet, so you may not find anything."

She shivered with the lure of the unknown. Would she

ever get tired of ripping open a new box of books and sifting through the treasures? "No worries. I'll go through
them if that's okay?"

The teen motioned toward the back of the store. "Help
yourself. It'll save me some work."

"Thanks." Kate walked down the deserted aisle and
into the storeroom. The cramped space held an array of
boxes, file cabinets, and papers in an extremely unorganized
fashion. The new shipment was clearly marked, though, so
she pulled it down from the pile and ripped it open with her
own hands, rather than with the box cutter. She'd never be
able to keep a perfect manicure anyway.

Kate sat cross-legged on the cold concrete floor and
pulled them out one by one. Romance. Biography. Some
dieting. She kept to the side a few that she wanted to try,
then found a great one on love signs that seemed several
years out of date. Hmm, you never knew what you'd glean
from the eighties. Could be helpful. She added it to her
growing stack. An interesting book on how males relate to
dogs. Definitely couldn't pass that one up. And then—

Her fingers closed on a fabric-covered book and she
pulled it out. Bright violet assaulted her vision. *The Book
of Spells*. Simple title. Small, square, not a novel but more
of a how-to book? She cracked the binding a bit and
glanced through the first page.

A low hum vibrated to the tips of her fingers. Her belly
wobbled, as if she'd just seen a hot male prospect rather

than a simple book. The hum grew stronger as she flipped through, making notes of an ancient love spell and a chant to Earth Mother. Fascinating. She'd never seen anything like it; there wasn't even an author noted. How was that possible?

Definitely a keeper. Maybe something fun for her clientele.

Kate dropped the book on her pile.

A crackle of electricity shot through her body like a wet plug in an outlet. She yelped and yanked back, staring at the purple cover. What the hell was that? Maybe the fabric gave some type of shock. But damn, that hurt.

"Need any help back there?"

Hector's voice echoed through the store. Shaking her head, she pushed to her feet and set the box back. Careful not to touch the purple book, she scooped up her treasure pile and made her way out of the storeroom.

"Got everything I need. Hector, I took six books. Charge it to my account, please!"

"You got it. Have a good one."

Feeling a bit better over her new purchases, Kate headed toward her car and the typical Saturday night with her books and her dog.

Good-bye, number one hundred. That date belonged in the record book of disasters.

It was going to be a long time before she had the stamina to even think about one hundred and one.

one

"I'M MOVING OUT."

Slade watched his sister drag her oversized floral pieces of luggage down the hallway and drop them at the front door. A strange panic roared through his system, but he stood frozen in the foyer, watching the scene unfold. Hell, no. She wasn't ready to go anywhere on her own yet, but somehow he needed to convince her without looking like a crazed control-freak brother. He kept his voice gentle and firm.

"Jane, I don't think it's a good idea. I know you want a place of your own, but I don't think you're ready. Besides, I'll get lonely by myself. Give it some time, and I'll help you find an apartment."

Jane turned fast, hands on hips, that furious female scowl he knew well. Bottom line, he'd screwed up his words again. "First off, give me a little credit. I'm ready. I appreciate you letting me live here, but I should've moved out a year ago. And the only reason you're lonely is your refusal to stay with a woman past one night."

Slade winced. Unfair. He was always discreet when it came to women, not needing his sister to try to bond with any of them, since long-term commitment was doomed from the start. The statistics alone of marriage breakups caused a shudder.

She marched into the open living room and headed toward the bookcase to grab a few off the shelves. Crap, was that *The Chew*'s new cookbook? He hadn't even looked at the pictures yet. "Be reasonable, Jane. You have nowhere to go, and I don't want you staying at a crappy studio in Manhattan. It'll cost a million dollars and won't be safe. Are you still upset over your breakup? We can go slash his tires, get drunk, and watch chick flick movies. That's what women do, right?"

Jane tipped her head back and laughed. "God, Slade, if I didn't love you so much I'd murder you. I have a place already. I rented an apartment in Verily on the river. I quit my job and lined up a new one at the local community college there."

The room spun. He stared at his normally shy, logical, steady sister and wondered what she'd drunk to turn into Mr. Hyde. "Quit your job? You were working on tenure!"

"And I hated it there. Stuffy, pompous, and boring. I hate Manhattan, too. It's crowded and hurts my head most of the time." Jane dragged in a breath and walked over, stuffing the books into her tote bag. Her long jet-black hair sprung into a whirlwind of curls, and her cocoa-brown eyes peered at him sadly from behind thick black glasses. "I can't do this anymore," she said. "I need a fresh start on my own terms. Verily is small and quaint, and the college focuses on using creativity in literature. I can grow there. Maybe meet a man who won't wring me dry and dump me." Her laugh was totally wry, and Slade's heart squeezed in sheer fear.

He couldn't let her go. If something happened, it would be his fault. Again. At least if she were under his roof, he could easily gauge if she was down-spiraling. Slade swung into lawyer mode. Being one of the top divorce lawyers in the state had to be good for something other than money. "I understand you want to be on your own. I agree it's time, but quitting your job and running off to a town you don't know is dangerous. I'll go with you to Verily this weekend. I'll help you look, maybe meet some people there so you're not alone, and we'll figure it out together."

Her voice rose to a dangerous level. "I don't want to figure it out together! I want to figure things out myself. Oh, for God's sake, look at this place." She flung out her arm and gestured to his expensive loft apartment situated in the coveted location of Tribeca. The huge open space was split into two levels with a sleek glass staircase connecting them together. Windows lined the walls and overlooked the city of Manhattan. Pricey art, bamboo floors, edgy glass tables, granite counters, and huge leather recliners completed the look of bachelor in the city.

"What's wrong with it? We have plenty of room here."

"This is your place! I haven't had anything for myself in

the past three years. I'm twenty-eight years old. It's time I do things on my terms without anyone worrying if I'm going to emotionally lose it when something goes wrong."

He winced. Jane was extremely sensitive and had always struggled in such a brutal society. He watched a long line of men crush her like a gentle flower under their heels until there was nothing left but a few stray petals. He'd sworn never to let anyone hurt her again. He had to make her stay.

"Sweetheart, I know you're much stronger now. Don't ever think I'm waiting for you to implode. I just think it would be better to wait."

"I don't." Jane opened the closet door, grabbed her black wool coat, and stuffed her arms into the sleeves. "When I get settled, you can bring the rest of my stuff and visit. I think you'll like it in Verily. And I won't be lonely for long. I've decided to sign up with a matchmaking agency."

Yep. She'd definitely slugged the Mr. Hyde punch. "Are you kidding me? Do you know how many of those get closed down for fraud? There's no such thing as the perfect match, and you know it. What is going on with you?"

She stuck her chin out. "I'm tired of being afraid and meeting the wrong men. Kinnections is a well-respected company. I like the women I met there, and I trust them. So don't worry about me holing up in my apartment and getting depressed. I'm going out there and meeting people. I'm different this time."

"This place is going to take your money and give you false expectations. What if it doesn't work out and you crash? I'm not going to stand around helplessly while you're destroyed again by some ruthless people out for your money."

She let out an outraged squeal. "Are you listening to yourself? God, stop protecting me. I'm a different person than I was three years ago and you're stifling me! Mom and Dad wouldn't want me to live tucked away in your man cave while I watch life happen to other people."

"Mom and Dad never found you on a bathroom floor overdosed on pills. Mom and Dad didn't hold you in their arms, praying you wouldn't die!"

The silence shattered around them. Slade closed his eyes briefly, grief cutting out pieces of him. The words entwined with a blame and a plea that twisted his stomach. The memory of finding her suicide attempt changed him. He wanted her safe. Couldn't she understand?

His voice broke. "I'm so sorry, Jane. I didn't mean to bring that up."

Hurt carved out the lines of her face, and her lower lip trembled. "Yes. You did. I'm sorry I put you through that. But I'm not the same person anymore. I deserve happiness and I'm going to take it. Yes, I may get hurt along the way, but I can handle it now, Slade. I'm stronger." She tossed her tote over her shoulder and grabbed the handle of her suitcase. "I don't blame you for not trusting me. But I'm going to prove myself. You're not responsible for me any longer."

"For God's sake, let me help you. I'll buy you dinner and we'll talk more about this."

She threw open the door. "No. The doorman is meeting me downstairs."

"But I need a number, an address, something."

"I'll call when I get settled. Love you."

She left. This time, he didn't stop her. Part of him recognized it was important she carve her own way. The other half decided he'd rip apart anything that tried to hurt her. Or anyone.

With a low curse, he stalked to his computer and typed in the words.

Kinnections. Matchmaking. Verily.

He stared at the screen for a while and made his decision.

two

SLADE STOPPED IN front of the glass door of Kinnections and took in the festive white lights and artistic sign. Scrolled in purple and silver, it promised passersby a "happy ever after" rolled up in excitement, hope, and mystery.

Temper snapped his jaw up like a well-trained karate kick. A bunch of con artists selling dreams that didn't exist. To him, it was worse than those emails promising a cut of a million dollars for a small standard fee. Worse than identity theft. In his estimation, the true evil lay not in stealing money, or goods, or even services. No, this was theft of the heart—a blatant lie to the lonely and broken to heal them with a ghost image of the perfect man or woman.

He wouldn't allow such scum to tear his sister apart.

Slade pushed open the door and strode in.

The woman at the main desk seemed surprised to see a client, as if the cheery bell warning her of his entrance hadn't worked. His gaze dismissed her as the receptionist, but he refused to waste his time moving up the chain. He switched into his lawyer voice that brooked no refusal. "I'd like to see the manager, please."

One brow arched. Yes, she was perfect for the first appearance of a matchmaking agency. Her hair was magnificent, so blond it was almost white, hanging past her shoulders in pin-straight strands that shimmered like corn silk. Her wide blue eyes assessed him with a thoughtful air, as if deciding whether or not to call her boss. Not a deep blue like the ocean, but more of a cornflower, so light her features seemed to blur in a type of angelic radiance. He shook himself out of his trance and wondered what the hell he was doing thinking in corn terms about a woman he didn't intend to have a conversation with.

"Can I ask what this is about?"

Smooth and mellow, her voice teased his ears like a wisp of smoke before vanishing. He wanted to hear more, but the whole meeting was beginning to freak him out. He cleared his throat and looked over his gold-rimmed glasses. "None of your concern," he clipped out. "Please get me your manager."

She crossed her arms in front of her and studied him with a thoughtful air. "If this is regarding a client, we won't be able to give you any information. We adhere to confidentiality agreements."

He snorted. "Convenient way to try to avoid lawsuits, huh?"

"Having a bad day, sir?"

Was he amusing her? He drew himself to full height and leaned over her desk. His court presence was well known to be deadly, but this slip of a woman dared mock him? "Now I am. I'm sure it will get better once I speak with your boss."

"Okay. Go ahead."

He let out a short breath. "Can you please get her?"

"I'm already here."

He barely concealed his jerk but fought through giving her the satisfaction. Slade knew two things well in life: the law and the way people worked. He'd used both to live quite successfully and remain mainly unscathed.

He blanked his features to hide any emotion. "I see. Somehow I'm not surprised."

Her pale pink lips tightened. Ah, good-bye amusement. Hello irritation. Much better. "Why do I suspect you're rarely surprised?"

Her correct assessment threw him off. "Because I'm not. People are quite predictable if given certain circumstances. Take love, for instance. The promise of something Disney has made into a fortune with kids' movies is like the Holy Grail. They'll fight, steal, and pay money they don't have for the opportunity of believing in a mirage."

He waited for a feminine temper tantrum and got . . . nothing. A gleam of interest sparked in her eyes. She waited him out, taking her time studying his appearance and making her own judgment. Oh, yeah, this one was good. There wasn't a man alive who wouldn't put himself in her hands, and not a woman who wouldn't want to be like her. The perfect combination to sell love.

"You seem a bit jaded for thirty, sir."

"Thirty-three."

"Ah, I see. Well, let me try to clear something up immediately. At Kinnections, we use a wide variety of services to help a person find a companion. What that means to him or her is subjective. Some want friendship, some want sex, and some want the crescendo of music playing when their eyes meet. I'm not here to judge. Our job is to try to get our clients what they want in a safe, consensual environment."

He clasped his hands in front of his chest and tapped his thumbs together. A favorite position with the jurors, giving the appearance of relaxation with full control. He eased his voice to a conspiratorial tone. "A lofty ambition. And if it doesn't work? Do your clients get a refund?"

Her chair squeaked. "No, they sign a contract up front agreeing to the terms."

"Convenient. I must give you credit, *ma'am*. You have a nice setup here. The businessman in me respects it. But I have one question I'm dying to know the answer to."

"What?"

"How do you sleep at night?" Finally. Her muscles tightened, and Slade circled his prey for the kill shot. "You're selling something that doesn't exist. Do you take responsibility for the broken relationships and hearts you created along the way? Is there a disclaimer clause for divorces that occur from your matches? Do you like taking a lonely woman's hard-earned savings while she keeps pouring money into a search that never gives her what she wants?"

The blond half rose from the chair, fists clenched, anger pouring from her figure in choppy waves. Triumph coursed at finally breaking the hard shell of pretense. Get someone angry, push their buttons, and you get the truth. Tricks of the trade. Slade waited for the long tirade with a bite of enjoyment he rarely experienced out of the courtroom.

Those luscious lips opened. Then shut. She dragged in a deep breath, closed her eyes, and seemed to do some type of meditative thing. When she opened them, she seemed calmer. Her hypnotic voice sang in his ears and promised him earthly and heavenly delights. God, what sounds did she make during sex? Moans? Husky whispers? Screams?

What the hell was that thought?

"You're good. You almost got me to lose it, but I'm working on my anger management skills, so I win this round. I'm very sorry."

"Sorry for what?"

A touch of gentleness lit her eyes. "For what happened to you. You were obviously hurt by a partner. Man or woman?"

Slade yanked his hands up and broke his position. "You think I'm gay?"

She clucked her tongue. "No need to be embarrassed. We match all kinds of sexual interests at Kinnections."

His breath choked him. "I'm not gay! And stop poking around in my head—I'm a master and know all about manipulation games. No wonder my sister fell for this charade."

She frowned. "Sister?"

"Jane Montgomery. She signed up with your agency last week. I'm sure you remember her."

The hot blonde tapped her finger against her lips. Slade noted the lack of stylish nail polish in favor of clear. A definite contradiction to her American cheerleader looks. "Of course. We're very excited about working with Jane."

"And she will no longer be working with you. I came here to tell you personally to shred her file and do not contact her again."

She had the audacity to look puzzled. "Why would you do that? We've already spent some time going over her wants and needs, and she's enthusiastic about starting to date."

Obviously this woman needed therapy. Or reality counseling. He spoke slowly, as if talking with one of his dim-witted clients strung out on too much extramarital sex. "Jane is sensitive and quite emotional. You may have a misguided idea of helping, but you will shatter her self-confidence, and I won't allow that. She's had a hard time in the past. If you continue to see her as a client, you will destroy her."

The woman crossed her legs like she had all the time in

the world and was contemplating what to order for lunch. Slade noted the sleek black pantsuit, tuxedo jacket, and stylish low-heeled boots. No nonsense, but chic comfort. The silver hoops flirted with her hair, and the silver cuff bracelet gleamed. He wondered what type of underwear she preferred, and then sliced off the thought as cleanly as with a surgeon's scalpel. Holy crap, he needed to get laid. It had been way too long.

"You seem quite protective. But I'm sorry I'll have to decline your request. Again, our client information is confidential, and I think we can help Jane here. I do appreciate your concern and promise to go slowly and carefully with her dating experiences."

Slade clamped down hard on his impulse to circle around the desk and tell her just how dangerous screwing with his sister's head would be. Instead, he turned on his inner switch and fell back into business. Cold, clinical, and dependable. He'd tried to be nice. Now, he'd get what he wanted the hard way.

"I think you misunderstood. I'm not asking you. I'm telling. You will shred Jane's file, inform her you will not be able to help, and never contact her again."

Fury shimmered from her figure. "Make me."

Again, surprise hooked him on the chin. Huh? Make her? Was he trapped in a bad Western? He lowered his voice to a silky drawl. "I can, you know. Make you. My sister has had enough heartbreak in her life, and I'm not going to allow you to deceive her with a mirage. If you don't willingly cut off her account, I'll draw up a legal suit to sue. I'll publicly drag out all your secrets and make sure you're buried so deep in papers, Kinnections will be bankrupt by the end of the year."

He ignored the pang of guilt for stooping to threats, but he needed to protect his sister at all costs. Slade watched the stream of emotions flicker over her face. Anger. Frustration. Fear. Resolve. Good. At least he'd walk away from this encounter and this woman who disturbed him and get on with his life.

"Ah, shit, you're a lawyer."

She spat out the word like it was dirty, but he was immune to the standard reaction. "Correct."

"A divorce lawyer, no less. No wonder you're screwed-up."

How had she known? He stiffened and adjusted his suit jacket. "Now, will you agree to my proposal?"

She tilted her head and studied him. Used to being on the opposite end, he tried not to squirm and held her bright blue gaze. "No."

He blinked. "Huh?"

"I don't negotiate with terrorists, Mr. Montgomery. This includes bullying divorce lawyers who think they're God. I'm not stupid. I have a team of my own lawyers who will match every paper for your paper. Sure, you may get us some bad publicity, but all PR is good for business. There's another issue you haven't considered: Jane's wishes. I don't think she'll forgive you for overstepping your brotherly boundaries and telling her what she can and can't do. She may be a bit shy, but she's not a pushover. How do you think she'll react when I tell her the truth about this little meeting?"

The tables tipped, curved, and readjusted. She was much feistier than she looked, and damned if she wasn't right. Jane already kept him at a distance, determined to show him she'd make it on her own. This may break the final, fragile bonds holding them together. Slade recalculated his loss-to-profit ratio and thought quickly. There had to be another way to help his sister without alienating her and keep his eye on Kinnections to make sure they didn't screw up. The idea took root, and though he searched for any other options, Slade realized he was truly screwed. There was only one way left, and it was a wooded, thorny path he wished he didn't have to travel.

"It seems we have reached an impasse, Ms. — "

"Seymour."

"But you must understand I don't intend to walk away until I know Jane is safe."

Her features softened. "I didn't get in this business to hurt people, Mr. Montgomery. I came here to help them. Hopefully, to put them on the path of love and happiness. Unfortunately, if one opens up to love, it can mean heartbreak. But it won't be because we didn't do our best and try."

His lips tightened. "Lofty ambitions don't make screwing with people's heads acceptable. There's only one way I'll be able to test your theory and your business model."

"What's that?"

"Sign me up as a client."

She jerked back. Satisfaction coursed through him. Finally. He was back in control, just the way he liked it. "Excuse me? That's impossible."

"No, it's not. If you can find me love, you win. I'll back off and be your biggest advocate. Hell, I'll use your agency to help my own clients, and Kinnections will explode."

She lifted her hands in the air in supplication, then let them drop back down to her thighs. "Our clients need to be open and willing to find their soul mate. There's a lengthy process, and you'd fight us every step of the way. It'd never work."

"I can try." A sense of calm settled over him. "I've dated endlessly and can never seem to find the woman meant for me. If she's out there, I'd like to find her."

"Why?"

He considered her challenge. "I'd like to have children one day," he said slowly. "A companion. A friend to grow old with. Who wouldn't? I don't believe it's out there, but I'm willing to let you prove me wrong. If you think you can handle it."

She tucked a wayward strand of hair behind her ear, and for the first time since he walked in, she looked completely scattered. About time. "You'd need to go through relationship counseling. Have intensive interviews and screenings with me. Be willing to engage in social events. This is ridiculous, Mr. Montgomery. And I have no time to waste."

"Neither do I." He locked his gaze on hers and refused to release her. "Take it or leave it. If you don't, I'll know you're a scam artist and I won't care about Jane's reaction. I refuse to let her get hurt so that you can put money in your pocket. If you do take me on, and I see the value in this matchmaking agency, it's a win-win for both of us. I'll help you grow your client list and tell everyone I know. What do we have to lose?"

"How about my sanity and sense of humor?" she grumbled.

"Funny, I figured you'd lost those a while ago."

She glared at him with suspicion, as if suddenly wondering if he had a real sense of humor. Slade wondered why he was enjoying this conversation so much. He was getting tired of being around two types of women: angry and bitter or needy and clingy. Hell, his work had become his full-time lover, and wasn't that sad in the prime of his life? Of course, he didn't expect Kinnections to work, but maybe he'd get out of his rut and mend his relationship with Jane. If they both were going through the process, he'd be able to keep a close eye on her. Yes, this was definitely a win-win.

"You'll need to fill out paperwork and pay the fee."

He raised a brow. "Of course, Miss Seymour. I didn't expect anything less."

"Kate." Her name spilled reluctantly from her sulky lips. "My name is Kate."

It suited her. Strong, classy, and full of punch. Simplicity on the outside and complexity on the inside. He reined in the poetic thought, half humiliated at his ridiculousness, and cleared his throat. "Slade. I'll be looking forward to working with you."

She fumbled with the stack of papers and shoved them into an envelope. Wrote a few things down on her pad. Then handed it to him. "Fill these out and get them back by the end of the week. I'll need to schedule you a session for a one-on-one with me by next week."

"How much is the initial fee?"

"One thousand dollars. All fees are clearly stated in the contract." Her tone came out slightly mocking. "I'm sure you'll study the clauses carefully and inform me if there's a problem."

He took the envelope and wondered briefly why she didn't want to shake his hand. Then shook off the thought. Whatever. He needed to get out of here.

"I'll be in touch. Good-bye, Kate."

The roll of her name on his tongue was sweet and spicy

hot. He hurried out the door without a glance back and wondered if he'd just made the biggest mistake of his life.

KATE UNCLENCHED HER FINGERS and let out a breath. The aftereffects of all that male energy still swarmed around her. What had she agreed to? The man was completely critical of the process, ornery, and had the potential for lethal charm known to good lawyers. She couldn't believe that Jane came from the same pool of genes, though her brother's protective instincts toward family gave him extra points.

"Now that one is gonna be a challenge." The husky purr drifted toward her ears. Her close friend and co-owner of Kinnections, Kennedy Ashe, strolled on her four-inch heels without a wobble, her smart pink plaid business suit screaming elegant perfection. She tapped a matching pink nail against bow-curved lips, her eyes dancing with humor. "The fun I can have with him. You did good, Kate. I sensed the violence within, but you never broke. Arilyn would be so proud. Are those meditation techniques to control your temper working?"

Kate grabbed her bottle and began to fill it from the cooler. "Funny. Don't mention I never watched the DVD; you'll hurt her feelings. My instincts screamed for me to turn him down, but I don't want to risk a lawsuit."

"Smart. We just broke a hefty profit, so let's not screw it

up. And the man is a drool-worthy specimen. Our female clients will be clamoring to secure an introduction."

She pressed the button and watched the icy stream trickle into the jug. "I know. We're right on target, it takes about three years for a business to solidify and begin making money. Of course, all the PR and ten weddings helped. Those are solid percentages in this industry."

"Maybe Bravo will finally give us a show instead of *The Millionaire Matchmaker*?"

Kate laughed. "No, thanks. All I need is the world focused on why the owner and head matchmaker can't seem to keep a relationship. Hell, I can't even get to date three. It's the curse."

Kennedy rolled her eyes and examined her cuticles. Her rich dark hair sparkled with subtle caramel highlights. "This drama again? Your family's not cursed. Your mom was happily married until your dad passed, and she never lacks for a date. You're just stubborn."

"I'm past sad and diving into pathetic. My last date was a nightmare. I set him up with the busboy and now they're happy."

"You did it again? Girlfriend, what is it with you and restaurants? You drove Paul into the waitress's arms last week."

Kate guzzled the water and tucked her hair behind her ear. "I have no choice. When she handed me the menu, I got the sizzle thing and saw how they looked at each other.

They were perfect together. I needed to be the bigger woman."

"He was a gorgeous doctor who wanted to settle down. Next time, be selfish. Setting them up for a late-night drink was creepy, Kate. And you didn't even charge him!"

Gloominess hovered. "I know. Sorry. Anyway, I made a decision. No more dating. I'm done."

Her friend tapped her foot against the polished floor. "Don't be ridiculous, we'll go bankrupt if our poster child is the crazy cat lady. Or dog lady, in this case. Maybe you can start wearing gloves. That'll stop your impulses."

"And look like an OCD germaphobe? No thanks. Madonna and Michael Jackson are the only ones who sported that look, and I have no wish to morph back to the eighties."

Kennedy shuddered. "Yeah, you're right. The fashion was a complete crime against humanity. And the hair."

On cue, the bell chimed again and the third member of their crew floated in. Arilyn Meadow was the symbol of a walking fashion disaster Kennedy worked hard to transform. Unfortunately, their friend was quite happy and centered living in organic cotton, yoga pants, and animal-free dyes, which excluded most makeup. "Hi, guys. What are you talking about?"

Kennedy gave her a pointed look. "What not to wear."

Arilyn laughed. The delicate sound matched her soothing voice, perfect for her counseling career with their clients. She was a flower child stuck in today's society, but still managed to turn heads with her hip-length strawberry blond hair and soulful green eyes.

Kate looked at her friends and down at her usual outfit. Black pants, black tee, jacket, and boots. It was easy, professional, and comfortable. One clotheshorse was enough in the group, and Kennedy pounced on any designer items she could snatch up for a deal.

Odd, the three of them were so different, yet the moment they all connected in college, it was as if they were meant to be together always. Like a family. Completely dysfunctional. In a good way.

Kate spent most of her life running from her family gift/curse and trying various jobs that never worked out. Something always seemed unsettling, as if she wasn't meant to be there, so it was easy to move on to the next project. But when her friends grouped all their skills and backgrounds together, the idea of a matchmaking service in their town took root and flowered. Plenty of nasty thorns and weeds along the way, of course. But Kate could honestly say they had found their foundation and Kinnections was growing fast.

Kennedy used her talents as the main social events coordinator. She ran all the events and functions within the company, handled makeovers, and was in charge of all marketing. Arilyn used her degree in counseling to carve out a niche as relationship advisor, meeting with all the clients to deepen their experiences and counsel them on a variety of issues holding them back from love.

Good thing she had the touch, or she'd probably end up being the weak link in the group. Of course, she preferred to complete a match based on a variety of their services rather than a random shock along the way. Other than her partners and family, no one knew about her secret, and she intended to keep it that way. The moment news of a witchlike skill went public, they'd be stalked by the press and discredited in their own town.

She shook off her thoughts and leaned her hip against the desk. "What's on the agenda for today?"

Kennedy ticked off the items on her mental list. "I have makeover screenings with two of our clients. Need to meet with the Purple Haze bar about our next cocktail party. Then I'm jumping out early for my date."

Kate raised a brow. "Anyone good?"

"We shall see."

"Did you find him through Kinnections?"

"Nope. I did this on my own and damn proud of it."

Arilyn sighed. "First dates are so rich with hope and intention."

Kate snorted. "And awkwardness, drama, and disappointment."

"Remember the code. Never use negative energy when speaking about dating. It could leak back into our company."

Kate would have liked to laugh off her friend's comments but learned early that Arilyn's sense of positive vibes was key for success. Maybe they were all witches after all. "Sorry. What do you have going on?"

Arilyn stretched her long arms out and flexed her fingers. "Counseling Gary on his social fears. Then I need to work on some of the computer programs and update our client base. Some of our clients made connections with profiles they found interesting and want a phone call arranged."

It always amazed her that Arilyn had the brain of a geek god when it came to computers, tucked neatly behind her holistic image. It was a lethal combination that drove Kinnections to compete with some of the high-profile match agencies.

"Sounds good. I have a light load also, so maybe I'll catch up on the endless paperwork and get out of here on time tonight."

They floated to their respective offices. Kate tried to concentrate on paperwork and not think about Slade Montgomery. Instinct urged her to take the chance on a lawsuit because the man radiated danger. But she'd never been a coward, and she wasn't about to start now.

No problem.

She'd handle him.

three

KATE WATCHED HER new client shrug off his jacket and take a seat in the chic plum chair. He glanced around the room, taking note of the clean lines and soothing decor. Arilyn had taken control with decorating Kinnections, choosing to pair tones that enhanced the heart chakra and encouraged openness and connection. The layout consisted of bold purple and violets, pewter and silver accents, and luxurious fabrics and textures. The counseling room boasted both chairs and sofas, with plump slate-colored pillows, bamboo plants, and a calming water fountain with flat rocks lining the base. The desk was small and tucked in the corner of the square room. Today was about bonding with the client, learning likes and dislikes, and formulating a dating plan.

She couldn't believe he'd actually shown up. A deep suspicion gnawed at her bones, which was going to make working together difficult. A sense of belief and vulnerability were needed in order for her to figure out what he really wanted and guide him in the right direction. Instead, two emotions warred for dominance. Distrust.

And lust.

She pitied his clients. The man was all muscle and towering length, easily topping six four with massive shoulders, and a tight chest clearly shown through his white dress shirt. He didn't just walk, he prowled. His tawny locks were a mass of thick messy waves her fingers itched to touch, and those jungle-green eyes pinned a woman to the wall and did bad things to her. The gold frames of his glasses only accented his gaze. Probing, heating, diving deep without apology or politeness. He'd be deadly in a courtroom, mesmerizing the jurors and dominating the judge. Finding women wasn't part of his problem. Neither was getting them in bed. She'd bet once dawn broke over the horizon, he was long gone and there was little morning playtime.

Somehow, he reminded her of Matthew McConaughey from one of her guilty-pleasure movies, *Ghosts of Girlfriends Past*. His long face and craggy features were cut to inspire women to rip off their clothes, and his strong presence lit up a room. But he had an arrogance that cloaked him, as if he were above love and emotion and messiness. Above the poor humans he shared the pavement with.

That was the part that pissed her off.

Kate swore to break through that armor by the time she found him love. Then he'd be ready.

"That look is scaring the hell out of me."

He crossed one ankle comfortably over his knee. His leather Italian loafers and cashmere socks told her he enjoyed his money and wore it well. The tight design of his navy blue suit screamed Calvin Klein. His tie was conservative pinstripe for his occupation, but her instinct screamed that there was an untamed wildness in his core desperate to come out. She scratched a note on her pad for a reminder when she was looking for a good match. "What look?"

He cocked his head and his lip quirked. She fought to keep her gaze from studying the sensual curve of his mouth and the fullness of his lower lip. "Like you're about to dive into a project and get dirty."

The word *dirty* buzzed in her ears and stroked between her legs. *Mother of God, was she wet?* She clenched her thighs and thought of war-strewn countries. Hungry children. Puppies trapped in animal shelters. *Much better*. Kate decided there was only one way to move forward without losing her mind. Show him who was boss.

She frowned and spoke in her prim, no-nonsense tone. "Let's go over the basic rules first, shall we? You must be honest with me regarding all my questions. I'm here to help you and match up the woman best suited to your needs. You waste both of our time by misleading me. There is no embarrassment or judgment. I've heard many requests and have never gotten flustered, no matter what my client tells me."

"Never?"

She tapped the gold-embossed pen against her pad. "Never."

"Interesting."

Kate ignored his murmur and forged on. "There's a certain level of trust and respect we need to work together. If you feel that I'm not properly listening to your wishes, we'll discuss the matter openly. Communication is key. I may also ask you to do things outside your comfort zone. Again, we'll talk about your reservations, but I may ask you to try something you'd normally not be comfortable with. Sometimes, people get stuck in a certain way of socializing, and pushing past those boundaries ends up being a breakthrough. This is an organic process to satisfy the different needs of your life along with your heart."

Kate uncapped her water bottle and took a sip. So far, so good. He scratched his head in serious thought and seemed to be considering her words carefully. "Have you ever slept with one of your clients?"

The water got stuck in her throat and went down the wrong pipe. She choked on the bubble and fought for breath. He sat patiently through her coughing fit, grabbed a tissue from the box on the table, and handed it to her. She pressed it to her streaming eyes. "Why would you ask me such a question?"

His shoulders lifted. "Well, you're digging into my life. I figured if we're going to trust one another, I should know something about you. Makes sense. You're a type of counselor, and tight bonds form. Just wanted to know."

"I don't sleep with my clients. Ever."

"Is that a company policy or your own personal code?"

Kate stomped down on her growing annoyance. He was like a predator, circling his prey and planning out the best route to block any escape. "Both. Once I sign you as a client, there's a layer of trust that can't be broken. I wouldn't be able to give you what you need if I had personal intentions. And of course, if it didn't work between us, Kinnections could be at stake. We won't risk it."

"Pity."

She shifted her weight and studied him. Oh yeah, he knew exactly what he was doing. Throwing her off. Making her uncomfortable. Bringing sex into the picture so he could neatly take the reins and guide the conversation the way he wished. A gleeful cackle rose in her chest, but she managed to squash it in time. He had no idea how good she was at her job. "I see you don't have the same code with your own clients."

"Pardon?"

Kate pretended surprise. "Your clients. You are a divorce lawyer, and I'm sure you're well versed in the bonding that goes on when counseling a brokenhearted, angry woman. Do you contain it to just sleeping with her, or have you ever instituted a longer-term relationship?"

He jerked in his seat. "I'd never sleep with a client."

"Oh. Is that a company policy or your own personal code?"

His gaze narrowed at her sweetly posed question. "Nice volley."

"Thank you. Now, instead of trading barbs for the rest of the hour, let's go over some of the basics of what you need." She scanned the stack of papers, though she'd already memorized most of his answers. "Intelligence is key. A woman who can hold her own with conversation. Someone formally educated. Master's or bachelor's degree?"

"Master's preferred."

She checked off the box. "Business background, or are you open to the creative professions?"

He winced. "God, no artists or writers. Well, literary writers would be acceptable. No fiction. Especially not those romance novels."

Another check. "Family background also seems important to you. Let's discuss a bit more. Are you looking for a woman whose parents are still together? Or are you looking to avoid alcoholism, drug abuse, or disease within the family genes?"

He shifted his weight. The arrogant cloud misted away, and she caught the first signs of discomfort. "I'm up for partner at my law firm. I'd like a woman who has no skeletons in her closet or family members who could pose a problem. We'll be attending formal business dinners, functions, and most of the partners are conservative."

"Understood." She scrawled her pen over the page. "Personality is the other aspect that's quite important. Do

you enjoy a woman who's funny? Shy? Assertive? Colorful? Tell me a bit about your past affairs or relationships."

"I prefer a woman who is conservative in public. Loyalty is key. I dislike flirty women who crave attention. I
want her to be strong within herself, but follow my lead
when I need it."

"When do you need it?"

"Excuse me?"

Kate looked up from her papers. "When do you need
her to follow? Around your business partners? Your family? In public? Or in the bedroom?"

The air charged around her, but she ignored it. Talking
about personal preferences in sex was a ticking bomb, but
experience had taught her a few lessons. The more businesslike and unshocked she was, her clients ended up relaxing into the topic and usually confessed their innermost
wants. "You want to know how I like my sex?"

"Yes, I do. Sex is one of the most important aspects in a
relationship. If you want shy and virginal, tell me. If you
like BDSM and enjoy tying your partners up, it's a good
item for me to note, because I won't set you up with a
woman who may go screaming for the door. I make no
judgments or opinions. Just tell me what you want."

Why was her heart pounding so loudly? Her throat
constricted, and her muscles tightened anticipating his response. Wow, she'd been physically attracted to some of her
clients but had never experienced such a primitive pull

straight from her gut. She kept her gaze averted so he wouldn't catch her female weakness and exploit it.

His laugh exploded through the room. The dark, husky tones stroked her like fingers plunging between her thighs and urging her to explode. Kate concentrated on breathing slowly and went back to the puppies in the shelter. "You want to talk about sex, huh? Okay. Let's talk about sex." She pretended to be busy scribbling so she wouldn't have to look up. "I enjoy pleasure. I enjoy sex. I prefer a woman who asks me for what she wants so I can give it to her exactly the way she likes it, because one of the sweetest sounds in life is a woman screaming my name." His voice lowered, whisper soft and wicked hot. "I'm not into BDSM, but I've used blindfolds, scarves, and toys in pursuit of the ultimate experience. I don't like to be tied up but prefer to do the tying. And I don't need a woman on her knees unless she wants to be there. Does that help answer your question?"

Kate bobbed her head up and down in a frantic nod. Her power of speech disappeared, and fire licked her veins. She reached for her water, took a large swallow, and managed to gather her composure. "Yes, thank you."

"You're welcome."

She pretended to look for something in her file, since her voice threatened to be wobbly. After a few moments, Kate dove back in. "Let's talk past relationships. Have you ever been married?"

"Yes."

She paused and ventured a glance under her lashes. His previous amusement vanished, and a wall slammed down between them. Ah, she'd hit pay dirt. "Divorced?"

"Yep."

"What happened?"

"We broke up."

"Care to tell me why?"

She waited him out. This was a turning point, because information on his past helped her plan his future. "I plead the Fifth."

His wife had hurt him. Ex-wife. The knowledge softened her heart and beckoned for her to reach out and touch him. She'd avoided any skin-on-skin contact, afraid the attraction would be more difficult to fight, but his comment made her curl her fingers into tight fists to keep from closing the distance. Kate gentled her voice. "Slade, I don't mean to pry and upset you. Our past makes up who we are and what we want. It would help if I knew what happened so that I can avoid setting you up with someone who can hurt you again. Not that there are guarantees, of course."

He tapped his finger against his chin and studied her with brooding eyes. "How about we play truth for truth? Why aren't you happily married? Unless you are and you like hearing other people's horror stories to get your kicks and excitement?"

The familiar pain sprang up, but she pushed it back

down with an expert ease that should have scared her. "No, I'm not married."

"Kinnections not working for you?"

She lifted her chin. "The truth is, no man has ever wanted me enough to propose."

The silence pulsed and hummed. She'd learned early that fair was fair. If she asked her clients to trust her with their backgrounds, she owed it to them to do the same. He cleared his throat and spoke with no emotion. "She cheated on me. But it was my fault. I was too involved in law school and ignored her for too long. Classic formula for the classic divorcee."

Kate wanted more but knew how much the words cost him. God, how that must have affected him. He was obviously a strong man, and once trust was shattered, it took years to rebuild confidence in love. His profession was pretty deadly to any optimism regarding relationships. "Thank you. Makes sense loyalty and trust would be among your number one requirements. That will help me." She lightened the topic, switching back to easy territory. "Give me your celebrity crush."

"Huh?"

She smiled. "If you got to pick the celebrity female you want to sleep with, who would it be?"

"Angelina Jolie."

The name slipped out so fast from his lips he looked surprised. Kate laughed and made the note. "Nice choice.

But I must say a bit cliché. Do you know how many times men *and* women rattled off her name?"

"Now I'm embarrassed. Change it to Zooey Deschanel."

"Ah, better. So definitely brunettes with curves. Too bad my friend's sister is happily married. She always reminded me of Zooey."

"Do I have a chance at stealing her?"

"Nah, Alexa is madly in love with her husband. But at least I've got an idea of your holy grail."

"Get me Zooey and I'll take out a full-page ad in the *Times* for Kinnections."

She laughed again. "I'll work on it. I see you don't list many hobbies. What do you like to do outside of work?"

"I work most of the time. I run every day. Golf. Boring stuff."

"Would you be open to an adventurous type of woman? Someone who skydives, likes sports, scuba diving, that sort of thing?"

Another shrug. "Sure. As long as she doesn't think I'm jumping out of a plane for her. Screaming may take away my manhood."

"Duly noted. Religion? Nationality?"

"Open. Oh, no virgins."

Her pen paused. "Under any circumstances?"

"Absolutely not. I can't take the pressure of no sex before marriage, and a woman who hasn't had experience may have a false attachment to me just because I'm her first."

Kate's finger shook around the pen. "Got it. Now, just so I have a good background of your beliefs, what is your viewpoint on love? You enrolled with Kinnections to try to find a life partner or a woman you can forge a solid long-term relationship with. I'll ask you again: are you completely committed and open to finding this?"

"I'm open. I just don't think it exists."

Fascinated, she leaned in. "Why?"

He uncrossed his legs, stretched his feet out, and settled comfortingly back in the chair. "One word. Oxytocin."

Kate blinked. "What's that?"

"Simple science. The body excretes a chemical hormone at certain moments that emphasizes the need for closeness and comfort. This lowers fear and instills a calmness we believe and translate to feelings of love. The main time oxytocin is released is after sex. That's why many times lust will get us into bed, good conversation will give us hope, and oxytocin will cement such feelings as love."

Her eyes widened. Pride and certainty carved out the lines of his face. Holy shit, he believed it! Caught between laughing and crying, she studied his muscled length in all his glory and realized that Slade Montgomery was going to be her hardest client as of yet. The challenge sung in her blood. Matching and finding him love would be her greatest satisfaction. A test of her skills. If she did her job correctly, he wouldn't know how to even say the word *oxytocin* at the end of their time together.

"An interesting theory."

"One you obviously don't agree with."

"That doesn't matter. You believe it, so, therefore, it's my truth. Thank you for being honest with me."

Slade peered over his gold glasses in pure suspicion. "You're not going to try to convince me otherwise?"

She smiled. "No. But now I know what needs to happen so you're sure it's not a chemical hormone. You need to fall in love before sex."

"What?"

"Yes. I'll be setting up an event where you can meet some women. It will be small, extremely tasteful, and discreet. You'll be able to meet and mingle, and then choose one for your main date. It's a good introduction and doesn't waste any of your time. But there will be one rule you need to follow if I have any chance of success. No sex."

His brows slammed together. "You better be joking."

Kate tapped her pen in a steady rhythm and met his gaze head-on. "No, Slade, I'm not joking. No sex. You're caught up in the lust-hormone cycle, and until we break through, you'll never be open to admitting real feelings. You need to agree to this."

"Sex is a way we can find out if we're both compatible. This isn't Victorian England, for God's sake!"

She sighed. "I'm not saying no sex ever. You just need

to set an initial time period where you don't engage in physical intimacy. Let's say, no sex until you're ready to begin seriously dating. Monogamy. Trust me, if you're not interested enough to want to have dinner with her for a few weeks, you won't be able to forge a lasting relationship with her. Sex sometimes confuses things, as you've just pointed out. Take it out of the equation, and we balance the playing field."

He pushed a hand through his hair. "I don't like this."

"I understand. But I'm asking you to trust me. I know my job, and I know how to get you what you need. Will you give this a shot?"

"Fine. But if I don't think it's worthwhile and helping me, I'm yanking that rule. Got it?"

Kate grinned. "Fair enough. I'll set up your mixer for next Friday night. Seven. I'd like to hold it here in Verily, if that's acceptable."

"Sure, I can check in on my sister. How is she?"

"I can't discuss her status with you. Just as I won't tell her about you."

He cocked his head. "Fine. I see you ask your clients to give you a full year to make a long-term match. Isn't that a bit long to keep collecting the fee?"

His mild-mannered tone contradicted the judgment in his eyes. Kate reached deep for calm, refusing to lose her center. This man knew how to goad and press buttons she never knew existed. Her smile oozed sugar and syrup.

"Funny, I think the exact opposite. An agency that guarantees results in three months for $19.99 would make me quite suspicious. The journey should be fruitful, rich, and full of adventure. What's a year compared to love for a lifetime?"

He snorted. "What indeed? Just a cache of new clients for me after it blows up."

Kate crossed her arms in front of her chest. "Hold the cynicism until after the cocktail party, please. You'll also need to complete a session with Arilyn and Kennedy. Depending on their feedback, we'll schedule the proper classes for you."

"What classes? Like sensitivity training? Or How to Give a Woman an Orgasm in Less Than Five Minutes?"

Heat flooded her body as that delicious lower lip tugged upward in a half smile. God, what that mouth could probably accomplish. Her toes curled in her boots, but she held it together. "We'll discuss their recommendations once they meet you. Let's say Sunday afternoon? Completing the classes before the first mixer is more beneficial."

He let out an irritated breath. "Do I have a choice? As long as your colleagues realize I have sensitivity galore and I've already mastered class number two." He paused and drilled her with his gaze. "Many times."

"G-g-g-good. Then you'll be ahead of the game. J-j-just be sure you're open to all suggestions and the journey ahead."

Damn stutter. This man singed her nerves, and she hated lapsing into her familiar weakness. Kate concentrated on music filling her mind and rolling out of her mouth. A few deep, even breaths, and she regained her center.

He held up a hand in mock defeat. "Fine. I'll be open to love and let it all flow. Always hated country music and all that sap."

"You're not listening to the right kind, darlin'," she drawled. "Most are about cheating men and kick-ass women. Or don't you watch *Nashville*?"

"I surrender."

A silly giggle threatened. Damn, he was funny. She loved a droll, sarcastic sense of humor. Too bad he was everything wrong in a man, and she was the exact opposite of what he wanted in a woman. At least it would save her a bunch of heartbreak, because once a woman fell in love with Slade Montgomery, she'd bet it was for a life sentence. Oxytocin, or whatever the hell it was called, be damned. Kate rose to her feet and walked with him toward the door. He shrugged on his jacket, flicked the button closed, and faced her.

"Thanks for the session, Kate Seymour."

He put out his hand, but she jumped in front of him and rushed out the door. Not yet. She wasn't ready to touch him and get slammed by any raw, sexy energy she might pick up on. She'd save it for matching him with the right woman.

He followed her and almost bumped into the two assessing females blocking his path.

Arilyn and Kennedy broke into bright, welcoming
smiles. Kate knew better. They were stalking him, assessing,
and couldn't wait to get him on their couch. A flare of appreciation lit both her friends' gazes as they took in his
trim physique and gorgeous surfer hair. Kennedy stepped
in front of him. "Hi. We wanted to introduce ourselves
since you'll be working with us. I'm Kennedy. I'll be helping with social events, makeovers, and anything you need
to make your experience better. This is Arilyn. She does relationship counseling and is our internet guru. Welcome to
Kinnections."

Slade quirked a brow. Oh yeah, the man was not dumb.
He knew they were checking out the fresh meat, and he
seemed amused at the concept. "How nice, a welcoming
committee. Slade Montgomery."

"Related to Jane?"

"Her brother. Older brother. How is she doing, by the
way?"

Arilyn gave a warm smile and completely ignored
Kate's obvious throat clearing. "Wonderful. We already
have her set up with her first date and she seems much
more comfortable with herself."

"Seems a bit quick, doesn't it? She just enrolled.
Doesn't she need more advice or time to find the right
one?"

"We feel she's ready."

"When is it?"

Kate stepped in front of him and gave Arilyn a glare. "None of your business. We do not discuss our clients with other clients. Right, ladies?"

Arilyn bit her lip. "Oh, I'm sorry. I just thought since they were family . . ."

Slade flashed a confident smile, all gorgeous white teeth. The top one was slightly crooked and kept him looking more rugged rather than pretty. "My fault, no harm done, Arilyn. It was nice to meet both of you."

He strolled out of the office. Kennedy leaned way over to watch him disappear. Then slumped against the wall with a hearty sigh. "Damn, he has a fine ass."

Kate winced. "I swear, if any of our clients heard you speaking like that we'd get sued. We have to be super careful with him. He's out to prove us to be frauds and thinks we steal money from the innocent and use love as the bait."

Kennedy whistled. "Interesting. Well, he's protective of his family, smart, and hot. A perfect trifecta. Why don't you take him for yourself?"

"I don't date clients, Ken. You know that. Besides, I'm done with men."

Her friend clucked her tongue. "Breaking a rule or two won't hurt anyone if you're both interested. You're the one who made that ridiculous law, so you can change it. Maybe you need to mix up your usual boring bread-and-water type with a pizza supreme."

Kate burst into laughter. Arilyn frowned in disapproval. "Though I do love pizza, I'll pass. Anyway, we just went over his list, and I'm the opposite of every trait he desires." She ticked them off. "He prefers brunettes, curvy, conservative background, solid family with no skeletons, master's degree—oh, and no virgins."

Arilyn widened her eyes. "No way. He actually said no virgins?"

"Yep."

Kennedy laughed. "Why are you guys so shocked? Other than our Miss Kate, there are hardly any virgins left in New York anyway."

Arilyn came to her defense. "There's nothing wrong with it. Kate just hasn't met the right one yet. She's not one of these innocents with dreams of picket fences. She only wants a connection."

Kennedy rolled her eyes. "I think you're both nuts. Kate needs to get laid, and you need to eat some meat. These affairs with your yoga teachers are warping your mind." Red color flooded Arilyn's face, but she made a good show at looking offended.

Kate groaned. "It's just a technicality! I've done plenty of foreplay. It's just when it came time, something wasn't right, so I chickened out. No big deal."

Kennedy huffed. "It *is* a big deal. Foreplay is nice, but

you're missing out on the culinary event. You just got a bunch of yummy appetizers but no prime rib dinner."

"Are you hungry? What's up with all these clever food analogies?" Kate asked.

"Stupid diet. I'm getting crankier by the minute."

Arilyn clucked in sympathy. "I have an organic granola bar with dark chocolate. You'll feel better. And leave Kate and her poor virginity alone. She's a pioneer."

Kate groaned and rubbed her hands over her face. "Nightmare material. So, do we agree I'm completely the wrong choice for Mr. Hot Divorce Lawyer?"

"I love lawyers. But yes, I agree. I'm thinking we hook him up with Hannah. Or Emma. They're physically his type, classy but funny."

Kate nodded. "I was thinking the same thing. I'm arranging his cocktail party for next Friday night. Check the site and let me know who you can get, and I'll approve it."

"Got it."

"Oh, and one other thing. Slade committed to the full Kinnections experience in all formats. I think we need to give it to him."

Arilyn grinned. "Oh, yeah. I have some wonderful things lined up for Mr. Hot Lawyer. And trust me, if I sense things correctly, it will revolve around heat."

Kennedy lit up. "He doesn't need much in the makeover department, but I'll take him to the next level. Bring it."

Satisfaction pinged in Kate. "Done. For now I need a

glass of wine, music, and distraction. Wanna head to Mugs?"

"Sure. Has anyone heard from Genevieve?"

Kate shook her head. "She was supposed to stop for coffee this morning but never showed. I'll text her to get her ass down here. She's working herself to death at that hospital. I swear, interning is *not* like they show it on *Grey's Anatomy*."

Kennedy snickered. "Yeah, but she did land her own Dr. McDreamy. Or was that the other hottie who died? What a waste."

Kate laughed, grabbed her purse, and headed out with her crew.

four

SLADE FLICKED THE Play button on the remote control, closed his laptop, and reached for his Sam Adams. The cherry wheat taste left a pleasant flavor in his mouth and should have satisfied him. He glanced around his home, perfectly decorated and detailed to fit his lifestyle. Luxurious but not overdone or fussy. The sixty-inch flat-screen television gave a nice feel to his man cave. The beverage holders and remote-controlled, heated recliners added to his complete comfort. A fully stocked tiki bar showcased rows of crystal glasses in various styles depending on the drink. His classic favorite comedy, *Office Space*, boomed from the HD sound system. A bag of chips lay to his right.

Perfect. After years of unrest, drama, and compromise, he finally achieved everything he'd dreamed. The space thrummed with a deep silence he coveted.

The nasty voice stirred and issued a cranky question. *Then how come you're bored out of your mind?*

Screw you. Leave me alone.

He turned up the volume and took another swig of beer. Women hated *Office Space*. They never got the humor. They hated messy chips in the living room and clothes that missed the hamper, and the obnoxious old heavy metal music he preferred. Hell, he didn't even have to worry about a pet to feed or walk. He was completely content and alone.

Again.

An image of Kate tumbled past his vision. What was it about her that stirred his interest? Sure, she was the all-American blonde most men lusted after, even more so because she didn't realize it and didn't overdo her natural beauty. She seemed comfortable in her own skin, which was an even bigger turn-on. Yes, his body definitely responded, but if he hadn't, that would've confirmed he was dead.

Besides, she definitely wasn't the type to inspire such basic needs. Fiercely independent, physically distant, with a chilly demeanor that said "Back off, this is all business."

Getting involved with the owner of a matchmaking service was pure doom and stupidity.

Not. Interested.

The cackling voice rose up and mocked his thought, but he figured he'd drown it in alcohol and salt.

Just another Friday night.

His cell beeped. He scooped it up, checked ID, and clicked the button. "About time you called me back. Are you okay?"

The deep sigh on the other end held a twinge of irritation he'd never heard before. His overprotective instincts toward his baby sister overrode his instinct to back off.

"Just because I don't check in with you on a daily basis doesn't mean I'm lying dead in the gutter. Mom."

He winced and tucked the phone under his chin. "Ha, ha. Look, cut me a break. You moved out of my house, quit your job, and signed up with a matchmaking agency within a month. I'm still trying to catch up."

"I know. But things are good. I love my new job, and I'm excited about my experience with Kinnections. The women there are so nice and approachable."

Kate's image flashed in his mind. More like sexy and frustrating. "You don't think they're a bunch of crazies stealing your money? You know, statistically, matchmakers gain no results and only offer an empty illusion. I surfed the net. Numbers never lie. Most of the marriages they arrange end up in divorce within three to five years."

Uh-oh. Her tone took on the higher pitch of a woman ready to lose it. "Enough with the statistics! Just because your marriage didn't work out, and your clients get divorced, doesn't mean I need to pay by being lonely."

The pain stirred, but he wrestled it back. Yes, he'd failed his marriage, just as his ex-wife had. But Jane didn't understand. How could she? He was the one who protected her from a bunch of crappy men who thought they could take advantage of her. The revolving door of brokenhearted individuals barely keeping their sanity was his daily reality. Jane's sweetness and fragile ego were prime targets of con men, and they'd already been through too many. He had to pay the last guy off to walk away. At least the asshole couldn't claim to be a starving artist anymore and hit up his sister for money.

"I don't want you to be lonely. I just don't want you to get hurt."

She sighed and her voice softened. "I'm sorry, Slade, that was a rotten thing for me to say. But I don't want you to chaperone me. If I get hurt, so be it. At least it will be on my terms. I won't hurt myself again."

The image of that night rose up and choked him with emotion. He'd almost lost her. He'd promised himself in that hospital room he wouldn't let her down again. Jane needed one person to count on, and by God, he'd spent the last years making sure she was protected. "I know. I'm proud of you."

"Thanks."

He dragged in a breath. Time to spill the truth. "In fact, I was so intrigued with the idea I actually paid them a visit. Decided to sign up myself for the experience."

His casual tone contradicted his unease. Put himself in the hands of Kate and her female crew? Meet a bunch of women he didn't know in the pursuit of some type of affair that wouldn't work out anyway?

Yes. He'd do it for Jane. To keep an eye on her and Kinnections.

Silence hummed over the line. "Are you kidding me? Why would you sign up with a matchmaking agency? You don't want to settle down!"

"Maybe I do. Maybe I'm looking for a companion to share my life with. If this place is as good as they say, I'll find someone, too. Hey, we can double date."

A strangled laugh echoed. "You are so screwed-up. I can't believe you'd really go through with this. The screening is intense. Are you getting a makeover?"

Hell no.

"We'll see. Did you get your first date yet?" he asked.

"Soon. Kennedy is taking me to the salon this weekend to freshen up my appearance. Then she gave me some guys to peruse online to get an idea of my taste."

The meat market atmosphere gave him the chills. Did people really do this shit just to get a date? For God's sake, why? "Hey, I'd appreciate it if you kept me in the loop. I'm a bit nervous about the whole thing. It'll help to know what you're going through, too."

Suspicion laced Jane's voice. "Kate will take good care of you."

An image of Kate on her knees unzipping his pants flashed before him. Sweat prickled his skin. What was wrong with him? "Maybe."

"When's *your* first date?"

"I'm getting a mixer next Friday night." He drained the beer dry. "Why don't you come?"

"What? Are you crazy? It's the first time you're meeting these women."

"Who cares? You can find out how Kinnections works,

and I can get your opinion. Besides, I never see you anymore, and they're setting it up in Verily. It's out of my element. I've never seen so many weird pottery shops in my life. How many pots can one person own?"

She gave the familiar snort she had since childhood. "Nothing's out of your element, Slade. That's your problem."

"So, you'll come?"

"Sorry, I can't. I'm buried deep in research for my new article and won't surface for a week."

"Lunch this weekend, then? I'll give you the rundown on my experience."

"Sure. I'll take you to Mugs, they have great burgers."

"Fine. I'll see you at one on Saturday."

They exchanged good-byes and he terminated the call.

He was in perfect position now. Jane wouldn't be suspicious, and he'd be able to watch her and monitor the company.

He hit the remote on the chair and eased back another inch, trying to concentrate on Milton's speech regarding the moving of his desk, squirrels, and his precious red stapler. What made a woman decide to start a matchmaking business on her own? Was she just a savvy businesswoman looking to make a buck on a good sale? Or did it run much deeper? Her probing questions stirred a nest of emotions he had no interest in exploring.

The knowledge of love wasn't enough, would never be

enough. There was pleasure, and enjoying the moment, and respect. Sometimes there was even friendship.

But not love. At least not long-term.

He thought about Kate and her own personal confession. The words rang in his mind like a mantra.

No man has ever wanted me enough to propose.

Her raw honesty touched something deep inside him. A part that ached to soothe the hurt and prove her wrong.

Yeah, a matchmaker and a divorce lawyer. That's got success written all over it.

His lips twisted into a smile. Probably the universe punishing him for his sudden craving to seduce her. Hell, he knew why he'd gotten into his career. To help guide the heartbreak and messiness of America's favorite pastime: screwing the ones they loved. He helped a few people and made a ton of money. Sure, he wasn't respected, and when he told people his career, they looked as if they'd gotten a piece of gum stuck on their sole. But who cared? No way was he messing up everything by chasing after a love do-gooder.

He was happy.

Life was perfect.

"ROBERT, I'M HOME!"

The scramble of feet on the ground filled her with a quiet joy. Her roommate, companion, and best friend appeared around the corner and headed straight for her.

Kate dropped to her knees and waited. His nonworking back legs didn't slow him down a bit as he scooted over the floor and stopped right before her. She touched her forehead to his smooth fur. The gentle lick to her face was the only sign of deep affection her dignified dog allowed himself to express. She petted his back and checked his bladder. Almost full. Another hour and the poor thing would've had a problem. "Sorry, baby, I was late. Stayed to eat with the girls. Let's go."

Kate reached for the scooter beside the door and hooked it up with an expert ease that made her proud of how far they'd come. Together. She ignored the leash and led him outside to the perfect patch of grass meant for him. The whip of the frosty air caused her to shiver, but Robert twitched his nose, took a deep doggy breath, and ran.

She laughed at his outright joy and freedom, the wheels of the cart spinning rapidly as he raced over the lawn to his favorite tree, and began to do laps round and round the gnarled trunk. A deep sense of peace settled over her. Her bungalow-type home might be small, and her yard less than half an acre, but she'd managed to create a home and a family she loved on her own terms.

Robert did his business with perfect restraint, hiding in his own private alcove. When she'd first met him, he'd been run over by a car and lifeless. She found him at the side of the road, a mangle of dead limbs and a hollow look in his eyes. Kate rushed him to the vet and was immediately advised to put him to sleep. No shelter would take him. No owner would want him. He was a pit bull—the worst dog for adoption. Surgery was possible but expensive. Better to let him go in a cold world that had no time for imperfect humans, let alone dogs.

She agreed and went in to say good-bye, to at least allow him to slip to the other side with a friend beside him. He must have been in wretched pain, but when Kate laid her hand on top of his head, he swiveled to look at her.

Brown eyes so full of regret. Maybe for the life he had. Maybe for the life he always dreamed of but didn't get. Human eyes, wise, accepting, and yet still full of kindness, though she knew his owner decided he was worthless and disposable.

I'm better than this fate. I'm worth something more.

The voice expressed from his eyes hit her hard. Kate knew in that moment he was her dog. Meant for her. A low hum of energy tingled her palm, as if she had met part of herself. And she turned to the vet and gave the order. "Save him. I don't care how much it costs or how you do it. I love him."

The vet's startled gaze changed to compassion and a determination to win. "Then I will."

It was a turning point for them both. Even though they were both damaged, they were worth loving. How many times had Kate cried herself to sleep, thinking of herself as a freak no one could love because she couldn't speak like everyone else? The torturous years in school, ashamed to read aloud, to say hello, to be teased mercilessly on the playground and bullied nonstop. But she'd risen above it all and made a success from her life. Just like Robert. The rest of the world could go to hell.

It took weeks for the healing, a ton of medical bills she guessed the vet helped her out with, and a wonderful charity that donated the scooter so Robert, now paraplegic, could learn to walk again without using his back legs. Kate learned to empty his full bladder when needed. She took him to physical therapy, learned new skills of how he could lead a full life, and hired someone to come in a few hours per day when she was at work.

She had regrets in her twenty-six years. She'd never traveled. She'd hung her head in shame for things that weren't her fault.

But never Robert. He was the only decision that made her proud.

He finished his run, and she undid the cart, giving him a quick kiss on his head. "I'm exhausted. I snuck out on the crew and I don't even care. Kennedy will be so pissed."

Robert's deep brown eyes gleamed with understanding. "Why don't we go to the dog park this Saturday and you can meet Arilyn's new rescue? I think you'll like him. He's got a long road to travel, like you did, but I think if he saw you he'd be more inspired to heal."

Robert cocked his head and nodded.

She headed toward the small galley kitchen painted red. "Cool. Meaty bone or chewy bacon strip?"

He barked twice. "Bacon it is." He politely tugged the strip from her fingers and wheeled off to his orthopedic mat to settle and treasure the treat.

She headed toward her pj drawer when the knock stopped her. Kate peeked through the window and flung open the door to see her best friend. "You missed Mugs."

Genevieve MacKenzie dragged herself over the threshold, still in her scrubs. "Extra shift. Forgot to eat. Help."

Kate shook her head and returned to the kitchen. Robert scurried from his mat to greet his second-favorite person, pushing his nose into her palm as Gen rubbed his head and gave him a kiss. "How's my favorite boy? Good day or bad day?"

Kate opened the refrigerator and pulled out a variety of lunch meats. "Good day. Bladder is emptying fine lately. No bedsores."

"That's my baby," Gen crooned, rubbing behind the ears. "I'm sorry I barged in before pj time."

"Don't be ridiculous, you live right down the road." Kate stacked ham, cheese, lettuce, tomato, and mayo on a big roll and set it on a plate. "Sit down and eat. What the hell are you doing to yourself lately, babe? You can't save the world if you collapse on me."

Her friend dropped onto the red stool and began shoving the food into her mouth. Kate grinned, poured her some water, dumped out a few chips, and slid onto the seat next to her.

"David sprang a research article on me to complete. We were supposed to be collaborators, but I discovered that means I do the work and he gets the publishing credit. Part of the resident torture."

An odd sensation settled over her as she studied her best friend. They'd met at NYU just like Arilyn and Ken, but when Gen moved down the road, they'd become like sisters. Kate adored Gen's big Italian family and always accompanied her to functions. They finished each other's sentences, liked the same things, and both had the same crazy ambition to succeed.

"Doesn't sound fair to me. You're pushing too hard."

Gen moaned around a bite. Her springy dark hair escaped her ponytail and curled wildly around her heart-shaped face. Navy blue eyes focused wholeheartedly on the meal in front of her, but Kate had also seen that gaze assess a medical emergency, soothe a scared child, and calm down a parent with the heart and soul of a true surgeon.

"So good. Will you make me coffee?"

"No, drink your water. You'll never sleep."

Gen gave a sulky pout but drank the full glass, then dove into the chips. "How was Mugs?"

"Good. We missed you. You never come out anymore. What's up?"

A strange expression flickered over her tired face. Gen

studied her plate. "Just work. David's been telling me I need to focus more on my career and getting ahead. And he works such crazy shifts, we rarely get to see each other. I just need to cut back on some of my socializing for a little while."

David, aka Dr. McDreamy, was Gen's boss, drop-dead gorgeous, charming, and one of the top pediatric surgeons. He spent half of his time at Westchester Medical and the rest at Albany. Kate knew her friend crushed on him for years, like all the other interns, but this past year David finally noticed her. They started an affair but kept it from going public, and for a while Kate watched her friend glow with a deep-seated happiness.

But she was changing: withdrawing from regularly scheduled social get-togethers, working nonstop, and spending all of her free time at David's place. Kate tried to sort through the emotions, wondering if she was just envious of Gen's complete focus, or if she just missed her best friend. She shook off her thoughts and forced a smile.

"I understand. Just make sure you take some time to rest and have fun."

"Yes, Mom." Gen slumped on the seat, looking sated. "God, that was good. God, I love you."

Kate laughed and scooped up the plate. "At least someone does."

"Another bad date?"

"Yep. But I'm done, Gen. Look at this." She looked around at her bungalow which she loved, from the trendy red kitchen, to the open living room with massive wooden shelves holding her fave movies, music, and books. Gorgeous hardwood floors shone to a bright polish, and it was all cheerfully decorated in yellow and gray. The oversized bay window and seat looked over the tiny patch of lawn and the edge of the Hudson River. "I love my place. I love my job and Robert, and I'm happy. Every time I come home from a date I get depressed, so I'm taking a break. Maybe a year. I'll focus on growing Kinnections and enjoying myself."

Gen grabbed her hand and squeezed in sympathy. "Bad dates suck. But I believe you're meant to find that special person. Sure you don't want to use your own company to snag someone?"

Kate shook her head. "No, the lines are too blurred as the owner. I'd rather use my energy on my clients. Especially the difficult ones." Slade's face drifted past and racked a tiny shudder. Maybe this was the key: focus on proving to Slade that Kinnections works and matching him up. Then she'd go back to her lackluster love life.

Gen slid out of the chair and kissed Robert good-bye. "What's that awful cliché stuff they always throw at women who are frustrated? You'll find love when you're not looking."

"I hope not. That theory puts me into bankruptcy."

Gen laughed and hugged her. "Thanks. I needed a little girl talk and food. Love you."

"Love you, too."

She shut the door behind Gen, turned the deadbolt, and immediately began to strip. She grabbed her favorite ratty flannels, which were faded and soft, and within seconds was curled up on her battered chair. Damn, she'd love one of those cool recliners with the heat and remotes. Maybe she'd treat herself next year for her birthday. Feet propped up on the scratched coffee table, she flipped through her DVR collection of recorded goodies. Robert settled in the pile of blankets next to her, already dozing.

She slipped over to comedies and found it immediately. Her fave. No matter how many times she watched *Office Space*, it always seemed funny. A sheer classic. She hit Play and settled back.

Yep. Everything would work out.

Perfectly.

five

SLADE WALKED INTO the small gym Verily boasted and headed toward the back room. He had no idea what to expect, but a good round of workouts was a great way to start a Sunday.

He made his way through an array of hand weights, bench presses, and treadmills, looking longingly out the window at the outside track. He'd much prefer a hard run, his favorite way to exercise, but Arilyn had a different idea.

Slade grudgingly admitted she didn't strike him as a used-car salesman. She probed with a pure intention, her melodic voice as graceful as her hip-length strawberry hair and smooth movements. Before he knew it, he'd sunk into the plum chair, soothed and relaxed, and began telling her stuff he'd never confessed before.

Humiliating. She'd gotten him good and scheduled him for a special workout that released negative toxins and got him cleared and open for love.

Yeah. Right.

Still, he signed the contract and was determined to uncover every ridiculous, misguided attempt to take his sister's money. He pushed through the glass doors and entered a small studio.

Crap. It was hot.

Sweat immediately formed on his brow and it wasn't just the temperature. Kate stood next to Arilyn, dressed in black yoga pants and matching tank. The Lycra cupped her ass like his fingers itched to do and emphasized the full thrust of her breasts. Her hair was clipped high on her head and gave him full access to the smooth, white flesh of her nape and upper back.

He flicked his gaze quickly away as he hardened. Talk about embarrassing, like a teen sporting a boner from his hot teacher. He turned, thought of his last client, a woman weeping in his office because her husband left her with three kids for his secretary. Biggest cliché of all. Thank God, he got back to normal and crossed the room.

"Morning. Is something wrong with the air?"

Kate grinned. Arilyn cleared her throat and motioned toward the other two men in the room. A large, muscled African American guy sported a shaven head, bulging biceps, and tree-trunk thighs exposed in shorts. The other one was on the skinny side, with red hair, pale skin, and covered from chest to ankle in sweats. Slade perspired more just looking at him.

"Gentlemen, if you'll join me in a circle, please."

The men obeyed as they all glanced at each other, obviously uncomfortable. The big guy grunted, his face pulled into a good imitation of Mr. T.

"Let me introduce you quickly. Slade, this is Meat."

Slade's eyes widened. "Meat?"

Meat glared. "Got a problem with the name?"

"Nope. Just confirming. Nice to meet you."

Meat nodded.

"And this is Trent." Slade greeted the younger one, who looked terrified of what Arilyn would do to him. What kind of counseling was this?

He glanced at Kate, but her bright blue eyes danced with glee, confirming this was going to be bad.

Real bad.

He concentrated on Arilyn's lilting voice. "Each of us has some issues we need to work through in order to be our better selves. The happier and more satisfied we are, the better our relationships. The body holds stress deep in the muscles and blocks many pathways, especially to our heart chakras. Today, we're going to engage in a session of hot yoga, which will break down some of the barriers we erected. Kate is going to help me assist as I guide you through different postures. Concentrate on your body and your breathing. If you feel the need to rest, please do so. I've filled water jugs for each of you and mats are already set up. Any questions?"

Trent made a strangled sound of horror. "I don't like taking my shirt off in front of anyone," he said.

Arilyn nodded. "I understand, but that's one of the blocks I'd like to work with today. There's nothing wrong with your body. You've been used to hiding behind clothes in order to keep women away. It's time to let go a bit."

No. Fucking. Way.

This was not happening to him. Hot yoga? Issues? Yep, Kinnections was as crazy as they come. And he paid one thousand dollars for this?

Slade cleared his throat. "Umm, no offense, but I doubt one session of sweat is going to clear up long-term problems."

"I agree," choked Trent.

Arilyn and Kate stared at him. Hard. He refused to shift his feet, even a little. No way would he be intimidated by one slip of a woman. Or two. He demolished cold-hearted jurors who judged him to be the scum of the earth without a blip.

"I understand your concerns," Arilyn answered. "I'm asking just to have an open mind and give this a chance."

"I'll do it."

Slade jerked back as Meat stepped forward. He left the circle and walked to his purple mat, lowered himself to the floor next to the crazy yellow cushion, and waited for further instruction.

Trent bit his lip and followed.

This was going to be a bad day.

No way was he wimping out. He'd do the silly stretching and report back to his sister they were all loon bugs. He hit the mat, stripped off his shirt, pulled off his socks and shoes, and turned to face them.

Bring it.

Kate grinned.

The session started easy enough. A few salutations to the sun or moon or whatever it was. Some easy push-ups. Backbends. Yeah, it was definitely hot, but his muscles actually eased a bit and the tightness from his neck leaked away. Hmm, maybe he was missing this in his normal workout. Soothing flute music drifted from the speakers and wrapped him in calm.

Then it changed.

Arilyn began transitioning into rounds of postures more quickly, and the flute music disappeared to some earthy, urban beat, automatically urging him to pick up the pace. Push-ups melted into crazy half-assed sit-ups, to plank, to backbend, and back again. Over and over, she pushed harder, until his muscles stretched and rivers of sweat trickled down his back.

Grouchiness hit. What was she doing? Why did she look so frickin' graceful and stronger than the three of them put together? Slade glanced over at his partners. Meat had his eyes closed, panting for breath as he tried to keep up, and Trent moaned and groaned in agony, trying to unstick his sweatshirt from his soaking skin, red hair flopping over his brow.

"A bit faster, gentlemen. Kate's turning the temperature to the highest setting to release all toxins. Your mind will fight you, but allow your body to surrender."

He muttered a curse under his breath and tried to ignore the quivering muscles in his biceps. He'd die before he quit. Hell, he'd melt in a pile of goo before they beat him.

"Ahhhhhh!"

A primal shout echoed through the room and jolted him out of his posture. Trent gasped, eyes wild, and ripped off his sweatshirt. Slade prepped himself for something horrible—why else wouldn't the kid strip. Maybe a third nipple? Scar tissue? But when he sneaked a look Trent looked—

Normal.

A bit lean, but nothing to stop him from going swimming or anything.

The kid seemed to have freed some inner demon, because then he surrendered to the workout, moving like a demon and making low noises that made Slade uncomfortable.

Well, at least there were two real men left in the room.

"Very good, Trent, let it all go. We're going to start holding our asanas for longer periods to really dig deep."

Oh, goody.

Meat scowled at Arilyn, and Slade figured all those muscles weren't too good for continuous, rapid stretches because his foot got stuck by his leg and didn't make it to the front of the mat. He groaned and tried to inch it forward, looking pissed off and irritated. Slade waited for the explosion, patting himself on the back that they wouldn't break him.

Kate appeared at Meat's side and whispered something in his ear. She eased his leg and placed a purple block under his hip. Meat grunted, closed his eyes, and breathed.

Slade decided to amuse himself by mentally reciting landmark cases and the court judges' briefs. His leg was on fire. So was his skin. He'd never been so uncomfortable or hot in his life, and when he glanced at the clock, he realized he'd only been in the room for fifteen minutes.

They moved out of that torturous position, where he gave a silent prayer of thanks, and Arilyn announced they'd do balancing. Piece of cake.

He'd seen warrior pose in some photos before, and it did look pretty manly. Slade followed her lead, lifting his foot and leaning forward with strength, agility, and confidence.

Then fell on his ass.

Meat and Trent didn't seem to notice. They held the pose like statues. Kate appeared by his side. "Do you need some help?"

Slade scowled. "Of course not. Mat's slippery from the heat."

"Balancing is difficult. Concentrate on your breath and relax."

He glared. Relax when he now knew what being in the center of a roaring volcano with hot lava was like? They should be arrested for torture. But he didn't say a word. Just sucked it up and redid the pose. Over. And over.

"Moving into deep backbends, gentlemen. Follow my lead. Go slow, no reaching or pushing ahead. This is not a competition."

She did something erotically graceful, bending way back and gripping her ankles. Chest up, hair streaming, he figured that was easy enough. He glanced over and saw Trent and Meat a quarter of the way there. Slade hid a smirk and went for it, pushing his back as far as it would go and grabbing his heels.

Which he couldn't find.

He toppled to the right, off balance, and fell over. Meat snickered in manly competitive code, though he pretended to be deep in the moment with his eyes closed. Trent had a proud smile on his face, his bare, gleaming chest arched in symmetry.

Bastards.

He tried it a few more times and kept falling. Usually he would've lied or faked weakness to get Kate's hands on him in any intimate way, but since it was real he was too stubborn to enjoy her touch until he got hot yoga right.

"Let's fire it back up and then cool down. Sun Salutation, Ashtanga style. And begin."

With each round, his mind roared with a bunch of emotions all mingling together in a complete mess. Anger and frustration. Physical discomfort. Ripped pride. A sense of loss. And slowly, something else.

Quiet.

The last five minutes, his body wept sweat, but his mind cleared and seemed almost . . . empty. How odd. His muscles stretched and moved to the music, beyond listening to any rational thought or yelling demand, and sank into the rhythm. As he was guided into some dead pose, lying flat on his back, wondering if he'd ever be able to walk again, a lightness flowed through his body and his breath came way deep.

For the first time in his life, a feeling he'd never experienced invaded his body and soul and mind.

Peace.

Slowly, Arilyn brought them back and they sat in a circle. Sucking down water, exhausted, he waited for some weird type of chant, probably an om, and then he was getting the hell out of Dodge.

"It's sharing time. Trent, will you go first?"

Slade choked on the water. This was going to get him a relationship? If he had an ounce of energy left, he'd tell them all exactly how nuts they really were and walk out. And he would, as soon as his calves stopped shaking.

Trent nodded. "I got so uncomfortable and crazed that my barriers seemed to break down, and all of a sudden I didn't care if anyone saw my chest. I was freed. I ripped it off, and I realized it was never important."

Arilyn smiled. "What a wonderful realization. That is exactly what I wanted you to feel in this session. You're definitely ready for the next step, right, Kate?"

Kate nodded. "I'll begin setting up some dates we spoke about."

"Does anyone want to say something to Trent about his experience?"

Meat turned to him. "Good job," he said in his low, rich rumble.

Everyone looked at Slade. He shifted slightly. "Umm, you have a good chest, dude. Be proud of it."

Trent beamed.

"And Meat? Your turn."

Meat rested his hands on his knees, deep in thought. "Everyone thinks I'm a mean person because I got these muscles and I'm black. That type of prejudice hurts me because I'm judged before I open my mouth. But during that balance pose, I realized I can only present who I am. Some people will judge, some won't, but I need to be happy with me."

Slade's mouth fell open.

Trent grinned and pounded him on the shoulder. Arilyn and Kate practically exuded kindness and love within the circle. "I'm amazed at your insights, Meat, from just one yoga session. We're all beautiful and struggle with others' opinions and concepts. You have a true yogi lying within."

Meat wiped at his eyes. "Thank you."

Slade watched in horror as four gazes were trained on him. "Slade?" Arilyn prodded gently. "Anything to share?"

Panic hit. Kate cocked her head, but a shred of cyni-cism gleamed in those baby blues. She didn't think he'd do it. She assumed he'd chicken out, rant and rave about the ridiculousness of the session, and stalk out. Anticipation hung heavy in the air, as ripe as the body odor of the men next to him.

He cleared his throat and searched madly for some-thing to top them. Something deep and sensitive and mind-boggling. Something to wipe out Kate's doubts and confirm he was open to this whole nutty experiment. He was an at-torney, for God's sake. "I felt a lot."

Silence. "Like what?" Arilyn asked gently.

He scratched his head and pushed back damp strands of hair. "I learned that being alone and pushing people away is a mistake."

Kate lifted a brow. Arilyn sighed. "Please don't say something that sounds good but isn't true. There is no judg-ment in the circle. No right or wrong. What did you actually feel during the session?"

Frustration beat in waves and simmered in his gut. They didn't believe him? Why didn't they question Meat or Trent's heartfelt stories? That's it, he was so done.

The words tumbled out of his mouth in very un-lawyer-like fashion. "Fine. I felt pissed-off, hot, sweaty, and misera-ble. I couldn't do half the poses I should, and I hated every minute."

"Better. What else?" Arilyn probed.

He let out a breath. "Ah, hell, I got nothing for you. The only thing I noticed was at the end of the session my head was empty. I'm always thinking or planning or hear this noise, and for the first time, it was quiet. Almost peaceful. But it was only a flash and then it was gone. That's it."

He tried not to sulk, which was so beneath him, but suddenly everyone smiled and nodded and Meat clapped him on the back.

"Nice work," Arilyn said. "That's what I wanted. You see, as a lawyer you're used to controlling aspects of a situation and expectations of a certain outcome. It's a part of your daily life. By ripping away that control, stripping you down just for a while, your mind surrendered and let barriers down. That flash you got was important. It was your true self dying to get out."

Her words crashed over him. He had little time to process, because everyone did a group om—at least he was right about that—and then it was over. Slade chugged the rest of his water, dragged a towel over his face, and watched while Kate chatted with Trent and Meat.

Arilyn packed up and left the studio. After a solid fist bump to regain their manhood, he watched Meat and Trent drift toward the weights, and the glass door shut behind him.

Kate dragged the mats over to the pile, her perky ass high in the air on perfect display. A wave of lust grabbed him in a chokehold, and suddenly he knew the session wasn't over.

He headed across the room.

KATE CONCENTRATED ON CLEANING up the studio so she wouldn't have to face the sweaty, irritated, gorgeously sexy client behind her. When Arilyn told her the plan, she had little faith Slade would even participate. Halfway through the grueling class, one glance at his face confirmed he'd never make it. Arilyn was wicked smart when it came to knocking down barriers. Kate had been the recipient of many of her sessions when her frustration with her stuttering caused her to shut down. Kate figured she'd get a kick out of watching Slade's confident charm slip.

Instead, he'd impressed the hell out of her.

He never quit, and his honesty in the circle was dead-on. He told the truth, after first trying to tell them what he thought they'd want to hear. She'd seen many men storm out during these sessions, not ready to go deep.

Of course, what really pissed her off was his body.

Slade Montgomery was sheer perfection.

Every muscle was lean and defined. Golden hair sprinkled over brown skin reminded her of delicious Honey Nut Cheerios, and she craved a taste. Even sweaty and irritated, he held a core center within him that told her this man knew who he was and didn't apologize. He liked to win. He liked to get what he wanted. He didn't apologize for his beliefs and never backed down from a challenge.

Her body wept, so she kept far away, careful not to touch him.

The door shut behind her and she sagged in relief. Finally. Kate dropped the last mat on the pile, pushed it neatly in the corner, and turned.

"Hi."

She jerked back. He stood before her and dominated her personal space. Hair damp and lying over his forehead, T-shirt sticking to his chest, he smelled rawly masculine and delicious instead of yucky. Damn, the man even sweats musk. How was this fair?

"H-h-hi. Thought you'd left."

"Not yet. Interesting session. Do you torture all clients equally or just ones you don't like?"

She fought the smile and tried to ease back, but there was nowhere to go. "There's no discrimination at Kinnections. You should see some of Arilyn's other sessions. You got off easy."

"She's scarier than a drill sergeant 'cause you don't see her coming."

"You did good," she admitted. Forced herself to hold his gaze, though she felt stripped and vulnerable. Her skin prickled with awareness as the heat surged between them, strangling her air.

"I held my own. Bet you lose a lot of clients forcing them into one-hundred-degree heat."

She lifted her chin a notch, but he still towered over her. Damn bare feet. "Some do. But if they're not ready to do some hard stuff in search of love, they're not meant to be with Kinnections. Relationships aren't all fluff and fun. It's tough work."

"At least you're preparing them to be strong when the divorce happens."

Ah, they were back on solid terms. She smirked. "You know, the divorce rate is actually decreasing due to couples living together for longer periods of time. Afraid you'll be out of a job with me in business?"

He threw back his head and laughed. The growly roar stroked her ears and between her legs like a rough caress. "Statistics can be manipulated to present any conclusions you'd prefer. But the simple fact is first marriages end at a rate of forty-one to fifty percent. Children of divorced parents are four times more likely to divorce, so the numbers will skyrocket. I'll end up retiring a rich man."

The verbal sparring leaked into the physical, her body sparking to life as quickly as her brain revved up. Her nipples twisted tight and poked against her Lycra tank. "If everyone lived their life by stats, or fear of taking a chance, we'd be a nation of robots. Love is the only mysterious magic in the world that gives us hope."

He studied her face, leaning in an inch. Two. "I agree. But magic is an illusion, Kate, just like love. Friendship lasts. Family. But romantic love is just a mirage—a glass of ice-cold Coca-Cola in the middle of the desert. You stumble and reach to quench the thirst, then find the glass vanishes right through your fingers."

"If you don't reach and believe in the glass, you'll die anyway."

His eyes darkened to a deep forest green. Kate froze, helpless to fight the crazy electric jolts between them, like a magnet forcing an object to cling. His husky whisper wrapped her in intimacy. "At least you die knowing the truth. On your terms."

She dug deep and rallied. "On your terms, yes. But with a cowardly pride and alone. Don't you want more than that?"

He leaned in. Kate licked her lips in typical romance novel cliché fashion as if waiting for the kiss. God, how humiliating. She fought for sanity, but her head swarmed with a cottony daze that kept her feet pinned to the ground, helpless under his spell. *He was a client. A client. A client. This was bad . . . bad . . . bad . . .*

"Why are you so innocent?"

"Why are you so hopeless?" she asked.

"Because my job taught me the truth."

"So did mine."

They stared at each other, not moving, barely breathing. Slade muttered something under his breath. She opened her mouth to stop the insanity, step away, and go back to business.

Too late.

He closed the last few inches between them, snagging her around the waist and lifting her up to meet his lips.

Snap.

Crackle.

Pop.

Like Rice Krispies gone berserk, a live jolt of electricity hit her hard, wringing a gasp from her lips. Her insides shuddered, and raw, burning heat poured through her body, lighting her up like the Rockefeller Center Christmas tree.

His fingers tightened around her waist, and his tongue dove deep between her lips, devouring her in a hungry kiss that drove every other thought from her mind except the need for more. Kate moaned under the sensual assault and reached up, stabbing her fingers into his surfer hair and twisting. The kiss devoured her whole. He tasted of coffee and mint and hot masculine need, and like a drunk, she took it all and demanded more. It went on and on, drowning her in pleasure and ratcheting up the lust and drive to get him naked, climb on top of him, and take him between her thighs, turning her into a wild animal she didn't recognize.

The door opened and a strange voice cut through the air. "Oh! Sorry, dudes, didn't know you were making out."

Kate yanked back, her whole body shaking. The charged air shimmered with electricity.

"Holy shit." Slade looked down at their broken connection. He blinked and shook his head. "What the hell was that?"

Oh. My. God.

The touch. The curse.

Him.

Kate had no time to decipher the crazy flood of emotions that pumped through her. She almost fell backward in a rushed attempt of retreat, stumbled, and madly dashed to the side when he tried to steady her. "N-n-n-no, don't touch me. T-t-t-that was a mistake."

Her words caught, tumbled, caught again. Kate scrambled for her center as her stutter grabbed hold and threatened to dominate.

"Kate, wait."

He put out his hands, palms up. A frown creased his brow, and he didn't make a move toward her, but panic reared. If he touched her one more time, she'd crumble beneath the crazy need to have him without consequence.

"I h-h-h-have to go. Let's just forget this happened."

"Kate!"

She took off and didn't look back. Scooping up her shoes, she headed through the gym barefoot, shoved her feet into her moccasins at the door, and raced to her Ford Fusion like the last survivor in a horror movie running from a serial killer.

As she pulled out of the lot, Kate realized her lifelong dream of meeting the man meant for her had just occurred. For more than four generations, the touch had bound male to female over and over without fail, confirming a true match of a love slated to last with the right man.

Until now.

Because he was the wrong man.

Six

SLADE SAT ON the sleek pewter-colored couch in Kennedy's office and tried not to scowl.

He was in a bad mood.

After the hot yoga session, he figured he was done with Kinnections' torment. Seems that he also signed to a mandatory makeover meeting, which besides getting his man card pulled, he didn't need. As a lawyer, appearance was key, and he made sure the jurors and his clients always saw a crisp, clean image. He tried to remain patient and stared moodily at Kate, who flanked Kennedy's side and looked as miserable as he felt.

The kiss haunted him.

Caught up in their banter at the gym, Slade decided to test the waters. Just once. He ached to kiss her, glean if her lips really tasted like the cotton candy he adored, and put to rest some of the crackling sexual tension.

Instead, he'd been electrocuted and shredded to pieces by a clawing hunger to have her. Mate, claim, possess. It was as if his inner caveman sprang to life and he'd sunk to an animal instinct. Her taste was like pure sugar, and once he got a sample he was afraid he'd be addicted.

He expected teasing, warm, and satisfying. He got hot sex and pure need.

They hadn't spoken since she ran away. He figured they both needed to process in order to decide the next step. Not that there would be a next step. She refused to date clients. He intended to prove her fraudulent. She said love was real, he said it was an illusion. Just because the sex would rock didn't mean any type of relationship would. He agreed it would be smarter to leave her alone, let the tension settle a bit, and move on.

But he didn't want to.

She wore her usual black, a sexy lace T-shirt, silk trousers, and those delicious spiked black boots. Her hair was pinned back today in a sophisticated twist thing that only made him long to rip out the pin and thrust his fingers in gold silk. Her no-nonsense manner and cool gaze told him her position without a word.

Get over it.

He wished he could.

When he heard about the mandatory makeover, Slade insisted Kate be there. She tried to escape by citing Kennedy as the expert, but he insisted she be present to oversee the whole thing. He needed another shot at trying to figure her out and this crazy connection thing.

"First off, don't think this is all about tweaking your appearance to make you hotter. You're pretty much already there, as you well know."

He fought off a blush as they both stared at him. "Uh, thanks. I think. So what are we doing?"

"Appearance is the first impression we give on a date. You have a public job so you need to keep a certain persona in the courtroom. But I wanted to ask you a few questions. What do you wear on a first date?"

Kennedy pursed her lips. The man in him recognized she exuded lust in her lush, sensual manner, from her full red mouth to her ripe curves. Funny, he just didn't ache to touch or taste her like the woman who stood beside her. Slade refocused and tried not to sigh at the ridiculous question. He was wasting valuable time here. "Standard stuff. Usually pants and a casual jacket and tie."

"Always a tie?"

He tamped down on his impatience. "Of course."

"Shoes?"

He tried not to roll his eyes. "Dress shoes."

"Hmm." She made a note on her pad. "How do you dress on the weekends?"

"Khakis. T-shirt. Loafers."

"Got it. Do you need the glasses to see?"

He touched the gold-rim frames. "These? Mostly reading, but I tend to wear them all the time now."

"Interesting." She scribbled something else. He tried not to crane his neck to peek. "Do you prefer certain colors?"

Slade glanced at his Cartier watch and blew out a breath. "Black, gray, and blue. Classical."

Kennedy smiled. "Thank you." She stood and walked to the far side of the room, sliding open pocket doors to reveal an enormous storage closet. As she hummed under her breath, he heard her sifting through hangers, pulling a variety of items and slinging them over her arm. He tried to catch Kate's gaze, but she pretended to study her friend's notes, refusing to look up. Frustration twisted his gut.

"Here we go. Try all these on." She dumped a pile of clothes, shoes, and belts in his lap.

Slade stared. "What's all this?"

"Your makeover. Glasses off, please."

He flung up his hand like she was a demon. "I like wearing my glasses."

"I know. You use them as a barrier to keep yourself removed and distant. Like looking out to the world through a pane of glass. If you don't need them to see, they're not needed. Hand them over."

He studied her determined expression with growing horror. They were all nuts. Maybe not legally fraudulent, but the inane things a client had to go through to get a date were unbelievable. Slade ripped them off and pushed them into her palm. "Fine."

She pointed to the right. "Changing area is over there. We'll wait."

His lips twisted in a sneer. Slade grabbed the clothes, walked out the door, and changed. With every minute that passed, his temper grew. He was a Harvard graduate, a well-respected attorney, and never had a problem getting a date. How dare they judge him? He was always open and charming on a date. He elicited information from his companion, used humor, and always listened attentively. Slade belted the jeans, shoved his feet into the shoes, and yanked on the shirt. Refusing to glance in the mirror, he marched out like a penguin on parade and simmered with temper.

"Here. Satisfied?"

Kennedy grinned like the badass she was. But it was the look in Kate's eyes that froze him to the spot.

Hunger.

He dragged in a lungful of air and drank in her expression. Eyes wide, she ate him up with her gaze, a feminine appreciation gleaming deep within ocean depths. Kennedy strolled over, adjusted his shirt collar, smoothed out some wrinkles, and turned him toward the mirror.

"Want me to tell you what I see now? I see a man who works hard but knows how to take it down a notch. A man open to the unknown, ready to be a bit vulnerable and give a bit of himself to his date. You see, Slade, I think your clothes were used as a type of armor. A suit and tie scream business dinner. Formality. But this shows your true personality and allows your date to feel as if you are as engaged as she is."

Slade almost snickered at her speech over a silly outfit. Until he saw himself in the mirror.

He looked . . . different. The dark jeans clung to his

thighs and gave him a rougher edge than his usual polished look. The shirt was black and holy mother of God—pink. Pink cuffs and a stitched collar open at the neck molded to his chest. The shirt was left loose and not tucked in. The shoes were low leather boots that he never would have tried, thinking them too European, but they gave him an understated polish yet brought it up a notch. Without his glasses, his face seemed more vulnerable, and he blinked at his image, trying to take it all in.

He never wore jeans, but they were both comfortable and gave him a freedom he didn't realize he was lacking. In some half-assed way, Kennedy was right. He did keep himself distant in a lot of ways. His thoughts flashed to Jane and the steps she may be going through.

"Did my sister go through the same process?"

Kennedy's face softened. "I meet with Jane this week. We've had plenty of sessions together, and I know her vulnerabilities. I promise you, Slade, your sister is in very good hands. I would never hurt her."

His throat tightened and he managed a nod. Somehow, someway, he actually believed her.

"What do you think, Kate?"

Slade slid his gaze to meet hers in the mirror after Kennedy's question. A low hum buzzed between them. Seconds ticked by. The tension cranked another excruciating notch, until he locked down his muscles in an effort not to grow to full staff under her heated stare.

"I think he's ready."

Her husky drawl broke the spell. Kennedy nodded in agreement. "Wear this to the mixer. I'm going to take a shopping trip with you later on in the week and make sure you have a few outfits. Of course, it's on Kinnections, part of the package experience."

"I have to go, I have a meeting. See you Friday night, Slade."

Kate hurried out of the room.

Kennedy cocked her head and studied him for a moment. "Hmm. Something tells me Friday is going to be interesting."

Slade nodded. "I'll tell you one thing. Since I signed up, I haven't been bored."

He went to change as Kennedy's laughter floated through the room.

KATE WALKED THE FLOOR of the elegant Italian restaurant, satisfied with the backdrop for Slade's first cocktail party. The back room was reserved for Kinnections and the social mixers they tended to run on Friday and Saturday nights. Cosmos boasted great food, an intimate atmosphere, and a premier wine bar. The huge brick oven wall and high counters showed the chefs at work, a fun visual for the crowds. Her boots tapped on the polished marble floors, taking in the Tuscan decorations of bold red, gold, and earthy creams. She met Kennedy halfway to the back room.

"Is he here yet?"

Kennedy shook her head. "Sorry. Hope he's not a no-show. Those suck."

Kate tried not to fume at the idea of Slade wasting all their valuable time just to refuse the main event. Her crew put everything into his counseling and makeover and picking the right women. If he didn't show up, she'd—

Well, she didn't know, but she'd come up with something really evil. The image of his kiss mocked her thoughts and screamed her a liar. She wanted to do something with him all right. Preferably naked, dirty things that shouldn't be imagined. Why, oh why, did he have to elicit the awful curse/touch? She needed to be firm tonight and not get too personal. Kate bore down and focused. She was his matchmaker and had an important job ahead of her. Find him a love match and do it quickly. "He works in Manhattan, so traffic is a mess. Let's give him fifteen more minutes."

"Got it." Kennedy leaned over the bar and winked at the chef behind the table. Her generous cleavage caused the next throw of his pizza dough to almost miss. "Hey, darlin'. Any way to get a drink around here?"

His gaze misted over. Kate watched as her friend worked her female magic to make every man before her go into idiot mode. She grabbed her arm and dragged her back. "Give him a break, Ken. Go order your drink at the bar like a normal person."

Kennedy flipped her hair in artful style and grinned. "But this is so much more fun. And that way I don't have to wait on line."

"When have you ever waited more than five seconds for a drink?"

Her lips pursed in a pout. "Never, I guess. You're no fun. I like torturing the male species. Give it a try."

Kate pulled her through the restaurant and into the private party. "Behave. You meet with Jane tomorrow, right?"

"Yes. I'm taking her to the salon for the works. I think she's ready."

"Good. And make sure to keep Slade away from her. He's nosy and wants to poke around in her love life. The last thing she needs right now."

"Hmm, I'd let him poke me anytime. Anywhere."

Kate rolled her eyes. "You never change."

"Hope not. What fun would this threesome be if all of us weren't getting any?"

She was saved from answering by the sudden appearance of the guest of honor.

The room fell into a short silence.

Holy crap. He was beyond hot. He actually wore the outfit Kennedy picked out, his jeans cupping his ass and thighs in all the right spots. The black and pink shirt gave him an air of edgy sexiness women loved, and his wavy caramel hair was a delicious shaggy mess around his head, framing those suspicious sage-green eyes. He took in the room with one sharp glance, obviously taking note of the occupants and his dates for the evening. Assessing. Commanding. Lord, he had alpha stamped all over him, and a tiny shiver bumped through her body.

The other women seemed to have the same reaction. Their gazes lit up with anticipation and roved over his figure like hungry she-wolves ready to feast.

And mate.

Kate pulled her professional demeanor around her tightly and walked up to him. "You're late," she whispered. "Why don't you come with me before I introduce you to the four women I picked."

"You're not gonna announce 'Meet my millionaire,' are you?"

She shuddered with distaste. "This is not reality TV and not Bravo. We don't lead with money here. Why, are you a millionaire?"

"Why? Do you want to know?"

Kate led him to the far corner, where the table of cocktails was already set up with various finger foods. "As long as you have a steady job you enjoy, we don't care what your profit margin is. Neither will your dates."

He snorted and eyed the table hungrily. And with more interest than he regarded the women. "Obviously, you haven't been in the real world. I'm starving—are those mini pizzas?" He ignored her clucking and dove in, filling his plate with a massive amount of food. "Can I get a beer with this? Or wine. Whatever everyone's drinking."

She crossed her arms in front of her and tried not to huff. "In case you've forgotten, this isn't the quick service dining plan. You're here to meet your potential mate."

"Right." He chewed heartily. "This portobello is amazing. Smoky and full of flavor. Perfect with the bite of gorgonzola. Funny, I've never heard of this place. Want to try one?"

"No. Let's go over the rules again, shall we?"

"No sleeping with them on the first date."

She glared. "Of course not! Now, Kennedy and I will be here to help you mingle, and if you're feeling awkward at any point, just give us a glance and we'll be by your side. We can also help guide conversation. This is your party, and we want you to feel comfortable. You'll have alone time with each of the women, and then you'll let me know at the end of the mixer who you bonded with. Then we'll set up a one-on-one date to take it further."

He bit into a mini crab cake with homemade aioli and groaned. "Best crab cake ever."

"Are you listening?"

"Yep. The more I think about it, I feel like the *Bachelor*. I don't have to break up with any of them at the end of the night, do I?"

"Funny. Can you please take this seriously? These women have taken their precious time to meet you."

"Sorry."

"Now, you'll meet Hannah, Emma, Sarah, and Ann. Each of them have the look you seem to require, steady jobs, and all the qualities you seem to admire. Are you ready for the introductions?"

"Can I have another piece of bruschetta?"

"No."

He wiped his mouth with the napkin. "Fine. I'm ready."

She pasted on a brilliant, confident smile. "Then let's go, shall we?" He reached out his hand in politeness, but she pretended to miss the gesture and marched in front of him. No touching tonight. That had disaster written all over it.

She made the introductions and fell smoothly into her role. The women all seemed to have a special quality she believed Slade was looking for, but it was Hannah whom she felt the most strongly about. With her dark good looks, curvy body, and sweet personality, she had the whole package. Her career as an accountant brought a seriousness Slade would respect. Her father was a well-known family court judge, and her mother an elementary school teacher. Satisfaction coursed through her at the immediate ease of conversation as they talked law and business. Kate retreated to the bar to keep an eye on the scene and give them the privacy needed.

She nibbled on cocktail shrimp and watched Slade work the room. She imagined his presence in court brought him a huge asset. It wasn't just the breadth of his shoulders stretched under his shirt or the grace with which he prowled from woman to woman. It wasn't even his piercing gaze or charming smile. No, his aura pulsed with sexual energy and a physical awareness to which no female was immune.

Including her.

Kate slid onto the red bar stool and grabbed a glass of Merlot. Whatever. She'd be more worried if she didn't lust after Slade Montgomery. At least her hormones were alive and kicking. She just needed to redirect them.

"And who is that gorgeous man you're panting over?"

The teasing question snapped her head. Genevieve bumped her shoulder and slid onto the stool beside her. She looked beautifully tousled in her jeans, peach sweater, and loose topknot. Kate laughed and gave her a quick hug. "You made it! I thought you were working an extra shift?"

Gen wrinkled her nose. "No, thank God. I have to pull an all-nighter tomorrow so I figured I'd grab some time to see you guys. Though I should probably be sleeping, as David says."

"Can you tempt him with sex in the on-call room like in *Grey's*?" she whispered.

"Nah, I use the on-call room to sleep. Usually because I'm dirty, smelly, and exhausted. Sex doesn't tempt me."

"Bummer."

"So, who's the hot guy?"

Kate slid her gaze back to his perfectly formed ass. She cleared her throat. "My new client. Slade Montgomery."

"Why the hell does he need Kinnections?"

"See, that's why I didn't hire you: you suck at PR. Because he doesn't have time to sort through the reams of women looking to date him."

"He's definitely into the tall brunette. How do some women get the tall gene and I get the Hobbit one?"

Kate gave her a playful shove. "You're not a Hobbit, you maniac. You're petite and gorgeous. I'd find your mate if you hadn't already."

Gen pulled her brows in a slight frown. "I'm not ready to get married, I'm still in residency. We're just experimenting."

"Right. He's perfect for you. Your father and Alexa are mad about him, and you know they never approve of anyone."

"Yeah. I guess."

Her lackluster response made Kate pause. "You are crazy about him, aren't you, Gen?"

"Hell, yes. He's got the whole package and things are going great. I just don't want to jinx it."

Kate relaxed. "I understand. Is your sidekick coming out tonight?"

"No. Wolfe said he was buried in details for the new opening of Purity. It's coming up in a few months and he's working around the clock."

Wolfe and Gen had met at NYU and clicked immediately; he was now a close family friend who ran a five-star hotel in the city. He also frequented Gen's many family get-togethers.

"No wonder you guys are a pair. Ambitious workaholics unite."

"I don't see you painting the town red either."

She ignored her friend's astute observation and decided not to listen to any more cracks about her love life. Or lack of it. Slade disengaged himself from Hannah's side and headed toward the bar. His gaze burned with purpose and focus.

Her panties dampened.

Damn him.

Gen let out a low whistle. "Umm, I'm heading toward the bar to look for Ken. Good luck."

Her friend disappeared. Slade closed the distance.

Kate wet her dry lips and looked up. "How's it going? I didn't want to interfere when it looked like you had things under control."

He studied her face, focusing on her newly wet lips. Like he was ready to dip his head and kiss the moisture from her mouth. *Focus, Kate, focus.* "I'm fine. Did I mingle enough yet?"

She raised a brow. "You're done? If you don't need any more time to pick your date, that's fine. Who did you connect with?"

"No one."

"Huh?"

"I mean, they're all very nice. Attractive. Funny. I'm quite impressed with your picks."

She cocked her head. "But you didn't connect with anyone. Do you want me to hold another mixer and give you some other choices?"

"Nah. They're good."

Irritation itched at her skin. Kate clamped down on her emotions and reminded herself he was just another difficult client. No big deal. "Okay. So who would you like to pick for your date?"

He reached around her and scooped up a glass of Merlot. "You pick."

A strange roaring echoed in her ears. "What did you just say? You want me to pick your date?"

Those massive shoulders lifted. He seemed more interested in the wine, food, and hanging with her. "Sure. You're the professional. You know what I'm looking for and probably already sense who's the best for me. Who would you pick?"

"Hannah Easton," she said quickly. "Did you have any chemistry?"

"Sure. She's smoking. And nice. Great choice—set it up." He glanced at the empty table. "Damn, I was hoping for more of those crab cakes. Think we can get some from the chef?"

Kate clenched her fingers and breathed deeply. She

suddenly felt like a cheap broker rather than a tastefully skilled matchmaker. What was really going on here? "Are you really committing yourself to this process? You don't seem enthusiastic. You need to be—"

"Open. I know. I am." He shifted his gaze, studying her with an intensity that peeled away her lying exterior and exposed her bodily truth. The masculine scents of tobacco, spice, and a hint of grapefruit hit her nostrils and affected her like she'd dropped into a Godiva factory. What was he wearing? Reminded her of the bonding scent vampires threw off when they met their soul mates in her fave series, *The Black Dagger Brotherhood*. Kate locked her knees to keep from leaning forward and taking a big whiff. And biting his neck. "You seem ready to yank my membership at any misstep." Amusement laced his tone and softened the brackets around his mouth. "Do most men you set up easily fall for the first woman they meet?"

She stiffened her spine. "No. But I don't trust you."

He leaned in another inch. "I'm a divorce lawyer and a man who's attracted to you. You'd be crazy to trust me."

His outrageous honesty and droll humor stole her smart-ass answer. "Fine. I'll set up your date with Hannah. Kinnections pays for it, but you need to check with me. No private charter planes or trips to Vegas. Keep it simple and elegant. Dinner, drinks, dancing, intimate atmospheres to get to know one another."

"Yes, coach. Do you get rid of them now or do I have to?"

She smothered a laugh. "I will. Let's go tell the lucky lady, and I'll take care of the rest."

Kate tried to slide off the stool, but her boot heel got hooked in the ring. Slade reached out automatically to help, and his hand imprint burned into her upper arm, searing right through the thin silk material of her blouse and scorching skin.

Her body exploded in a riot of messiness. The sting of energy made her push him away in a frantic attempt to make him let go. The stool teetered, and she crashed to the floor.

"What the hell was that?" His shocked look as he stared at her in a crumple of limbs bought her a few precious seconds. He made another attempt to help her up, but she scooted back on the floor with her hands in front of her. "D-d-d-don't touch me. I-I-I'm wearing f-f-fur."

His brows slammed together over a blue storm cloud. "What type of fur do you own? It's more like eel skin that gives off electrical currents. For God's sake, let me help you up."

Kate got to her knees and scrambled to her feet. Like her legs, her tongue twisted in her mouth, and her past limitations roared before her and sped up her heart. "Th-th-thank you, but I'm fine. I'm s-s-sorry."

He tilted his head and studied her face as if she were an alien experiment meant to save the earth. Kate closed her eyes and pictured a blank white screen. Peace. Harmony. She breathed, concentrating on relaxing her muscles and her lips, going back to the safe place she had created to trust herself and allow herself to speak again. When she re-opened her eyes, her pulse had steadied. Slow, with a tinge of music to keep the sounds flowing. "I apologize for that. I must stop wearing these boots before I hurt someone." She forced a light laugh. "Now, let's put that embarrassing scene behind us and say good-bye to our guests."

"Not yet."

She froze. He eased over and blocked her path with one smooth motion. Jammed his hands into his pockets and rocked back on his heels. His magnifying presence kept her still, unable to do anything else but wait. He lowered his voice to an intimate pitch.

"Same thing happened when we kissed. What's going on?"

She stuck out her chin. "Nothing. It was the fur."

"You were barefoot. So unless you wear fur underwear, you're lying." A gleam of interest lit his eyes. "Do you wear fur underwear?"

"No!"

"I rest my case."

She panicked and lost her patience. Desperate to get away and drop the subject, she hurled the words at him. "Fine, I'll tell you. I'm a witch. I cast wacky love spells on our clients, and I was practicing on you to see what I'd need to create to match you. Satisfied?"

That should do it. She'd read somewhere to wrap a little fact with a whole lot of fiction. He seemed to calculate, weigh, and judge her reaction. Her thighs quivered and moisture drenched her core. God, she loved a brainiac. Was there anything sexier than a man with a sharp mind?

"Know what scares me the most, Kate? I think some of it's accurate. You did cast some spell on me because ever since I met you, I keep dreaming of burying my face between your thighs and watching you come."

Her mouth fell open. An odd squeak emerged. "D-d-don't talk like that. Believe what you want but leave me alone. It was a strange, once-in-a-lifetime occurrence, and I don't intend to have a repeat. I need you to concentrate on your date with Hannah and move forward. There are no other options here."

Kate adjusted the buttons on her silk blouse, smoothed down her trouser pants, and turned on her heel, leaving him behind. His gaze burned into her back, but she ignored him and swore to get this whole debacle fixed.

She had no other choice left.

She needed to see her mother.

seven

SLADE WATCHED HER smoothly reject the other three women, set up the date with Hannah, and wrap up the entire mixer in a neat little bow. Normally, he'd be amused at his first foray into the love industry, but the lingering tingle in his hand distracted him.

Kate Seymour was hiding something big. And he was going to find out.

The woman intrigued him on every level. Her cool, composed appearance completely contradicted the lightning bolt her touch gave him and the obvious confusion and stutter when she was taken off guard.

Made him want to take her off guard in a variety of more . . . pleasant ways.

Like hard-core, no-holds-barred sex.

Her hips gracefully swayed, and he wrestled back his rapidly growing erection. Damn pants. How did she make them so sexy when she was all covered up? The peekaboo of her black camisole gave him a hint of delicate lace and a mouthwatering glimpse of cleavage. Then the black tuxedo jacket with the lush fur collar swung back and covered the whole thing up. The whole hide-and-seek game was starting to get him irritated.

He shouldn't have been so honest about his intention to get her naked, but the moment her skin slid over his, he exploded. As if he had no control over his body and the craving to take her. Not his smoothest moment, but he had plenty of time to recover.

He gave her credit, though. Slade expected to be underimpressed with the four choices at his mixer, but the women were everything he was looking for. Smart, funny, attractive, and independent. Weird, he didn't feel any type of physical charge, but his upcoming date with Hannah would give him a more intimate atmosphere and maybe something would emerge. Did he really want to keep chasing Kate when she didn't want to be caught? Better to try to focus on a woman who was eager to be with him and explore a possible connection. Even though he didn't believe in long-term love, an affair with a companion he enjoyed was something he missed.

But he wasn't ready to leave yet.

The ladies dispersed and Kate headed toward the bar. Slade picked up his wine and followed her. As if she sensed his stalking, she stopped short and he almost rammed into her. One arched brow rose. "Did you need something else?"

Ah, he was being officially dismissed. The humor of the situation made him want to push for more. This woman amused him with her bossiness and the way he seemed to underwhelm her. "Thought I'd hang with you for a bit. After all, it's a Friday night. Still early."

Pale pink lips tightened. "You could've continued the

mixer for longer. The women were quite impressed with you."

"At least they were. You seem to treat me like an annoyance."

Her startled jerk satisfied him. "That's ridiculous. I'm only trying to do my job."

"Excellent. Then you can babysit your new client and let me buy you a drink."

His delight at her obvious attempt to ditch him was pretty sick. Maybe he was too spoiled by women throwing themselves at him on a regular basis. She gave a cute little humph, but politeness interceded. "The drinks are free," she said grudgingly. "At least till ten. Part of the contract for holding our exclusive mixers here."

"Good deal. Another Merlot or Chardonnay?"

Kate shook her head. "Merlot."

He walked to the bar, scooped up two fresh glasses, and handed her one. He wondered if she intrigued him by her mystery. Maybe if he broke through some of that reserved demeanor, he'd realize she wasn't as interesting as he originally believed. After all, it happened to him all the time. "So, tell me a little background on Kinnections. Not many people have the guts to start a new business in this economy, especially such a risky one."

Her snort told him she wasn't buying his fishing expedition. "Hope you do better in court when you're trying to dig for information. That was pure amateur."

Slade threw up his hands in surrender. "I'm interested in your company. Sue me."

Kate chuckled. "Fine. Let's get this over with. Cross-examine me, counselor."

Anticipation charged him up. "How did you decide to launch Kinnections?"

"The three of us met in college at NYU freshman year, got assigned a group project in English together, and became close friends. We decided to room together during college and graduated together."

He shook his head. "The three hot amigas tearing it up at NYU. The poor guys must not have known what hit them."

Her eyes flashed with a memory and a bite of pain. "It was different than you think."

"How so?"

Discomfort oozed from her pores. She shifted her weight. "We didn't really fit in with the regular crowd. That's probably a big reason we bonded so quickly."

"Specifics?"

"You're not getting any."

His shark instincts flamed to life. Slade tabled the topic for a later discussion when she was off guard. "What was your degree in?"

"Business management. I always dreamed of being an entrepreneur but wasn't sure what I wanted to focus on. Arilyn graduated with a degree in counseling, and Ken in media and communications. We pursued careers for a while but found everywhere lacking. One night we got drunk on cosmopolitans and came up with this whole idea of a matchmaking agency."

"Women still drink those, huh?"

"We do." Her eyes sparkled with the memory. "We were hung over the next morning but still agreed it was the best idea we ever had. We pooled our resources, our talent, and moved forward."

He loved the gutsiness. Most grown men he knew sat around whining because they hated their jobs but were too afraid to take any risks. "Why Verily? I'd think you can make a hell of a lot more money in Manhattan."

"We didn't want to go head-to-head with some of the big names in the city. Spindel, Kelleher, and many others would blow us out of the water. Verily has the perfect mix of young, career-oriented twenty- or thirtysomething professionals. It gives us the majority of the market, introduces us to a new client base, but is still close enough to Manhattan so we can host events there and still recruit. Our focus is the twenty-five to thirty-five bracket, and we don't accept clients outside those barriers. Gives us a special niche."

He nodded. "Nice move. Here's to brilliant drunken ideas." He clicked his glass to hers, and her lips curved in a genuine smile. What was it about the angles of her face, the fall of her hair over her brow, the stubborn tilt to her chin? Separately they were nothing extraordinary. Together, they held him almost . . . spellbound.

Yeah, let's get married and have babies 'cause you like the way she looks. That'll work.

He ignored the *Ted*-type voice in his head. Somehow, he didn't get the image of a funny teddy bear. More like a gleeful devil boy with black teeth. He shuddered at his mental insanity and refocused on the conversation. "How successful have you been?"

"Ten marriages in three years. A good percentage of engagements. Not bad stats, and hopefully we'll have more good news this year."

"Divorces yet?"

She bared her teeth. "No. But if I get the call, I'll send them over. Try to leave the cynicism at home on your date with Hannah, please."

"Of course. I'm very good on first dates."

"Yes, I'm sure my challenge will be getting her not to dump you by the third. Statistically, that's when elements of a true personality begin to leak out."

"Ouch. Don't you need to believe in your clients?"

A shimmering lock of angel gold slid over her cheek. She pushed it back. "No. I just need to match you."

His gaze locked with hers. Raw heat slithered in his veins and scratched at his skin. God, he longed to back her up against the wall and kiss that haughty expression off her face. Make her moan while he slid his fingers between her thighs and torture her for mouthing off. If she shocked him again, would it be like pushing into fire? His pants tented and Slade controlled his breathing to stave off an embarrassing scene. He needed to remember why he was putting himself through this whole charade. Why hooking up with his matchmaker would be a disaster, chemistry aside.

His sister.

Prove them fraudulent and protect Jane. Though lately, the idea they were true con artists was drifting away. Lately, he'd begun to think they actually believed in this ridiculous happily-ever-after nonsense. And if they weren't straight criminals and just misguided, he had a bigger problem on his hands.

Because belief and hope in a concept that really didn't exist was neither a crime nor punishable by law.

Slade deftly changed the subject. "Are Ken and Arilyn married?"

"No."

He pondered the answer and jabbed off the cuff to try and wring out some truth. "So, if you're a witch and cast spells, how come you didn't find love for your two best friends?"

The air between them heightened. Kate gripped the wineglass so tightly he worried it would shatter within her grip. "They're not ready. I was only being facetious, counselor. Making sure you won't be able to sue me for any misguided claims such as love spells that fail."

"That's what you wanted me to think, but I still don't believe you."

She gave a delicate shrug. "That is your right."

He decided to push. "Do you light up most men you touch?"

Kate stiffened. "I don't know what you mean."

"Yes, you do. That was no regular kiss. It was something else, and you don't want to admit it."

Bingo. The distance shrank and temper lifted her chin. "Don't kiss me anymore and you won't have any problems."

"That is a problem."

"Why?"

He dropped his voice. "Because I like kissing you."

She jerked. "Trust me; I'm the complete opposite of what you need."

"How do you know what I need?"

His flirty tone seemed to piss her off. Sparks shot from ocean-blue eyes and reminded him of a tsunami of temper. "Because I interviewed you, remember? The only reason you're suddenly interested in me is some perverse masculine challenge to win me over because I don't like you."

Damn, this was more fun than his last court battle. "Why wouldn't you like me? I'm charming, successful, intelligent, and a great lover. Wanna test me out?"

Her gaze narrowed. "I know your game, Montgomery. You signed up for this thing as a joke and to keep an eye on your sister. You think you'll waltz through these dates, and I'll keep you amused while you poke at me and have your fun. But I've got news for you. I play by my own rules, and by the end of this contract, I'll rip down those neat little walls you built and show you what it's like to be in love. Real love. Not the kind of crap you play at. I'm gonna do it for two reasons. One, I'm damn good at my job."

"What's the second?"

She smiled, slow and deliberate, imitating the symbol of Eve and everything a man would give up just for a taste of a poison apple. "Because payback is a bitch."

His heart thundered at her warning, almost as if she had cast a spell on him like a hard-core gypsy. She put her glass on the bar and spun on her heel. "Where are you going?"

"Home. My party mood has disappeared and someone is waiting for me. Someone who reminds me that love and emotion are real, and not some mocking game played by arrogant lawyers."

A strange panic stirred in his gut. "You didn't tell me you were in a serious relationship! Who's waiting home for you?"

She threw him a pitying glance. "His name is Robert, and you're not worthy to say his name. Good night."

Kate stalked off and left him wondering if he'd pushed both of them too far.

Who the hell was Robert?
And why did he care?

"BABY, YOU'RE HERE!"

Kate stepped over the threshold and got smothered by

her mother's enthusiastic greeting. Strong, tanned arms wrapped around her neck and squeezed like a pumped-up boa constrictor. The familiar scents of incense and pot drifted in the air of the cozy lake house in upstate New York, luring pedestrians through the doors with a promise of pleasure.

Kate hugged her back and fought off the rest of the embrace in order to breathe. "Mom, what if you get busted by the police? For God's sake, at least close the door and windows when you smoke." Madeline Seymour laughed and shook her head in easy amusement. White-blonde hair similar to Kate's shimmered in the rays of sunlight.

"No one wants to arrest an old lady, darling. Want some? You're way too tense, I can tell from the set of your shoulders." Her mother's tall, elegant body was clad in hot pink yoga pants, halter top, and her usual bamboo beads to promote health. Her bare feet padded over the worn wooden floors toward the back of her makeshift workout/meditation/drug studio. Kate had been raised in the hippie era where free love, peace, health, and spiritual kindness are the tokens of a good life. Madeline ate only vegetarian foods, wore organic clothing, grew an herbal garden to rival Vitamin World, and held retreats at her lake bungalow for women searching for their inner Goddess. When Kate was a teenager, she'd caught sight of her mother on a harvest moon night, naked and singing with a bunch of other females around a fire. That had ended in an epic battle with tears, rage, and a vow to never talk to her mother for embarrassing her like that again.

Kate respected the philosophies her parents raised her with but hadn't dealt easily with combining the real world she craved with her mother's cringe-worthy ideals. Arilyn, of course, adored her and said Madeline was the last great hippie left in New York.

Kate shrugged out of her coat and eased onto a purple-seated cushioned chair. The Buddha statue dominated the room, with wildly painted murals on the wall to inspire relaxation and flow. "No, thanks. Sobriety is a goal of mine."

Her mother floated across the room and settled on a plump gold cushion on the floor. She hit the Remote button and the sounds of chanting monks cut abruptly off. "I just finished my yoga practice and decided to meditate before my client tonight. He's having some problems with impotency, and I thought we'd try some controversial methods. I need clarity beforehand."

Even after all these years, knowing her mother was a sex therapist still had the same affect. Sheer discomfort. Then guilt. Who wanted to think of a parent having sex, let alone with a bunch of strangers in order to help them? Besides not being able to speak clearly, she grew up trying to hide her mother's occupation from the world. "TMI, Mom," she said.

"Sorry, dear. Now, what brings you? It's been a while."

Kate squirmed. "I'm sorry; I've been so busy with Kinnections. Are you okay out here? You'd tell me if you needed anything, right?"

Madeline smiled. In her late fifties, her face glowed like a younger woman's, unlined, smooth as glass, soft as butter. Deep blue eyes lit up her face, reminding Kate of Michelle Pfeiffer, a beautiful presence most people couldn't stand to look away from. "I'm fine. Seeing someone new who's wonderful and making me happy. Are you having sex, dear?"

Kate sighed. "Sure, Mom. I'm having lots of sex, thanks for asking."

"Don't lie. You're so stopped up with emotion my skin is tingling. How many times have I told you a good orgasm is a release of toxins in both the body and mind? Did you get the vibrator I sent you last week?"

This was so not happening. No wonder she never visited. Kate fought for calm. "I got it. There are so many speeds and buttons it's taking me a while to go through the instruction manual. Umm, can we focus here?"

"Of course. Tell me the problem."

"I j-j-just had a few questions. About Dad. About the touch."

Madeline nodded in encouragement. "You can ask me anything. You know how much I loved your father and I'd never hide anything from you."

Yes. How many times had she prayed to not know certain information? Sometimes she felt as if she was born into a family she never understood or identified with until the touch had visited her and she realized she was blood. She was only fourteen when her father passed from a heart attack, and she'd been enraged at her mother's ability to move on. Until she came to understand later that it was the only way Madeline knew how to cope with the loss of her soul mate. The other men were mere distractions in a world that had seeped color and a desperate attempt to fill a void only her father managed to soothe.

For one strange instant, an image of Slade drifted past her vision. What was one of the requirements on his list for his perfect woman?

No embarrassing family secrets.

Good God, he'd go screaming for the hills of *The Sound of Music* if he got one good look at her mother and heard her history. And why the hell was she thinking of him again anyway? His date with Hannah tonight would be perfect. She'd left him a polite voicemail message asking if he needed any advice or support and he never got back to her. Obviously, he had everything under control. She just hoped he didn't break her ironclad rules and try to seduce Hannah.

"Kate? You said you had questions?"

She dragged herself back to the present and swore she wouldn't think about Slade Montgomery again. Ever. For real. "I know you used to tell me about how you connected with Dad immediately on contact. But now I want to hear specifics. Was it a gut feeling? Did you get dizzy? Or did your skin tingle?"

Madeline smiled with the memory. "Oh, no, it was much more intense than that. Your father and I went to shake hands and an electrical shock jolted us immediately. It was the strangest thing—almost like I stuck a wet finger in a socket. Benjamin Franklin's famous kite had nothing on us."

Shit.

Kate tucked her hair behind her ear and studied the whirling patterns of the bamboo floor. Just a coincidence. "After the shock, did you get a sense he was meant for you? Or was it just a physical chemistry?"

"Sure, it was sexual, but that type of buzz comes once in a lifetime. It always has for our family. Your grandmother experienced the same symptoms with your grandfather, and so on, dating back for generations. Don't worry, darling, when you feel it you'll know. There's no possibility of denying it. And when you do, it is literally the most earth-shattering sex you have ever experienced."

Kate ignored her own crazy staccato heartbeat and dove straight in. "It happened to me."

Madeline stared at her, eyes wide. Her voice dropped to an intimate whisper. "You met the one?"

No way.

Kate jumped to her feet and paced. She'd never wanted a joint so bad in her whole frickin' life. Kennedy would have a field day with this one. "No, that's the problem. He's not the one. *So* not the one. But I think it means something else that we missed. He's a client at Kinnections, and I think I'm meant to find him his soul mate. I'm convinced it's a weird third-party factor misfire."

For the first time in years, she caught a seriousness to her mother's face that caused her gut to free-fall. Why had she thought this would be simple? A quick explanation, an easy visit, and a return to her normal life? "There's never a mistake with the touch," Madeline stated firmly. "I know you've fought me on this, but it will be easier if you accept that this man is meant for you. What's wrong with him? Why do you think he couldn't be your match?"

"B-b-b-because he's everything I don't want!" The nerves rose up and choked her, strangling the free flow of words she needed as desperately as air. Kate took a breath, pictured the blank screen, and heard the faint sound of music to soften her syllables. When she spoke again, she had calmed. "He's not right for me. Once someone in our family experiences the touch, what happens if the person denies it? Or what if it's wrong? Has that ever happened?"

Madeline turned away. Studied the bright orange Buddha statue as if it could answer her question. "Well, it has happened once. Before your grandmother. A cousin of ours experienced the touch, but felt as if it was wrong. So she didn't marry him."

Finally. She stopped pacing and leaned forward. "Now we're getting somewhere. What happened?"

Her mother reached out to the small drawer with trembling fingers and slid out a joint. Kate stomped down on her disapproval and hoped breathing in the smoke would get her a contact high to calm her down. "I can't tell you."

Impatience nipped at her nerves. "What do you mean you can't tell me? You just said you'd tell me everything I asked. What's the big deal?"

Again, Madeline's eyes refused to meet hers. "It's just a rumor. You cannot deny the touch, a gift given by God. If you do, there are consequences."

A shiver raced down her spine. She felt as if she'd been dropped into a horror movie. "Mom, I don't have time for spooks. What type of consequences?"

"I don't know. I never learned the whole story of my cousin Rose. My grandmother told me it was a lesson not to deny the man meant for you."

Kate snorted. "Great, we are a bunch of witches. I'm not gonna get burned at the stake, am I?"

"Don't make fun. That was a tragic time in women's history."

"Sorry." She rubbed her temples and tried to focus. "Okay, so something bad happens if you deny the gift. I don't think I'm denying it. I think it's stopped up and I'm sensing a connection with one of our other clients."

Madeline took a hit. The smoke seemed to give her the courage needed to look up. "Be careful, darling. This is dangerous territory. No one in the family has used the gift as well as you do. You've been able to turn it into a pathway for people to meet their mates. If you deny your own fate, you don't know what you will unleash."

"Yeah, consequences we don't know or you can't tell me. Great. Thanks for the info, Mom. So, you're saying that everyone who experiences the touch for themselves just accepts it? How did you explain that to Dad? Or what if you connect with a random guy on the street? Do you chase him down, screaming if you don't get married, you'll get screwed by consequences?"

Madeline sighed. "Each situation is different. Of course, marriage doesn't happen overnight. Your father and I dated for almost a year before we married, but the connection helped open a flow between us that was vital to the relationship. Has this man pursued you? Shown any interest other than being a standard client of Kinnections? Do you have any type of relationship with this man?"

Kate remembered the way he trailed her at the bar. The way he stripped her mentally, challenged her snarkiness, and generally pissed her off. Remembered the stark beauty of his kiss, mouth to mouth, skin to skin, wringing away any rational thought except the need to be his. Was that a relationship? Or her own brand of crazy? "He's just a client," she said firmly. "Nothing more, nothing less."

Madeline nodded. "If there's no obvious flow, you should be okay."

"Define flow."

"Opportunities to see each other. Talk, share information. Each time an encounter of intimacy is formed, it makes the touch stronger and more vibrant. You never did anything other than touch, right?"

Ah, crap. "Well, we kind of kissed. But it was really quick and it'll never happen again."

Fear skittered over Madeline's features. "Was it electric? The best kiss you ever had?"

Yes.

"No," she said firmly. "It w-w-was good, but not the best." Her mother gave her *the look*. "Fine," she huffed. "It was the best kiss I ever had."

"This is very bad, Kate. Very bad."

Irritation kicked in. For goodness' sake, she didn't believe in witchery and spooks. She made a mental note to shift Slade over to Kennedy as his main contact. If she backed off, the whole thing would go away. "And if I decide to block this type of encounter?"

Her mother frowned. "You will cause the energy to be disrupted. And then cons—"

"Yeah, I know," she interrupted. "Consequences will form."

"Why is this man so wrong for you? Has he caused heartbreak to others?"

Kate eyed the joint with envy. "He's a divorce lawyer."

Her mother jerked back with sheer horror. "Oh, no! Negative energy probably invaded his entire aura. And I wished for so much more for your match," she moaned.

"He's not my match. I'm telling you it's a mistake. I'll fix it."

She sucked in a deep breath of the sweetly sick smoke and hoped she'd get a good contact high. At this point, no consequences could compete with the hell of spending more time with Slade Montgomery. He pushed too many buttons, and they were obviously wrong for each other. There must be another explanation for their connection. Her phone bleeped out Maroon 5 "Payphone" and she clicked the button.

"Yeah?"

"I need you. Now."

His voice leaked over the phone, all hot and creamy, like the favorite hot fudge and caramel sundaes she tried to avoid. Kate blinked through the smoke. "What's up? Don't tell me you're canceling your date with Hannah, that's just plain rude. And how did you get my cell number?"

He practically hissed at her through the phone. "Never mind, I'm in trouble and it's all your fault."

"I never even touched you, the baby's not mine."

"You're a real laugh riot."

Kate rolled her eyes and propped her phone up by her ear. "Listen up. Hannah canceled our date. She came down with the flu bug, was trying to make it 'cause she felt bad, but decided to pull out an hour beforehand."

"Well, that sucks, but it's not her fault. Did you re-schedule?"

"I don't care about rescheduling, I care about having a dinner date tonight."

She stretched out her legs and rested comfortably against the cushions. Her mother busied herself with pouring another cup of her Japanese tea. "Sorry, not understanding. You can't go out to dinner alone? Then order takeout."

She heard the gnash of his teeth over the line. "You're not listening to me. I need a date here, at my doorstep, in one hour. I'm about to walk into a huge business dinner where everyone has a date except me. I'm up for partnership, I need to make a good impression, and if I don't show with someone fabulous it'll take away some major points. I haven't worked this hard to screw it up now."

The true facts of his statement hit her in the gut like a sucker punch. Holy crap. His intimate, first date with Hannah was really a business function? Hot, pure anger pumped through her veins. "Wait a minute. Are you trying to tell me for your first date with Hannah you planned to drag her to a business dinner? No alone time? You expected her to dazzle your partners on your terms and used my company to do it?"

A short silence hummed. "You're twisting my words, and I have no time for this. I approached Hannah with the situation, and she agreed to help me out. Said she didn't mind at all and she handled business dinners all the time with her job and with her family background. It's not a big deal."

Her voice squeaked. "Not a big deal? Of course, Hannah said it was okay. She's sweet and always tries to help people out, but you used her just as much as you used Kinnections. Now, I'm thinking of kicking you out of our program!"

"Don't be overdramatic. Listen, you need to get here within the hour."

The phone almost dropped from her hand. "What did you say?"

"You heard me. I cannot show up alone, you arranged this date for me, and you're going to get me a replacement. Besides, it's in the contract. You don't give me this, I have legal grounds to sue."

Kate blinked. "That's an indemnity clause for a completely different reason. It states if you're not satisfied or get stood up on a date, Kinnections will find you a replacement date. It doesn't say that night!"

"Your lawyers screwed up and should've thought about it. Since the contract clause does not specify a certain time, it can be used the night of the date. I'm invoking my right to get a replacement date within the hour or I'll take you to court."

She gripped her iPhone like it was his neck. "You son of a bitch. You can't do that to me, it will never stick in court."

"Try me. You have my address on file. Wear something conservative, but pretty. And bring your A game."

"I c-c-c-can't get there in an hour! I have no time to shower, change. I have to check in with Robert."

"I can deal with an hour and a half. No more. And as for Robert, I don't care what he thinks—business is business. If he can't understand that, you should've dumped him already."

"You are a horrible person, Slade Montgomery. Pure evil. As bad as-as-as Megamind!"

His laughter rolled over the phone, hit her ears, and stroked between her thighs. "A little old, but still a great movie. My friend's kid made me watch it. And you must not have seen the whole thing. Megamind started off as the villain but he ended up the hero and saved the girl. Remember?"

"You-you-you—"

"See you later. Thanks for helping me out."

Click.

Kate stared stupidly at the screen saver picture of her, Ken, and Arilyn in front of the Kinnections sign, arms around each other, goofy smiles on their faces. Her mind sifted through the possibilities of his threat. She doubted he'd follow through, but as the owner of a company that meant the world to her, she couldn't risk it. And she had no time to begin calling random clients and begging them to meet a surly, arrogant man for a boring business dinner.

No. She had to do it.

Kate glanced at her watch, made calculations, and

crawled to her feet. "Mom, I'm sorry, I have to go. I have an emergency at Kinnections."

"Was that him, dear?"

She nodded. "Yeah, that was him. At least he confirmed once again he could never be the mate I need in my life. There's definitely something else going on, so I'm not going to worry. I'll stop by next weekend."

Madeline rose, gave her a strangling hug, and walked her to the door. "Have fun. I'll come visit you soon, I miss Robert. Oh, you forgot your purse, dear."

Her mother went back to the room and came back with her Coach bag.

"Thanks."

"Don't forget to use the vibrator to release tension and toxins!"

Kate stifled a crazed laugh. "I will, Mom."

Kate made her way to her car. She had just enough time to take care of Robert, change, and throw on some makeup. No time for shower, shaving, or primping. Of course, she showered this morning so she should be acceptable. She roared out of her mother's driveway and headed home, using every imaginable, colorful curse to describe what she thought of her pain-in-the-ass client.

eight

"YOU WERE FIVE minutes late."

Kate refused to give him a response. She stared stubbornly out the smoked-glass window of the Jaguar and watched the scenery whiz by. The Henry Hudson Parkway was gorgeous with no traffic. The massive ship, the U.S.S. *Intrepid*, dominated the port, and the water of the Hudson River threw a million points of light and flashed it back to the open blue sky. Snow-tipped mountains shimmered in the distance with an arrogant force. Usually, a night out at an exotic Brazilian buffet would've filled her with excitement. She had a good relationship with food and looked forward to trying new restaurants. But the moment he met her outside, dressed to kill in his hot designer suit that cupped his powerful thighs and ass like a lover, she realized he'd played her. Big time.

His gaze practically ate her up in all the right places, and she'd had to jump into the car before he put his hand on her. He'd turned her evening topsy-turvy, made her rush into the city, leave Robert alone for the entire night, and he acted as if it were no big deal.

"You wouldn't have sued me."

Again, his stare had literal heat and sizzle as her bare thighs tingled under the short dress. Why, oh why, had she worn this outfit? It was her go-to attire for a business/pleasure event when her usual black pantsuit wouldn't fit. But she felt more exposed than ever, with the hemline barely reaching the top of her knee, and the figure-hugging royal blue sheath emphasizing more skin than it concealed. She shifted in her seat with feigned nonchalance even as her core dampened and throbbed for the slide of his wet tongue. She'd never craved oral sex before as much as she did right now. Maybe she'd inhaled too much secondhand pot. The perfume and quick cleanup should've wiped out all evidence, but she still caught the slight traces of sweet smoke in her hair and clinging to her skin. Kate swore she'd never let her mother engage in such activities again. At least not when she was in the same room.

The devil actually grinned at her. "Probably not," he agreed. "But it wouldn't have been good business to take the chance."

She fisted her hands and held her temper. "Do you have any remorse from your actions? You ruined my Saturday evening and treated Hannah like a commodity rather than a date. Have you no shame?"

"Baby, I'm a divorce lawyer. I left shame at the door the moment I stepped through the doors at Harvard."

She sniffed. "Big Ivy school doesn't impress me. Even blond cheerleaders can get into law school there."

He sputtered. "If you're even trying to cite *Legally Blonde* to me, I will sue you. I barely made it out of that place alive, and I can assure you, there were no sorority girls there."

"Whatever." Kate gave herself a point. Seems the man was quite tender when his education was insulted. Something to remember for the future. At least he seemed to know his movies. "So, are you going to give me the rundown on the suits we need to impress?"

He eased the car toward the clogged city streets and got immediately snagged in traffic. "Bob Myers is CEO. Travis Hilton is second in command. They're the ones who make the decisions on who's going to join them in the penthouse. You'll meet their wives. My competitor, Samuel Flag, will also be there with his long-term mate. The partners are trying to decide between the two of us."

"Sounds fun. Like standing on the Department of Motor Vehicles line during lunchtime."

He tossed her a warning look. "Be warm but polite. They're known to prefer executives who get along with their wives, since they have tons of business dinners. You get along with other women, right?"

"Of course. Other than the occasional mud wrestling, I hold my own."

"Cute. I already told them you were an accountant, and they were impressed."

"Hmm, don't like the matchmaking types, do they?"

He slammed on the brakes as the car in front skidded to beat the red light. "Not a word about matchmaking—that will bury me. Your family comes from a solid line of accountants and court judges. You're now running your own business."

"This makes no sense. Why do you suddenly need to show up with a perfect date? Your coworkers must know you haven't been dating anyone steadily. You were the one who said you'd tout Kinnections if I found you a match. Did you lie?"

He gripped the wheel in a deadlock. "My word is law. I don't lie, but I screwed up. News got out that the partners want to recruit a solid family man for the job. Some crap about a divorce lawyer you can trust since he's committed in a personal relationship. I panicked, so I told them I was dating someone seriously."

"Sounds like a lie to me."

He glowered. "Since you're gonna hook me up with my future wife, it wasn't a lie. Just a foretelling of the future."

"Nice volley."

"Get me through tonight and I'll come clean later. I just need some time to impress them with my own credentials rather than some imaginary relationship they approve of. In the meantime, try to play the role of the intelligent, adoring girlfriend."

Steam billowed from her pores, but she dug her nails into her palms and the pain grounded her. "How Stepford of me. And how uncreative of this team you want to join. Is this type of stereotypical success so important to you? Do you want to create a perfect life that barely scratches the surface of messy reality?"

His lips tightened. "I deal with messiness every day, and I don't live in your world of rainbows and sunbeams. You focus on the beginning where hormones and dreams rule. I get the heartbreak and emotional riptide of kids, money, and hate. So, yeah, to answer your question, that's the exact world I want to live in. Here we are."

His words cut through her and touched deep. Kate fought the instinct to question him further. What type of childhood did he have? Were his parents divorced? She knew his ex-wife was unfaithful, but there seemed to be so much more than a simple betrayal. She opened her mouth to offer something . . . but suddenly he leaned toward her and sniffed.

"What's that smell?"

She ducked her head and grabbed her purse. "Perfume. Don't tell me your prospective partners are allergic?"

"Funny, it smells familiar."

"I've probably worn it before. Are we done with the cross, counselor?"

"Do you have a mint in that bag?"

She rolled her eyes, stuck her hand in, and caught the handle. The contents dumped out on the floor. Great. Shoving the stuff back, she handed him the roll of mints and then her fingers closed on a stick. Kate frowned, pulling it out.

And stared at a joint.

She tried to shove it back, but his sharp indrawn breath confirmed it was too late. Kate glanced over. A dangerous light gleamed in those emerald eyes. His brows slammed together. "I knew it. Holy shit, you were smoking marijuana?"

Thank you, Mom. She strove for cool, calm, and collected. Kate tossed her hair over her shoulder. "It's not mine."

The incredulous shock on his face was almost worth the humiliation. "You did not just say that to me. Are you denying possession or use?"

"Both." His gaze tore and pulled her apart, making her squirm with discomfort. How dare he judge her? "What's the matter, Mr. Goody Two-Shoes Hot Lawyer of Harvard? Never got caught on the wrong side of the law?"

His disbelieving laughter surprised her. Slade shook his head. "I don't believe I'm having this conversation. Who on earth would want to frame you with a joint?"

She shrugged. "My mother."

Kate didn't wait for his answer, opening the door and sliding out. She pulled her fake fur coat around her for warmth and teetered on her Jimmy Choo ankle-strap heels that had cost more than the coat and the dress together. Of course, she believed every businesswoman needed a good pair of designer shoes, especially on sale. Skipping the heating bill had been so worth it.

He spoke briefly with the parking attendant and strode over, pulling her to the side. Thank God, the cushion of fur blocked most of the electrical current. He stuck his nose close to her hair and took another whiff. "I'm taking you to one of the biggest dinners in my life and you're high. Is this what you do with your *Robert* on a Saturday night?"

"I told you, I'm not high and it's not mine." She clamped down on the urge to stick out her tongue. "And *Robert* is none of your business."

Frustration sparked from his gaze. A dangerous stillness settled over him, and her body roared to answer the call. A pure, sexual rush hit her hard. Her nipples pushed against the lace of her bra, and her pussy throbbed for relief. As if he sensed her reaction, he whispered his next words right by her ear. "Don't push me, Kate. Unless you want to see what happens."

Goose bumps broke out on her skin. Kate fought off the panic and pretended she was on the verge of a stuttering attack. She cleared her mind, reached down deep for composure, and breathed. When she steadied, she tipped her head up and met his gaze head-on. "I'm here to save your ass, counselor, so deal with it. Now, let's go. We're late."

She broke his grip and walked toward the restaurant. Churrascaria Riodizio was one of the most popular Brazilian buffets in the city. "Any last-minute advice before you throw me to the wolves?" she asked.

Streaks of caramel hair blew in the frigid wind and lay against his brow. His smoke-gray cashmere coat emphasized his elegant sense of style, pinning him immediately as a Wall Street broker or lawyer. She'd dated both and swore she wouldn't repeat the experience. "Be charming. And try to keep up."

Then she was inside the restaurant.

The host led them to a private back room. Kate admired the high ceilings, elegant crystal chandeliers, and massive buffet where an array of seafood chilled on ice among beautifully cut sculptures. Large parties crammed into tightly seated tables, and the roar of conversation and laughter echoed in the air. She took three steps down into a plush inner chamber where corporate met and ruled.

Showtime.

The men rose quickly to greet them, clasping her hand in firm handshakes that thankfully didn't set off any crazy electric vibes. Bob wore his distinguished gray hair cut close to the scalp, his skin well tanned. Probably from golf. He looked like a golfer. His razor-sharp gaze probed and assessed in record time, and Kate bet he'd been a literal predator in court. His commanding presence lured a jury to want to agree with the man. No wonder he was the owner.

Travis was his younger brother, and seemed a bit more

relaxed, but his lazy charm gave him a different ruthless-
ness she appreciated. Kate assumed they did a great job of
playing good cop/bad cop. She nodded her head at the
third member of the party, Samuel Flag. He seemed about
Slade's age, with reddish-brown hair, thin lips, and commanding features. His robust laugh mocked the charade of
seriousness at the table, but Kate knew he was more dangerous than maybe even Slade gave him credit for. His
gray eyes held the flat dullness of a shark's. What he wanted,
he got. And it seemed his companion felt the same. Her
red hair was lustrous and thick, and she packaged it well
with a curvy body draped in lime-green silk. She was strik-
ing but didn't overdo it, using subtle makeup, low-key jew-
elry, and demure shoes to balance her image. Like Samuel,
her probing gaze made immediate opinions and quickly
dismissed them as competition for possible partnership.
Kate smothered a laugh. She guessed she didn't own the
killer instinct that would have garnered this woman's respect. Samuel quickly introduced her as Melody, his current fiancée.

The other women seemed more welcoming. Linda and
Tanya greeted her with warm handclasps, which threw
Kate off for a few seconds. Odd, there wasn't a buzz of
chemistry confirming that they had married their soul
mates. Not even a slight tingle. She always received a jolt of
recognition when touching a married couple—or at least if
it was a true soul match. They both glanced at their hus-

bands with a deep affection and love from long-term marriage, past the point of crazed passionate encounters on the kitchen table, probably settling for the deeper emotions of the day-to-day chaos of true living. Kate bit her lip, wondering why she hadn't sensed any connection, but introductions were over and she had no time to process this new information.

She slid onto the cushioned seat, crossed her legs, and settled in for a lengthy evening.

The women already knew each other well, so Kate figured she had a long way to travel before being able to join in the group's conversation. Thankfully, this was not the life she'd have forced on her. Socializing for Kinnections was a very different thing, and she'd always hated the almost political, ruthless cliques in business, turning adults into scrambling teens looking to belong to the popular group. She forced a welcoming smile and focused her attention on the women.

The three of them smiled back, taking in her appearance and cataloguing it for future reference. Kate wondered about their reaction if she confessed the truth about being a matchmaker. Slade seemed to catch her thought and tossed her a warning look before the waiter came to take their drink orders.

Linda spoke up. "They have these wonderful signature drinks here I adore. Crushed basil with a bit of mint, it's almost like a mojito but better."

"Hmm, that sounds wonderful," she said.

"Kate doesn't drink."

The words were flung out at the table in a commanding voice that had everyone nodding as if they understood. "Too many calories, right?" Melody said.

Kate stared at his implacable face. Ah, her punishment for his belief she was higher than a kite. A giggle threatened, but she managed to smother it just in time. Did he really think he was dealing with an amateur?

"I'll have a gin and tonic. The lady will have sparkling water," Slade instructed.

She lifted her face up at the waiter and smiled sweetly. "It's a special occasion, right? I'll have one of those signature drinks, please. I'm off my diet for tonight."

Slade opened his mouth to contradict her, then quickly closed it. Round one to her. God knows, she'd need some alcohol to get her through. He jerked his head but managed to play off his irritation. Maybe this would be more fun than she thought.

"So, Kate, we hear you're an accountant. You're in tax season, now—it must be brutal," Linda said.

"Yes, I'm practically chained to my desk. Slade and I have been looking forward to this evening; we rarely get out this time of year."

Bob gave Slade a proud look. "A real power couple, huh? Ah, to be that young again with the future ahead. I remember when I started Myers, Inc., we had two offices, my brother and I, and a few clients. But we were hungry, and eventually we made a name for ourselves as the prestige firm in New York."

Linda placed a hand on her husband's shoulder and shook her head. "He always had great ambition to be the best. Fortunately, so did I."

"What do you do, Linda?" Kate asked.

"I'm a lawyer, too." Her eyes sparkled. "In fact, I'm Bob's biggest competition."

Kate grinned. "That must have been interesting after hours."

"Oh, yes, but we made it work. We both respected each other's ambition. I think couples who own their own businesses have bigger challenges, but they understand one another. They are sometimes a better fit."

Interesting. Kate wondered if that was another reason Slade was so keen on only being involved with a career woman who owned her business. She sipped her drink, enjoying the sweetness of basil, the chill of the ice, and the sting of alcohol blending together.

"What's your accounting firm called, Kate?" Travis asked.

"Kinnections."

She froze, the name slipping out too fast for her to backtrack. Travis cocked his head. "Odd name for an accounting company, isn't it?"

Slade tightened his fingers around his glass. He opened

his mouth to rescue her, but she'd always hated the formulaic princes on horseback. She preferred the princesses who slayed the damn dragons themselves. "Kind of like connect the dots to your refund. A play on words."

Everyone laughed. She took another sip. God, the drink was good. She ignored her companion's warning glance and ordered another. One more wouldn't hurt, especially with the amount of meat she was about to feast on. "Clever," Melody drawled. "And how did you two meet?"

"I needed an accountant, of course," Slade said. "Thank goodness it only took me two visits to get her to accept my dinner invitation. She's quite expensive."

"I bet she is," Samuel murmured.

Her gaze narrowed. He was sizing the two of them up, as if he sensed there was something underneath the surface of a newly dating couple. Kate sucked in a breath and vowed—no matter how much Slade pissed her off—to help him gain entrance into the inner circle for partnership. "It's like we're meant to be, isn't it, darling?" she cooed, staring up at him from under her lashes.

He quickly covered his surprise. "Yes."

"How long has it been?" Samuel asked.

"A month," Slade answered.

His brow shot up. "Thinking of going permanent so soon, Slade?" His voice rippled like an oily snake. "You always seemed to equate marriage with funerals. Or so you've said in the conference rooms."

Slade lifted a shoulder. "I never met Kate," he said simply. "One of the benefits of being older is when you finally meet the right woman, you don't need the same amount of time to figure it out. You just know."

A shudder racked her body. His words cut deep, with a need for them to be real that scared her on a gut level. What was happening to her? She acted so strangely in his presence, as if the false words that fell from his lips were real. As if they were meant for her. Kate forced a smile as the older couples nodded, as if reliving their own memories. She also noticed Samuel's features tighten. *Take that.*

Bob lifted his hand. "I'm happy for you, Slade. You know I believe my partners should have a solid family life, or the hours in the office chew you up and spit you out. And I may have good news for you, Kate. I've been looking for a new accountant. With retirement looming, I've gotten contradictory statements on IRAs versus mutual funds versus bonds. Some of my investors are telling me to buy gold instead of trusting the economy. What are you advising for your clients now?"

Kate froze. Holy shit. She didn't know a mutual fund from a checking account. She left the major math to Arilyn and her geekness, and rarely got involved with investments. Slade chuckled. "No worries, Bob. I'm sure she can give you the inner workings later. I'll talk with you about setting up an appointment."

"Sounds good. But honestly, what's your opinion on that, Kate?"

Everyone stared.

She cleared her throat. The hell with it. She tried to remember a few of Arilyn's musings on the financial world. "I've been pushing my clients toward the stock market lately. Plenty of risk factors which equal growth."

Bob frowned. "Now, that I haven't heard. I just got slammed on some cash cows, and I'm not happy about it. What are you suggesting?"

She twisted the napkin on her lap and reached for calm. "Matchmaking agencies," she burst out.

Melody leaned forward. "Like that woman on Bravo? The one with the reality TV show where she matches millionaires?"

Kate nodded. "Yes, but newer agencies are storming the market and will be the next big thing after social media."

Travis shook his head. "I took a hosing on Facebook. No more of that for me."

"Love is the biggest commodity people are searching for," Kate said. "People don't have the time to date or figure things out for themselves. Matchmaking agencies are the perfect vehicle to transcend the dating world, way beyond eHarmony and internet sites. A personalized approach is key, and very affordable. I think it's the next big thing."

"Fascinating," Bob said. "Slade, you've got a smart

woman here. I'm going to look into this first thing Monday morning, after I make an appointment to see you in the office."

Kate beamed.

HE WAS GOING TO strangle her.

Slade kept a tight grip on his calm which shook ferociously under the storm that was Kate Seymour. He ducked his head and concentrated on his meal in order to give himself a few minutes to recollect his sanity. When he called her, he realized he was taking a big chance but saw no other options. He needed a date, and she owed him. With their business relationship, he'd almost be guaranteed she'd go along with the charade without a hitch. Oh, she went along alright. He was in a shit storm of trouble on Monday.

She completely charmed everyone at the table. She wielded her razor wit and sarcasm with a polished edge of humor that his bosses adored. The women who initially stared with suspicion now seemed open and laughing. She encouraged them to ignore the calories and drink with her, and now Slade sat at a table with slightly intoxicated women. He worried Bob and Travis may think she pushed too far, but they seemed amused and delighted by their wives' too-loud conversation and revelry.

Course after course of meat was served in an endless march of vegetarian hell—pork, lamb, steak, and chicken,

all sliced lean, piping hot, and so fresh he would have
sworn the farm was in the backyard. Each customer was
given a place card, and when it was turned, the waiter
swooped in and refilled plates and drinks. Slade couldn't
believe the massive appetite Kate exhibited, consistently
roaring through plates and flipping her card so it became a
running joke at the table.

His charade had completely backfired. Instead of fighting him, Kate threw herself into the role of accountant, citing her fake famous father who ruled the courthouses, and
even promising Melody to get her out of a speeding ticket.
What the hell? How was he going to explain this week
when Bob couldn't find her office, and Melody had no idea
what court judge to go to? His temper stretched through
each course while she relaxed, ate, drank, wrecked his life,
and lied her way with enjoyment.

Yet, he wanted her.

Badly. From the moment she stepped out of the car and
glided his way with her usual frosty demeanor, he'd been
smacked between the eyes like a punch from a bad slap-
stick comedy.

She ruined him.

The legs usually hidden behind her pantsuit were
killer—all sleek muscle and length, with high sexy sandals
that had delicious straps crisscrossing up her ankle. The
simple dress did everything to be subtle, so it was the most
seductive garment to a man's gaze. The blinding blue of

draping silk fabric moved with every step, highlighting the full curve of her breasts, the swing of hip, the silhouette of her ass. Her shimmery blond hair hung pin straight with long curves of bangs that played peekaboo with her sultry eyes. She was fire and ice, hot and cold, onyx and pearl, and his dick rose to attention like a new recruit in the military saluting his commander.

He'd been targeted for seduction by much more beautiful women. Professional models, pampered socialites, and surgically enhanced actresses. His occupation, looks, and wealth cast a wide net, but never had he felt completely coldcocked as he did the first time he saw Kate. But it was so much more than looks. The moment he caught sight of her, a rocketing sexual energy flowed between them, refusing to be calmed. It was if the universe were forcing them together. Her taste haunted him: hot and sweet and melt-in-your-mouth spun sugar. Her feisty attitude challenged him, her humor entranced him, and he needed to dig deep until he solved the puzzle before him. Behind the shell was a shattering disappointment that awaited discovery. He knew it, accepted it, and still needed to pursue the path until satisfied. It was the only way to claim back his power, by reminding himself there was no such thing as perfection or a soul mate. For God's sake, she smoked pot. And she had the nerve to deny it, wrinkling her nose like he was dirt under her feet and she was the Queen of Sheba.

He loved every minute of her brashness.

Kate jerked his body inside out, but it was woven within her core. She had no idea of the sensual punch she gave out. In fact, she avoided him at all costs, not wanting to even play the game. And that intrigued him much more than anyone he'd ever met before. For the first time, he was the pursuer, and the old instincts sparked to life, hidden under layers upon layers of civility.

Own. Possess. Mate. Dominate.

Obviously, he craved the chase. So be it. Time to test her own resolve not to get involved with him, and see if he could change the verdict.

Unless the mysterious Robert became a problem.

Irritation bristled his nerves. He needed details. His gut told him they weren't living together, though she was quick to throw his name out when threatened. The idea of her sleeping with someone else made him want to howl at the moon and run around in circles. Quite primeval.

Slade laid out the rest of his plan for the evening. She may have started the game, but he was about to finish it. Her own actions of heavy drinking throughout the evening only confirmed the trap she'd now set for herself. And if Robert was up waiting for her, perhaps they'd have a chat.

Slade spoke up. "Darling, we'd better get going. It's late and I'm sure you're exhausted."

She caught his intent immediately and tossed him a cheeky grin. "I'm actually having a wonderful time. Must have caught my second wind. Another round, ladies?"

The women lifted their glasses. Slightly drunken laughter emitted from the table. Slade winked at his boss and played the man card. "As happy as I am that you're having a wonderful time, darling, I'm looking forward to getting you home. Now."

Her eyes widened slightly at his not-so-hidden meaning. Travis and Bob chuckled and shot him a knowing glance. "I think that settles it. We'll join you; I believe Slade has the right idea, ladies."

He didn't wait for Kate to gain the upper hand. With deft, economical motions, he helped her tug on her fur coat and led her out the door within the safety of his business crew. It didn't take long to say their good-byes and pick up his car from the garage. She remained silent by his side, and he took advantage of her docile manner to get her safely buckled in and headed out of the city.

"I didn't appreciate the way you ended the evening," she finally stated. Her voice held the prim tone of a purebred snob. "Your comment was quite crude."

He shook his head. "Funny, I didn't appreciate you showing up high, getting my bosses' wives drunk, and the endless stream of lies you spun at the table."

Her head jerked around. Those baby blues filled with hot anger and something else. Something he swore he'd push toward the edge to see what would finally escape. "I told you I wasn't high. And that's what you get for being a bully. Besides, I did everything you wanted. I played your respectable accountant, the doting lover, and got them to relax in the process. Too bad for you if you thought I'd be boring to boot."

"I asked you to pretend for a few hours, not live the role so my boss will be wondering where your Park Avenue office is, and Melody won't show up for court because your nonexistent father is dropping the charges."

Kate sniffed. "I was only doing what you ordered. No more, no less. Our agreement is now terminated, with your clauses fulfilled, and I don't want to hear any further threats concerning lawsuits."

He shot a glance at her. She seemed in control, but her fingers twisted in her lap like a gnarled tree branch. "Agreed. You technically held up your part of the bargain. So, how long have you and Robert been together?"

She stiffened. "A few years."

"Does he live with you?"

"I'm your matchmaker and you have no need to know about my personal life."

"Just curious. You seem worried about him being alone a lot. Does he keep you on a short leash?"

"No, I keep him on one."

"Maybe that's your problem. I wouldn't make that mistake."

She spluttered and turned a shocked gaze toward him. "You're outrageous. I wouldn't let any man control my actions, especially you. Wait a minute: you never said in our session you wanted a woman you can lead around. Have you changed your requirements? If so, I need to make some adjustments in your matches."

Ah, crap, he was officially nuts about her. The stubborn way she clung to business though her body showed all the signs of fighting her physical attraction made her even more desirable. She hunched into that fur jacket as if she could hide her hardened nipples. Instead, her rapid pulse and the way she squeezed her thighs together in punishment told him all he needed to know. "Let's just say I'd change the rules for you. You wouldn't appreciate a man to walk all over. He'd need to be strong enough to stand up to you."

He waited for her mouthy comeback, but her obvious surprise told him his words intrigued her. Would she be greedy and demanding and vocal in bed? Or would she melt into his arms and be sweetly submissive to every dark, dirty command he wanted to give her?

"W-w-w-well, we don't have to worry about that, do we? You'll reschedule your date with Hannah and give it a valid chance. No disguised business dinners. Why are we going on the bridge?"

"I'm taking you home."

"No! My car is parked at your house and I need it."

He merged onto the Tappan Zee Bridge and sped through the dark on a mission. "You've been drinking. I don't know what type of man you pegged me for, but I don't let a woman drive herself this late when she's tipsy. I'll arrange to get your car to you first thing tomorrow."

Her mouth opened, then shut. "This is out of your way. You don't know where I live."

"Of course I do. Close to Kinnections in Verily."

She bristled with indignation. "Stop nosing around in my life, counselor. You shouldn't know these things."

He dropped his voice. "I disagree. And I intend to know a hell of a lot more by the end of the evening."

She shuddered, wrapped her arms around her chest, and turned toward the window. Slade fought a smile.

They drove to her house in sulky silence. He'd done his research, and had no problem navigating the twisty streets of Verily, until he came to the edge of town close to the water. The small bungalow seemed to fit her. Even in the darkness, her home owned a slight quirkiness and strength he associated with her, with its crooked roof, cheerful yellow paint, and postage-stamp yard with a big weeping willow dominating the front.

He didn't spot another car in the driveway as he eased to the curb, but the porch and living room lights were on. "Here we go. Safe and sound."

She shot out of the car like a bullet, spilling onto the sidewalk in a tangle of limbs. "Thanks for the ride, talk tomorrow." She hurried up the front walk without a glance back.

Slade grinned. Shut the door, locked the car, and strode leisurely up the brick pathway.

She jerked her head around. "What are you doing?"

"Seeing you to the door. Can I use the bathroom, please?"

She narrowed her gaze. He wondered what those ocean-blue eyes would look like during orgasm. "There's a gas station around the corner."

He lifted a brow. "You're telling me I'm not allowed to come into your house to use the bathroom after driving you home? I'm also thirsty."

"They sell bottled water."

"Kate." Her name shot from his lips like a caress, though he intended it to sound like a warning. "Don't make me beg."

Her fingers clutched around the key and a vicious curse sailed past his ears. "Fine. Bathroom, water, and then you need to leave. I'm exhausted."

"Thank you."

She pushed the door open and he walked inside.

Slade prepared to meet an irritated man with a bad temper and a thousand questions. His adrenaline spiked, ready for a confrontation. Ready for some solid answers on the woman who was beginning to wreak havoc with his sanity. But no one greeted them. At least, no one human.

He caught sight of a blur of fur barreling forward and a joyous bark. Kate dropped to her knees, lifted out her hands, and caught the creature within her embrace. She nuzzled his ears, cooed in doggy sounds, and finally laid her forehead against the dog's as if they shared a secret, silent mental code.

Robert.

Son of a bitch.

The initial anger quickly gave way to relief. There was no one else waiting on the sidelines for her. The final obstacle melted away and left him with one conclusion that would not be denied.

Slade intended to claim her.

He studied the canine-human embrace and noticed Robert's back legs were lifeless. His launch toward his owner was completed on his belly, and his rear sagged to the ground. Half pit bull, half some weird mix. Brown, spotted, with a broken ear, homely face, and an assortment of wicked scars, including a bald patch of fur right on his chest. The exposed skin still looked raw, though he bet it had healed as well as possible. Cage fight? Car? Dog battle? The possibilities were endless.

He always had an inclination toward dogs but never had the time to pursue the interest. This one had to be a hell of a lot of work, especially for a single business owner. He pegged her for a classic, low-maintenance Lab to go running with and not a dog so obviously needy.

A strange emotion tightened his chest as he watched the raw love on her face. She was always so guarded around him. He ached to be the man who she looked at like that. Now where the hell did that thought come from?

"I'm sorry, baby," she whispered into his ear. "Are you going to be able to pee? Or am I too late? Mommy did a bad thing and stayed way too long. I should've had Shelly check in on you." With gentle, expert motions, she ran her hands down his flank, belly, and probed his bladder. "We have a shot, so let's try. Wanna go out?"

Robert barked once.

"Okay, here we go." She took out a contraption that looked like a cart, and quickly attached the straps to his body. Robert waited with dignity, staring up at him with the assessing gaze Slade had expected her live-in boyfriend to exude.

Kate rose to her feet and gave him a hard look. "Slade, this is Robert. I need to take him out. The bathroom is down the hall to your right."

In amazement, he watched the dog glide on his cart toward the yard, the wheels spinning madly where his back legs should have been. He had no idea those things had even existed, let alone see a dog use one.

Slade quickly used the bathroom, then stepped out onto the front porch and joined them. Robert seemed able to complete his business under the tree, then broke into a canter, running round and round the tree trunk. Kate's laughter echoed in the chilly wind.

"What happened to him?" he asked.

Her shoulders stiffened. "I found him half dead on the side of the road. Thrown from a car. Vet thinks he managed to crawl out of the ditch and then was hit a second time, crushing his back legs."

"And you saved him?"

She lifted her face up. The moonlight soaked her skin, illuminating it to the sheen of a pearl. Those pale pink lips pursed in the timeless symbol of a kiss. "No. We saved each other. I just helped get him the medical care he needed to stay alive. He deserved someone to believe in him."

He studied the stubborn tilt to her chin and wondered about her secrets. Why would a vibrant, beautiful woman such as her need saving? Something was locked up there he wanted to unbox. The lawyer in him screamed with the challenge of delving deeper. "Why? He wasn't your dog in the first place, right? Didn't the vet suggest you put him to sleep with those types of extensive injuries?"

The barriers dissipated as red-hot anger flared to life. She leaned in, her white-gold hair a hellish halo around her head. "Putting him down would have been the easy road, right? No medical bills, no responsibility, and no mess. Maybe people deserve more than what's easy. Maybe there are too many imperfect people out there, with disabilities and problems no normal, sane individual would ever want to take on." Her eyes glittered, and her pale skin flushed. Her voice trembled with the depth of her emotions. "But maybe we'd be worth a chance. When I looked into Robert's eyes, I saw more than a dog with a disability. I saw a beautiful spirit who needed someone to give him a chance, who'd been heartbroken so many times in the past but had enough courage to take a shot on me. He was willing to try one last time and trust me." She blinked as if fighting tears. "I didn't care about the money or the time or the sacrifice. Because what I got back was so much more. You don't need to be thrown away if you're partially broken. Robert made me believe again, and I don't care how stupid you think I sound."

Slade locked down on every impulse burning through his body to yank her into his arms and kiss her. To once again feel the burn of her skin, the softness of her mouth, the muskiness of her scent. He was humbled at the gift she'd given without any knowledge. Another layer shifted, settled, and revealed a piece of her inner core. This woman fought for what, and who, she believed in. She was a fierce mama bear who protected her dog and believed in the goodness of a soul. Her magnificence floored him, but she needed time to process what she'd admitted. And he needed time to regain his balance.

"I don't think you're stupid," he said softly. "I think Robert's gift in this life was meeting you. I think he's a lucky son of a bitch."

A flicker of surprise lit her eyes. She paused for a moment before speaking. "He is technically a son of a bitch, isn't he?"

"Funny." He tugged at a stray lock of her hair. "Can I

have that bottle of water now or are you kicking me to the curb?"

Her lip quirked. "One bottle."

The wheels whirred as Robert followed them inside. Kate removed the cart, freshened his water, and turned. "Bacon or peanut butter?"

Robert barked twice.

"Ah, a change-up tonight. Good choice." She plucked a peanut butter dog treat out of the bag and gave it to him. With a gentle motion like he took it from a baby, Robert closed his teeth around the treat and dragged his legs behind him to settle on the woven mat.

"Did he really understand you?" Slade asked.

"Sure. I ask him questions all the time. We have a code; one or two barks will be his choice." She opened the refrigerator and gave Slade a chilled bottle of Poland Spring. "It's a long drive back."

He took a long swallow, wiped his mouth, and grinned. "I know. Mind if I sit for a few? I'm tired. Wouldn't want to endanger my life and fall asleep at the wheel."

She snorted. "You're good. Maybe if you use that famous charm on Hannah you'll end up in a serious relationship. In love. Happy."

"Maybe. You called me hot in the car. Now you admit I have charm, huh?"

She blew out a breath, grabbed a bottle of water for herself, and headed into the living room. Slade followed and noted the character inside the house matched the outside. It was small, but held a cheery yellow love seat, worn recliner, massive entertainment center, and braided throw rugs over cherry hardwood floors. The curtains were delicate lace, and colorful artwork adorned the walls. One bookcase took up an entire wall from ceiling to floor. Piles of books fought for space with framed photos, strange ceramic vases, and an assortment of tiny full-bellied Buddhas.

Slade tried to be casual as he wandered toward the bookcase, intrigued by her reading habits. Damn, her DVD collection was respectable, with a bunch of comedies slanted more toward males, and some great HBO history series. "I like your place."

She remained standing at a respectable distance. "Thanks. It suits us. Why are you still here?"

He cocked his head. "Why are you always trying to get rid of me?"

Kate seemed to choose her words carefully, "Because I don't want you to get any ideas. About us. My job is to find you a satisfying, fulfilling relationship with someone else. I don't want you to lose sight of the goal."

He took a step forward. "What if I told you I have my goal clearly in sight?"

The connection between them surged like a live current. The air thickened, and she seemed to struggle for breath. She threw her hands out like she attempted to ward off a stalker. "N-n-no. This is one big test you set me up to fail. You want to expose me as a con artist, remember? You intend to save your sister from my evil clutches. Fine. But you have to prove my intentions, and so far you've been quite lousy at living up to your part of the contract. Seducing me is only a way for you to show Kinnections doesn't work. You're a master mind gamer and I'm not about to be your next victim."

He should have been mad by the insults. Instead, he had the craziest urge to laugh and lunge at her. Slade paused in his approach to give her a moment to settle. "Not giving yourself much credit, are you? What if I told you I don't want to keep ignoring the attraction between us? Why set me up with another woman when we may be good for each other?"

Her eyes widened in pure horror. "W-w-we're complete opposites. Unsuited for any type of long-term relationship. Trust me, I saw your requirements, and I'll never fit the bill. Besides, I told you over and over I don't date clients."

"Funny, I think we fit rather well. And as much as I respect your business principles, I think this thing between us is getting in the way of me finding the right mate. I'm blocked and I need your help."

Her mouth opened, then closed on an outraged squeak. "I may be the typical blonde, but I've been around the block a few times. And that doesn't mean sleeping around.

More like a ton of men trying to sell me the Brooklyn Bridge by assuming I'm stupid."

"I'd never insult your intelligence, Kate, and you know it. We have a problem that can be easily solved. We're attracted to each other, so how can I have an open heart with Hannah or any other woman if I'm stuck on you?"

"I'm n-n-not attracted to you!"

Her rock-solid composure was finally shot. Slade enjoyed a moment of satisfaction before his closing argument. "Lie. I bet if I put my hand on you—in you—I could get you to shatter in minutes."

"Arrogant lawyer."

"Confident. Maybe if you didn't electrocute me when we kissed, I'd believe you."

She remained stubbornly silent. Slade eased in another step, not taking his gaze from her face. Her breathing had turned to short little pants, as if imagining what he would do once he closed in. He vowed she'd find out. "Did you ever think why you felt the need to deceive me with Robert? I'm a bit embarrassed I fell for the old trick. Very cliché. Almost like believing a woman is a man by her nickname. But you obviously felt the need to protect yourself from me. Why?"

She seemed to simmer with pent-up temper. "I like my privacy, and you were poking around in my life too much. You're a client. No more, no less."

"Another lie. You're scared to be alone with me, but

this fear is getting in the way of business. We're two grown adults with a strong sexual attraction. Let's spend the night together. You say we're not suited for long-term. Fine. But don't we owe it to each other to try?"

Her gasp broke through the room. Robert lifted his head, studied them both, then dropped back to the mat. "Are you propositioning me for a one-night stand? Sorry, counselor, I'm not interested, though the argument was well presented."

He pitched his voice low and eased in another step. "Aren't you tired of running? No one gets hurt and all we gain is pleasure. And I promise you great pleasure, Kate. I'm not a selfish lover."

"So says every man on the planet," she sneered.

"I'll enjoy backing up my words with actions."

She shook her head and let out a strangled laugh. "How about I just take your word for it? My job is to find you a long-term mate, and I intend to do it. I'd like you to leave my house and we'll agree to wipe this whole conversation from our minds."

Slade gathered his forces and made a risky decision. Retreat with the idea firmly planted in her mind? Or push the physical connection so she couldn't deny it? A delicate balance was in play and the wrong move could lose his case.

He made his decision.

He placed the water bottle on the table, drew himself

up to full height, and slowly closed the distance between them.

She stood her ground to the last minute when panic seemed to hit. Eyes wide at his obvious intention, she hurriedly stepped back until her back hit the wall and it was too late.

"I don't want to forget this conversation," he said softly. He moved slow and deliberate, reaching out to calmly stroke her hair, enjoying the way the silky strands lifted and jumped under his touch. He used his voice to wrap her in a cozy blanket of security.

"Don't t-t-touch me."

"You're not afraid of me, are you, Kate?"

She lifted her chin and spat the words out. "Don't be ridiculous. I've dealt with bigger snakes than you."

His lips quirked and he kept stroking her hair with gentle motions. "Good. I don't want your fear. I can't seem to get you out of my head. I keep thinking about that kiss. Have you thought about it?"

"No."

"I have. Every single night. Wanting more."

She gave a tiny moan and seemed to try and muster the energy to fight him. Slade didn't give her the opportunity. He placed both hands on her bare arms in a firm grip so there was no barrier between flesh to flesh.

And then it happened.

Slade expected a slight tingle, but the explosion between them rocked his sanity. Burning heat raced through his palms and burst in his gut, as if the simple touch set off a crazy array of currents that blazed one by one. Her slight cry told him she felt it too, and immediately his brain shut down in a raw urge to arouse, possess, pleasure. His dick swelled to full staff and the blood thickened in his veins, driving every rational thought from his head.

This time, he was prepared. This time, he let the energy take hold and flow through every cell. Her scent swamped him, a delicious hint of sugar and musk that rose to his nostrils and made him want to stamp and snort like a Thoroughbred about to mate. Those gorgeous blue eyes darkened, and her pale pink lips opened as she fought for air, the stab of her nipples tempting him through the delicate silk. Her body shook and trembled, but he already knew it wasn't fear, but the knowledge she couldn't hide any longer.

"No," she moaned, in one last attempt to deny him.

He lowered his mouth and stopped inches from hers.

"Yes. Oh, yes."

HIS LIPS COVERED HERS.

Kate drowned. From the first sizzling touch, everything she'd been fighting to believe, to understand, fizzled away. She was ripped to the bare bones of a shaking need and lust that refused to be sated.

His mouth was the perfect combination of delicious

heat and greed that devoured hers. She opened for him without hesitation, and his tongue swept inside to take it all. He tasted of mint and cognac and chocolate. He used his teeth to nip at her bottom lip, soothed with his tongue, and dove deep to uncover every hidden secret she tried to hide.

Kate clutched at him, digging her nails into his shoulders, and he pressed his body against hers for full contact. She groaned with sheer relief, needing his firm strength to hold her up as her knees gave out. His hips cradled hers, his erection notched between her thighs, and a rush of liquid warmth pulsed between her legs. She tried to shift to get closer, to ease the empty ache that was slowly tearing her apart.

She'd been with other men on various physical scales. She may be a technical virgin, but considered herself adept in all the ways of lovemaking and foreplay, engaging in creative and intimate ways to satisfy one another. But never had she been completely overtaken by a fierce lust to mate: to rip off her clothes, climb on top, and bury his cock deep inside her wet channel. He feasted on her lips, then trailed downward to lick and bite her neck while his fingers worked up the hem of her dress to her waist. Kate thrashed her head from side to side, hitting the wall, not able to verbalize the reactions her body was experiencing. As if he knew, Slade cut through any conversation with pure action. Her dress hit her hips, and he jacked her up higher against the wall, hooking her leg high on his hip so she was spread open. His hands quickly reached around to unzip her dress until the front fell forward, exposing her black lace bra. His warm palm cupped the weight, rolling the nipple around and around, then gently pinching it between his thumb and forefinger as he watched her face.

"Oh, God!" The twist of pleasure/pain shot straight to her pussy. Her skin tightened and her breasts swelled, demanding more of him, everything he could give in every capacity he could give it to her. Slade lowered his mouth and licked her nipple through the rough lace, pulling the fabric taut so the hard tip rubbed and poked against the barrier. He never let up the frantic pace, as if driven by the same crazed lust she experienced. His fingers trailed along her inner thigh in a sensual threat that covered her skin in goose bumps.

"No more lies." The front clasp of her bra clicked open and her breasts sprang free. Cool air rushed over her prickling skin, and Kate let out a cry of relief, arching against him for more of his delicious tongue and teeth. "Tell me you want me. Now."

He sucked on her nipple, and his fingers danced over the thin fabric of black panties. She dripped with need, her clit so swollen Kate thought the slightest rub would set her off to orgasm. What was she doing? Dear God, he was a client, and all wrong for her. She fought off her body's reaction with a fierceness of sheer survival, knowing if he dipped her under the seething surface of sex she'd never come up for air again. Hell, she'd never want to.

"We can't do this," she moaned, at the same time another shudder racked through her. His index finger traced the swollen mound, playing with the edge of elastic that held all her secrets. "It will complicate everything. Let's talk about this like rational businesspeople."

His soft laugh hit her ears the exact time his hot breath streamed over her aching, swollen nipple. "I'm not doing my job if you're still talking business." He lifted his head and gazed directly into her eyes.

She sank into emerald depths so hot they turned to molten gold, full of power and masculine demand that battled past all barriers and smashed them to pieces. The raw need carved in his features told Kate she was past the point of no return, that this man was meant to claim her, all of her. She sucked in her breath, poised on the pinnacle of a massive change that terrified her to the core. "From the moment we met, I've been imagining your face when you come, my fingers inside you, my tongue in your mouth, my dick buried so tight in your heat we don't know where one of us ends and the other begins. I'm tired of being denied you. Now, come for me, Kate, show me what you've been hiding from me all this time."

She stared with helpless fascination, entranced by his voice and his words, and then his mouth crashed over hers and his fingers hooked under her panties and plunged.

He swallowed her cries, refusing to let her fight her response, using his body as a weapon to get her to give him everything he commanded. His thumb rubbed her swollen clit the same time his fingers thrust inside her clenching channel. His tongue battled hers, won, and claimed his bounty while his hips rocked back and forth, the dueling rhythm of his body and his dick and his fingers pushing her fast toward the edge until—

Kate screamed as the orgasm took hold, pleasure shattering in waves and breaking her into tiny pieces. He whispered her name in triumph, helping her ride out the orgasm to the maximum effect, gentling his touch but coaxing every last shudder as she slumped against the wall in complete surrender.

He nibbled on her swollen lips, pressing kisses across the line of her jaw and her neck. His arms held her tight and she felt wrapped in a cocoon of warmth and security, as if her body sensed he'd keep her safe, hold her, take care of her in a way no other man before him could ever attain. Kate let the odd thought flow past her, too far gone to even worry about the eventual fallout when her brain clicked back on.

"Magnificent," he murmured in her ear. "I could watch you orgasm for hours, challenging myself to bring you to climax in a thousand different ways." His erection pressed against the damp barrier of her panties. "I want to take you to bed and fuck you so many times you forget every man before me. That's how crazy you make me, Kate Seymour."

"Yes." She held on tight and gave him what he wanted. "Yes."

He let out a vicious curse. His jaw clenched, and he seemed to lock down every muscle, as if fighting for control. "But not tonight."

She blinked, trying to cut away the fog. "Why?"

He pressed his forehead to hers like she did so many times with Robert. The intimacy and tenderness of the gesture startled her. "Because I want more. And you're not ready for that tonight. I needed to show you what we can be together in bed, but you have to come to me, Kate. I have to know you want it just as bad as I do. And I don't want you calling foul play in the morning when you can hide behind alcohol, or exhaustion, or my dominance."

She managed to find her voice, but the words came out a bit slurred. "I make no excuses for my choices, counselor. Get over yourself."

He chuckled and took her mouth in a quick, bruising kiss. "I like the way you make *counselor* sound like a dirty word. I may make you beg with my title rather than my name. Would be an interesting battle."

The idea of the sensual challenge racked a delicate shudder, but she managed to sneer "Like that will ever happen."

"Oh, it will."

"Are you offering one night together? A relationship? What do you think this can be?"

He cupped her chin. "They're just silly terms to try to make sense out of human emotions that are uncontrollable. Affair, relationship, one-night stand. Pick a tag that makes you happy. But soon, Kate. I don't think I can wait much longer."

He didn't give her a chance to respond. Just eased her gently back to her feet, and walked out of the living room without a glance back.

nine

KATE ORDERED ANOTHER café mocha and kept a close eye on the corner table. The eclectic café was a popular place to meet friends and potential mates, and perfect for Jane's first two official dates. Adele crooned from the speakers, and the scents of coconut and chocolate drifted around her in puffs of steam. The battered oak coffee bar and mismatched tables cluttered the small space but gave it a cozy feel. It was known for its bakery goodies, and patrons feasted on buttery scones and decadent cupcakes and sipped a variety of brews, from holistic and organic, to calorie-induced sweet shakes to court cavities and false energy. Decorated in bright yellows and greens, the café was where local artists displayed their works on canvas to sell, so Kate's vision always blurred a bit from the vivid and odd collection of colors. Still, it was another part of the reason she wanted to settle in Verily. There were no outsiders here, because everyone belonged. She'd spent most of her life trying to hide and not speak, terrified of being laughed at and feeling completely isolated from the human race for too many years. Verily wrapped her in acceptance and forced her to mingle with all types of people. She'd grown so much here and was now completely happy with herself, who she was, and where she was going.

Well. Kind of.

The image of Slade flickered past her vision. Damn him. One full week since their episode, and he took her lead with a politeness that pissed her off. He was right to leave. When she woke in the morning, she blamed the kiss and her temporary physical weakness on a bunch of factors. If they'd spent the night together, she would've regretted her actions and probably blamed him out of her own crippling guilt.

Kate glanced down at her chic black-and-rhinestone watch. He'd be getting ready for his date with Hannah. She decided to put the incident behind them. After all, they'd both been curious, especially with the strange connection they shared. Kate figured she'd reschedule his date with Hannah and get him back on track. Of course, when she contacted him, all crisp and businesslike, he'd readily agreed and refused to even mention Saturday night. Like he'd never wrung an orgasm from her body, or whispered naughty things in her ear, or kissed her like he was starving and she was the only thing standing behind survival and death.

Over it. She was so over it.

She sipped the chocolaty brew and motioned over to Kennedy when she finally strode through the door. "Hey, babe. How's our girl doing?" Ken gave a subtle glance in Jane's direction. Slade's sister now sat with a bit more confidence, her gestures less jerky and nervous after the weeks of training under Ken's and Arilyn's hands.

"I'm so proud of her," Kate said. "She seems to be more secure within herself."

Ken shrugged out of her leather jacket, slid onto the stool, and ordered an espresso. "It was a brilliant move to pick out only two dates for her. She'd never be comfortable with a mixer, and she needs one-to-one contact."

"Yes, dinner would be too intense. I want her to have fun, not scare her the first round. Brian and Tim are the right choices."

"Is Tim next?"

"Yes, she has a few more minutes with Brian, a break, and then Tim. This way she'll get a better idea which man she's more attracted to."

"Hmm, well, I knew looks weren't her problem anyway. Funny, I think she's more beautiful than the obvious choices because of her simplicity. Her bone structure and skin are amazing. Another reason I love a good makeover. It proves over and over there's nothing wrong with us, just the choices we make to flatter what we own." A darkness flashed in her friend's eyes, then quickly disappeared.

Kate reached out and squeezed her hand. "You were always beautiful, Ken. Inside and out. Anyone who told you different is an asshole."

Ken laughed. "You're good for my ego, babe. Right back atcha."

"Thanks. Hmm, good body language between them. This may warrant another date. Without us as chaperones."

"Or you can just give them a quick touch and see if they're meant to be." Kennedy grinned. "You may call it cheating. I call it good business."

Uneasiness slithered in her gut. She tapped the edge of her cup in a random rhythm. No way was she about to confess her temporary loss of her gift that Kinnections was based on. It would only freak her friends out, and be harder for her to ignore the looming knowledge something was definitely off. Other than the explosion with Slade, she couldn't seem to even scare up a tingle, whether she was near a couple who was married or dating. Sweat prickled her brow, but she kept her tone light. "Sorry, no breaking the rules. If Kinnections is going to be a solid success, we base it on scientific research, hard work, and instincts. Not some magic witch spell I inherited."

"Fine. Just trying to speed things along. Speaking of Kinnections, how's it going with Slade? Are he and Hannah an item yet?"

Her fingers squeezed around the handle as a shot of rage licked her veins at the thought of Slade with Hannah. Kate cleared her throat. "Not yet. They had to cancel their date last weekend, but they're seeing each other tonight." She refused to blurt out the truth regarding their impromptu date and resulting kiss. At least, not yet. Her friends seemed to own an innate talent to pry every secret from her grasp, so it was just a matter of delay.

"Interesting. Why don't you seem excited about the possibility of matching him?"

She narrowed her gaze at her friend's obvious glee. "Don't start, Ken. I don't need any misinformed match-maker forcing us together for good intentions. I'm attracted to him, but it's strictly physical. Emotionally, I know he's all wrong for me, and I'm grown-up enough to recognize the limitations and move past them. I want a soul mate, not a temporary bedmate."

Kennedy clucked her tongue. "Pity. I'd take him as a bedmate any night. What'd your mom say about the touch thing between you guys?"

Kate prayed for forgiveness. Not lying to her best friend was one of her own personal ten commandments. "She didn't seem concerned. No worries."

"Good. Did you get me some good pot? Your mom has the best."

She rolled her eyes and laughed. "No. Now don't mention drugs, Jane's coming." They watched as Brian rose from the table, put his arms around Jane, and gave her a quick, intimate hug good-bye. Kate studied their interaction, noting the close body language, the open facial expressions, and the relaxed muscles. A solid match, one best suited for a more intimate date to see if a physical attraction could grow. Jane looked so different from the last time she had seen her. The ill-fitting clothes had been replaced by a pair of snug jeans, high-heeled boots, and a rich gold sweater that brightened up her face. Comfortable but fresh. Her normally curly hair had been tamed to fall into luscious waves and flirted with a pair of gold hoop earrings. Stained red lips was her only makeup, bringing a man's gaze to her mouth. The old glasses had been thrown away for a pair of trendy Coach tortoiseshells, giving her the sexy librarian look men died for. Brian whispered something in her ear, and Jane laughed, then turned and strode toward the coffee bar.

They waited until Brian was safely down the street and away from view.

Ken grinned like a proud mama bear. "Girlfriend, you rocked that date. Tell us everything."

Kate nudged her. "Anything you feel comfortable telling," she corrected. "Did us being here help or hinder the date?"

Jane's normally serious face broke into a smile. "Helped. I hope it wasn't dumb to ask you to be here. I hated to think Brian thought I couldn't handle a simple date by myself, but I just wanted to know you were here in the room. Some crazy reverse sort of Cyrano, but just silent."

Kate patted her arm. "No, many of our clients ask us to stay. And it's not dumb. The key is to make sure you're comfortable and relaxed in the environment so you can let go and really see if you have something together. Did you like him?"

Red bloomed over her cheeks. "Yes. We had a lot in common. He met my eyes when we spoke, and he seemed interested in my career and research."

"We thought since he taught poetry you both would have an immediate conversation topic. We still have a few minutes before Tim gets here. Here, I ordered some biscotti—let's share."

Kate bit into the honey-almond cookie, enjoying the crusty texture contrasting with the sweetness, a delicious combination of hard and soft that made biscotti her go-to snack to offset her coffee addiction.

"What happens if they don't like me?" Jane asked.

"Then you're not right for each other," Kennedy answered. "Remember what we spoke about? Just because a man isn't attracted to you doesn't mean you're unworthy of him. It's a give-and-take—the same elements work in a woman's favor. We do our best to pick the best suited and wait to see if anything takes root."

Kate nodded. "This isn't a sprint, it's a marathon. Too many women get so stuck on one rejection that it ruins their confidence and blurs the vision of a man who may be right beside you."

Jane sighed. "You're right. I suck at this."

Kate snapped a biscotti in half and slid it over. "You're new at this, Jane. We all have issues and hang-ups. We created Kinnections because we realized women should be having a lot more fun finding Mr. Right. Why be miserable during the journey?"

Jane pondered the thought, studying her fingers as her brain clicked away. Kate enjoyed Jane's company. Once she let go of her expectations of what society wanted her to act like, her natural intelligence and charm shone through. Kate wondered why Slade was so overprotective. Curiosity simmered within, and she fought the temptation to casually ask questions about her brother. She ached to know more about his childhood. Other than his ex-wife, had there been others who ruined his ability to trust? Arilyn counseled Jane on her past, but Kate never liked to probe just for curiosity's sake. They each had a role in Kinnections and tried not to overstep boundaries just because of their friendship. What Jane confessed to Arilyn was deeply personal and private.

Kate glanced at her watch again. Yes, they'd be at an early dinner now. Probably sipping cocktails while they waited for their table. Would he obey and wear a more casual outfit like they counseled? Would he rush the date to get more intimate, or enjoy her at leisure, unveiling each of Hannah's layers like removing tissue paper from an expensive gift? Would he even think about the kiss they shared or had he easily gotten over it?

"Earth to Kate? What's up? You look weird."

She shook her head and refocused. "Sorry, just tired."

"More like distracted." Her friend studied her face. "I

have a great idea. Why don't we all go out tonight? A girls' thing. We'll talk about men, drink cocktails, and wear ridiculous high heels. And dancing. Definitely dancing."

Usually Kate craved her remote, Robert, and her pjs on a Friday night. But the thought of Slade with Hannah could torture her this evening. Getting out of the house and being distracted would be the best thing. Jane looked surprised at the invitation.

"Uh, you guys don't have to include me to be polite. I have to work on my research."

"No work tonight, for any of us. You're coming with us, right, Kate?"

Kate gave Jane a smile. "Absolutely. We'll have fun, I need a night out. I'll text Genevieve, and you text Arilyn. We'll meet at The Grille for dinner and then go dancing at Mugs. Deal?"

Jane lit up. Odd, it was almost as if she didn't have the opportunity to socialize too much. Probably like her, Jane had become used to being alone, and it was hard to break the habit. "Okay, thanks for inviting me."

Tim walked through the door and glanced around. "Here's bachelor number two. Are you ready?"

Jane took a deep breath, adjusted her sweater, and nodded. "Yes. I can do this."

"Remember: be yourself. Relax. He's not scary, just an alien of the opposite sex that we'll never understand but must learn how to accept and mate with."

Jane laughed at Kennedy's remark and strode over to

Tim. Kate watched as they introduced themselves, then sat at the same table to share conversation. She was tempted to walk close enough to see if she got a tingle of awareness but besides cheating, Kate was afraid there wouldn't even be a crackle. And that would only depress her.

"If we're going out tonight, I need to head back to Kinnections, then get home to Robert. Can you handle this by yourself?" she asked.

Kennedy waved her purple-tinted nails in the air. "Of course. Wear something slutty tonight. If you keep insisting you don't want to hook up with Mr. Electricity, then you need to find someone else. I swear if you hit thirty without losing it, Kate, I'll hire a gigolo for you."

Kate sputtered a laugh. "Stop threatening me. I promise to dress like a tramp if you'll get off my case."

"Done. I want to see lots of skin."

Kate stuck out her tongue, grabbed her purse, and headed out.

SLADE SMILED AT THE exquisite woman across the table from him. He had to admit, Kate had hit all the facets he always desired in a woman. Besides her physical attractiveness, Hannah Easton was an accomplished businesswoman. Intelligent, successful, with a kind of humor he enjoyed and admired. If he drafted up all the qualities of his perfect mate, Hannah's photo would be right beside it.

Except . . .

He didn't want her. Didn't crave to back her up against the wall, lift her skirt, and bury his fingers between her thighs. He didn't want to devour her mouth, suck on that lower lip, and bask in the husky moans he ripped from her throat. She didn't piss him off, turn him inside out, and make his soul shake with need.

Ah, crap.

Hannah offered to pay part of the bill, which he quickly squashed. As they walked out of the restaurant, he took her elbow to guide her over the slick sidewalks. Not even a slight tingle of awareness between them. He distantly appreciated every quality she could bring into a relationship, but knew he wasn't the man for her. Should he tell her now? Wait to break the news to Kate? He hated this part. No wonder he despised dating.

He stopped at her car. She tilted her head, staring up at him with an eager anticipation in her pretty brown eyes. For a kiss? He avoided the whole trap by moving fast. Slade swooped down, kissed her on the cheek, and took a step back. "It was lovely meeting you, Hannah. I had a wonderful time with you tonight, thank you."

She blinked. "Oh. Yes, I did too, Slade. Hopefully, we'll see each other again."

He nodded like a dimwit, desperate for escape. The big bad millionaire lawyer scared of hurting a woman. He was such a dweeb. "Yeah, I'm sure we will. Drive safe. And thanks again."

He stumbled away and headed toward the parking garage, cursing Kate and Kinnections and his damn hormones the whole way. He hated disappointing a sweet woman, but better now than leading her on later. He wondered if he would've been attracted to her if he'd never met Kate. Not that it mattered. He was a goner.

The idea of one night in her bed seared his brain and his dick. If he could just spend hours with her naked, he may be able to exhaust his hormones enough. Maybe even get rid of that intense connection they seemed to share. Of course, he hadn't called her all week, giving her time to stew and think it over. He hoped knowing he was on a date with Hannah had driven the point home.

Slade got in the car. The idea of heading toward his empty home was suddenly depressing. He could call a few friends and go for a drink. But even that didn't hold his interest. Maybe he'd check in on his sister. He'd been trying to give her the space she wanted, but he always worried. He punched in the number on his Bluetooth and eased the Jag into traffic.

"Hello?"

"Jane! It's your long-lost brother. Have you forgotten me? Or replaced me with some hot stud?"

Her laughter made him smile. "Funny. Actually, I'm on my way out tonight."

"Date?"

"Girls' night out. Kate and Kennedy invited me to hang

with them. We're on our way to Mugs. I forgot how much fun being with other women is. I think I avoided it too long."

The memory of her shattered and lying lifeless on the floor flashed in his mind. Slade shifted in his seat. Was it a good thing they invited her into their group? Or bad? No, Kate would never hurt Jane, but did anyone ever realize their actions until it was too late? He kept his tone light and easy. "Dancing, huh? Sounds like fun. How's the matchmaking going?"

A pause. "Are you fishing?"

"Yes. Look, throw me a bone. You're my baby sister and I'm going through withdrawal. I have nobody else's business to nose around in."

She blew out a breath, but he knew she was laughing. "Okay. I met two nice guys today, and I'm going on a one-on-one date with Brian. He teaches poetry."

"Good. I want you to be happy."

"I am. What about you? Dating?"

"Yeah, just got done with one tonight. She was nice but not for me."

"Poor thing. She's probably half in love with you already," Jane teased.

"I'm sure Kate will find me another match. Is she going with you tonight?"

"Yep, she's dressed to kill, and Kennedy wants to hook her up with a man tonight. Says she hides in her house with her dog too much. Sounds like you, huh?"

He grunted. "I don't have a dog. Listen, do you mind if

I swing by for a drink? I'm not ready to go home and I'd like to hang out."

"Well, it's kind of a girls' thing, but I'm sure it will be okay. You know where Mugs is?"

"Yep. On my way. Be there in half an hour."

"See you later."

Slade clicked off, turned toward the Thruway, and headed to Verily. The hell with it. There was no way he was letting Kate distract herself with some other man. Not while he was suffering with torturous sexual dreams and a boner that wouldn't go away. It was time he reminded her of their attraction.

If another man touched her . . .

Slade cut off the thought and punched on the gas.

KATE SIPPED HER CHOCOLATE martini and relaxed into the feminine chatter that was as soothing as a spa massage. From harmless celebrity gossip to the endlessly fascinating topic of men, the subjects whirled in a dizzying array and made her happy to be a woman.

Mugs was overflowing, but they held the prime table at the edge of the dance floor looking out. Pink belted out her moody lyrics, and people swung their hips to the beat. The atmosphere was perfect for a variety of needs, from dancing and pool and darts to large tables to congregate at. Kate ducked her head and took one last glance.

Yes, his date was definitely over. Unless he had continued it at home. Of course, that was against the rules. She'd preached over and over the mantra he must follow: no sex until he wanted to actually date the woman. The idea that in a few minutes they'd been ripping at each other's clothes humiliated her, but she swore to move past it. Just a mishap. One mistake. Would never happen again.

"What about that guy?"

She directed her attention to Kennedy's subtle headshake toward an attractive man staring at their table. When Kate looked up, the man raised his glass and smiled. She automatically returned the greeting before their gaze broke.

"Oh, yeah, he's the one," Kennedy drawled. "Why don't you go over?"

"Why don't you?" she teased back.

"Because I'm taking the night off from men. But you, my dear, need a night off from just women."

She made a face. "I love you, Ken, and lust after your shoes, but, don't want to sleep with you."

Jane giggled and hiccupped. Obviously, she rarely drank, so her two cosmopolitans gave her a rosy, happy glow. Kate made a note to make sure she got home safe.

"Cute. Right now, I'd sleep with you anyway. You look hot, Kate."

Kate grinned. She kind of did look hot. It had been a long time since she had slipped into her usual black but kicked it up a notch. The skirt was ultrashort and chic, with cutout flaps that sneaked glimpses of her bare legs. The sequined tank top emphasized her cleavage and shimmered under the lights. But the shoes were deadly. Four inches of black strappy leather that climbed up her ankles gladiator style. They were fuck-me pumps meet badass boots, and worth every penny.

Kennedy leaned in. "Girlfriend, don't waste the outfit on us. Go and talk to the guy. I'm begging you."

Kate glanced over. The guy was definitely staking her out, but he didn't have the lust-filled scary face that usually freaked her out. More like a deep appreciation for her appearance. After all, that's exactly why she wore the outfit, for attention, not to fade into the woodwork.

The image of Slade and Hannah pressed tight together, kissing hungrily, blurred her vision. Slade dragging her into his open door, ripping at her clothes. Hannah moaning as his talented tongue danced over her skin.

Kate got to her feet, picked up her drink, and faced her friends. "I'm going in."

The low whoop gave her confidence. She eased over to the stranger, ignoring her nerves, and went for the honest approach.

"Hi. I'm Kate."

The guy smiled back. "I'm Bruce. Nice to meet you, Kate. Girls' night out?"

"Yeah, blowing off a little steam from the week. Do you live around here?"

"I'm actually in Nyack, but a few friends of mine love coming to Mugs so I figured I'd check it out. I'm meeting them later. But right now, I'm thanking God they're late."

She laughed and eased into the give-and-take of the initial mating conversation. His buzz-cut hair emphasized a strong face, and meaty arms under his button-down shirt and jeans. Maybe military. When she brushed against his arm from the bump of another patron, there was a distinct lack of any tingle. Still, she was so over the touch thing. Tired of judging herself and every man she laid her hands on. For tonight, she wanted to be silly and girly and let go. With Bruce.

The sexy R&B strains of "Blurred Lines" blasted from the speakers. "Would you like to dance?" he asked.

She tilted her head in surprise. Rarely did she meet men who were comfortable on the dance floor after the first meeting. "I'd love to."

He placed their drinks on the bar, took her hand, and led her to the floor. His body was rock solid, but she topped him in height with her crazy heels. Still, he didn't seem to mind, not afraid to hold her close but still retain a modicum of modesty. Kate relaxed into the mating call of the dance, her arms on his shoulders, content for a while not to engage in conversation but to let their bodies mingle and move.

A woodsy fragrance drifted to her nostrils. Kate sighed, letting go of the tension, content to enjoy the physical touch of a man without any demands. Maybe this is what she really needed. A man who could help her forget, maybe give her physical pleasure, maybe more. A crazy touch meant nothing and had only gotten her into trouble, giving away her mates to other women and leaving her alone.

"Hi." The familiar voice jerked her head around. She stared at Slade, who danced right beside them holding Jane. "How's it going?"

She blinked. His inane words buzzed her brain like a fog. "What are you doing here? You have a date."

He grinned and dazzled her with those perfect teeth. "It's over."

Bruce turned her slightly, probably dying to get away from the chatty guy, but she leaned her head to the side. "How did it go?"

"Amazing. Wait till I tell you about the dinner."

Hope crashed. Ice slithered down her spine, and she fought off her initial reaction like the survivor she was. Good, he was finally going to move on. With Hannah. Not her.

Awesome.

"I'm so glad," she forced out.

Jane gave a sigh and shook her head. "Slade, let poor Kate enjoy her dance. Give her some privacy."

"Oops, sorry. I'll catch up with you at the bar."

She nodded, forced a smile at Bruce, and tried to enjoy his embrace. Unfortunately, she kept sneaking glances at Slade and Jane, wondering about the details of his date.

Did he fool around with her? Kiss her? Make another date for tomorrow? That would be too soon, and she'd advise against such a move immediately.

"That guy a friend of yours?" Bruce asked.

Focus, Kate, focus. "Just a client. Sorry I was distracted."

"It's okay. I'm willing to be one of your distractions."

She laughed at the half-lame line but gave him credit for effort. His hands tightened around her waist and she leaned in, determined to relax. They moved well together, but the song ended and turned into a pounding club rhythm with JLo and Pitbull's "On the Floor." Kate waited for him to pull her off, not used to any men she ever met actually dancing, but Bruce tossed her a grin and threw himself into the dance.

Enjoying his enthusiasm, she moved her hips to the grindy tempo and let herself go. Bruce was going up a few notches—any man with solid dance moves deserved credit.

Suddenly, her rear was bumped. A hand closed around her upper arm and burned her skin.

Kate jumped back in a twist and faced Slade. "Sorry. Don't you love this song?" he shouted. In sheer astonishment, she watched him expertly mimic some major hip-hop moves, his jeans emphasizing the tight curve of his ass, his designer white shirt catching the light and flinging it against her gaze like an explosion of fireworks. Jane matched his moves with no self-consciousness, free for a little while with the music and darkness and crowded floor.

She raised her voice over the music. "I didn't know you danced."

"Most women love dancing. Mom taught us both when we were young. Counseled me a man needs to know how to move if I have any chance of catching a woman."

Kate laughed. "Smart woman."

"Umm, Kate? How about I buy you a drink?"

She looked up with guilt. Bruce shot Slade a dirty look, obviously not happy about the shouted conversations over the dance floor. "Sure." She waved at Slade and Jane, and stepped off the floor to follow Bruce.

Where she belonged.

He guided her back into a cozy corner and tried to get the bartender's attention. "Your client seems determined to talk to you tonight," he said. "What kind of business are you in?"

"I'm a matchmaker."

Bruce lifted a brow. "Like an escort service?"

"No, more like eHarmony but not online."

He lifted his hand, but the bartender ignored him. "You go out on dates with a variety of men?"

Irritation hit. She shifted her feet. "No, I'm the owner."

"Ambitious little thing, aren't you?"

His teasing question seemed way too chauvinistic, but

she decided to move on. "Yes, I guess I am. What do you do?"

"Air Force. I was in Iraq."

Most military didn't volunteer their service so quickly, but she reserved judgment. "Was it very difficult?"

"Yep. I'm ready to get back out and kick some more ass. Better concentrating on the enemy than my cheating ex-girlfriend who dumped me while I was away."

Hope plummeted. She looked at his angry face, now not so teasing and instead full of a bit of resentment and a whole lot of mess. "I'm so sorry you had to go through that. Your service to our country humbles me."

"It should. Maybe you'll be more respectful than the last woman. Where the hell is that bartender?"

"Chocolate martini?"

She whipped her head around. Slade held the drink in front of her, a wicked grin curving his sensual lips. "Y-y-yes. Thank you." She took the drink and glanced at Bruce, whose face now resembled a thundercloud.

"Sorry, dude, I didn't know what you were drinking or I would've bought you one too," Slade said. He eased himself into the small notch between them and clinked his Sam Adams to the rim of her glass. "Cheers. Are you having a good time?"

Kate battled the urge to giggle. He was completely and overwhelmingly arrogant, charming, and frustrating. How did one fight such a force? Still, she arranged her face to relate disapproval. "Yes, Bruce and I were having a wonderful time together."

"Good. You look amazing, by the way. The shoes are killer."

Pleasure bloomed. "Thanks."

"Welcome. So, I finally tried Carbone near Hell's Kitchen."

She gasped. "Is that where you went on your date? I've been dying to try that place—it's impossible to get reservations. Did Hannah enjoy it?"

"I think. I had the lobster black tie pasta. The sauce nearly knocked me sideways, and with the Chianti, the richness of the tastes combined perfectly in the mouth."

"What did Hannah have?"

"Veal parm."

"And how did the date go?"

"Good. For appetizers, I ordered the mussels. Fresh and soaked in a spicy tomato broth. I swear I've never had anything better."

"Did you share your appetizer with Hannah?"

He frowned and seemed to think hard. "I offered, but she doesn't like shellfish. Pity."

"Sharing a meal is a good way to increase intimacy on a date. Even a bite. Tell me more."

"I ordered the espresso and tiramisù for dessert. Top rate."

Kate let out a breath. "Stop talking about the menu. I want to know how the actual date went."

He took a slug of beer. "Good."

"Did you get along well? Did you have a connection? Do you want to see her again?"

"She's really nice. Accomplished. Intelligent. You did your job perfectly."

Her blood turned icy, but she forced a smile. "I'm so glad. When did you set up the second date?"

"Oh, I'm not going to see her again."

She choked on her martini. He pounded on her back, which made it worse with the electrical currents shocking her system. "What are you talking about? You said you liked her!"

Blazing emerald eyes grabbed and held her in the merciless grip of his gaze. Her breath squeezed in her chest and she froze.

"I do. But she's a bit too perfect. I don't want to hurt her feelings, but there's no spark."

"You said you wanted a companion, a friend, a long-term mate. I'm trying to keep you away from using sex as a tool to distance yourself. Hannah can give that to you. Many times the spark grows later."

"I don't want Hannah."

The softly spoken words singed her ears. The undertones of his real meaning hit her hard. His body heat radiated in waves and her body loosened, opened, craving his touch and just one more kiss. Within minutes he changed from casually charming to dangerous lover. He lowered his head to speak against her ear, his warm breath rushing into the sensitive shell. "I want you."

"Don't."

"Can't help it. How long are you going to torture both of us? I forgot the reasons we're even trying to fight this."

So did she. Almost. Then she remembered his focus was to expose Kinnections, and her, as a fraud. He required everything she wasn't in a mate, only believed in sex without love, and he was a client whom she had promised to find a match. It was wrong on every level, but her body didn't care as it hummed and purred by his very voice.

"It's a mess we both don't need. Better off trying to ignore the physical connection and concentrate on the better good. Finding you a true match for your future. Helping your sister. Proving Kinnections can succeed for you both."

"Yeah, how's that working for you, so far? Total bust for me. God, you smell good."

"We can't keep doing this," she whispered.

"So let me take you home. We'll end it now. Tonight."

A strangled laugh escaped her lips. "Sex won't end it. It'll only make things messier. Haven't you learned anything yet about God's sense of humor?"

"Not thinking about God. Wondering how you'll taste when I finally slide my tongue between your thighs."

She shuddered, teetered on the edge of giving him the

win, then fought back. "No. You need to honor the contract. If Hannah wasn't the right fit, I'll find you another."

He lifted her chin and forced her to meet his gaze. Temper and lust swirled in an edgy mix of green gold. "Are you that determined to send me to another woman? Ready to take such a risk? I'll only take so much, and then I'll go after what you're offering. Then we both lose."

She swallowed past the pain, past the knowledge that if she slept with this man, he might take something much more precious than her body. Her heart. Her soul. Her sanity. He'd leave her behind, sated, challenge over, and she'd need to pick up the pieces. Hell, no. Not in this lifetime.

"Or we both win," she said softly. "You find your mate. I prove my point. Jane finds her happiness. A perfect circle."

"Fine. We'll do it your way."

"Don't you want to pick the woman?"

"No. You seem to know everything about what I need and want. Prove it. Show me the woman who'll make me walk away from you without a glance back."

Her gut lurched at the thought, but she rallied. "Fine. Now can you give me some privacy so I can speak with—"

"He's gone."

Kate turned. Bruce chatted up a pert blonde perched on the opposite barstool. Both of them held a beer. Her plans for the night withered. What pissed her off the most was she didn't even care. She clenched her hands and glared at Slade. "Stop running off my own dates, please. Next time keep it professional and stop stalking me."

He eased back to charming companion and threw his hands up in surrender. "I was just talking some business and dancing with my sister. Besides, he's got way too much hidden anger. Arilyn would have a field day with him."

She gritted her teeth. "Thanks for the opinion."

"Any time."

"I'm going to the ladies' room. Thanks again for the drink."

Kate quickly moved past his rock-solid figure, weaving her way through the crowd to the restroom. She locked herself into the stall, sat on the toilet, and put her head between her legs. *Breathe. No need to get this upset over something that was never yours. Or someone.*

He rattled her with just a look. It didn't bode well for their future working relationship. She might have to step back and force him to deal with Kennedy.

Kate took her time to regain her control. Washed her hands, checked her hair, and strolled out.

It happened so fast she had no time to react.

Someone grabbed her hard, lifted her, and dragged her deeper down the hallway. Into a dark corner by an abandoned coat closet no one used. The smell of wood and must hit her nostrils, along with another familiar scent, calming the instinct to scream.

"Are you crazy?" She shoved against him, but he barely moved. "You scared the hell out of me; I thought you were a rapist."

"Maybe I need to show you again what you're trying to give away."

The warning was all raging male hormones and a sexual claim. Kate fought between the dark thrill and sheer panic, knowing if he kissed her, she'd lose it. "I need to change your intake form. Seems there's a bit of the dom in you."

"Funny, lately I've been feeling like the slave in this relationship."

She ignored him, though the image of her on her knees, servicing him in all ways, left her hot and tingly. "We don't have a relationship. I think you should give Emma a try. You enjoyed her company at the mixer, but she's a bit different from Hannah, less serious. She's a college professor, like your sister, so you may have a lot in common. She's also your perfect physical type."

Slade actually grinned, reminding her of a really pleased wolf about to show his mate who's boss. "You drive me crazy. Shut up, Kate."

His mouth covered hers. She waited for the drive of his tongue, the spark of being completely out of control while he commanded the embrace, but he only ran his lips lightly over hers, his tongue licking lightly at her bottom lip. The teasing gesture played with her sanity. She softened under him, all bark and no bite, but he made sure to punish her well. Never putting the pressure she craved into the kiss, he plucked at her nipples stabbing out from the delicate lace top and seesawed his thighs between hers.

Kate moaned and reached for more.

He moved back a precious inch and twisted her nipples.

Red-hot lust shot to her pussy. She lifted herself up on tiptoes, damned to eternity to be his sex slave, her breasts swollen and aching. "You have to let me in," he murmured, nibbling on her bottom lip, keeping barely any contact with their mouths while his hands left her breasts and slipped behind to cup her rear. He dug his fingers into her ass and rocked his hips against hers. "Tell me what you want and I'll give it to you."

She tried to force him to kiss her without the words, sliding her tongue between his lips, but he refused entry, pressing gentle, nonsatisfying kisses across her jaw, her cheeks, while his hand lifted the back of her skirt, and his finger slid underneath to trace the wet lace of her underwear. Her clit throbbed for relief, and she twisted for more, knowing one dip of his finger could bring her off to a shattering release.

He laughed low and dirty, teasing her through the damp material. "Oh, no you don't. I'm not letting you come this time until you beg. Invite me in so I can remind you what you're missing by sending me to another woman."

Rage and frustration mingled and rushed like a choppy

tidal wave through her body. "Fuck you and your games, counselor." He pushed his knee in the center of her pussy and her legs gave out.

"Oh, I intend to fuck you all right. All day and all night, making you come in so many ways you beg me to stop. But I won't stop, Kate, I'll use my dick and my teeth and my tongue to make you scream."

The shock of his words ripped a shudder from her weak muscles. She cursed him and hated him but gave him the words. "Kiss me. Put your tongue inside my mouth and kiss me properly."

"About time."

He ravaged her mouth, his tongue sweeping and licking and conquering every slick corner. He drank in her essence like a vampire draining her soul, and Kate tilted her neck back and gave him everything he wanted. She surrendered to the dark embrace with no thoughts of holding back, his raw male need a complete aphrodisiac to the empty, lonely corner of her soul. Her fingers dug into his scalp and tore at his hair. He ground her against the wall, into that musty corner, and showed her everything she was lacking and everything he intended to give her.

Then stepped back.

Her breath shuddered. A hazy mist of lust clouded her vision. His erection strained the fabric of his pants as he stared at her, jungle eyes wild with desire, a sheen of sweat evident on his forehead.

She opened her mouth to tell him she made a mistake. That she wanted him, would take the chance, but it was too late.

"Set me up with Emma for Friday night. Good night, Kate."

He walked away.

Kate turned her face to the wall, fighting back tears, and wondered why getting what she wanted was so painful.

HOURS LATER, CUDDLED UP in her favorite chair, she stared at the television droning with infomercials. Robert snored beside her on his orthopedic mat, his doggy grunts and mild moans confirming some heavy dreams. A restlessness nipped endlessly at her nerves, driving her from her spot to her bookshelf. She couldn't sleep, and needed to get her mind off sex. With Slade.

Kate grabbed a bunch of books she'd purchased from the secondhand store a few weeks ago and brought them back to her recliner. Maybe she'd do some research for Kinnections. She found many books with kernels of information that helped her clients or gave her a fresh direction to explore potential relationships. She skimmed a few, making mental notes, until an electrical shock jolted her fingertips. Kate jerked back, annoyed, and revealed the purple, fabric-colored book.

The Book of Spells.

She remembered discovering it in the stack, and the weird electrical thing had happened before. Strange. It had occurred before only when she met people, never with inanimate objects. A bit wary, she gingerly reached out and opened the cover. A mild tingle traveled up her arm but no pain.

Kate relaxed and flipped through the book. The few illustrations were beautiful, and only one strange spell was contained within the faded pages. An odd scent of incense and smoke drifted to her nostrils, and she shook with a sudden need she couldn't make sense of. Crap, what if this thing had belonged to a real witch? It held some sort of spooky power. But the spell seemed . . . well . . . pure. Stripped down to the essence of what a woman craved in her lifetime mate. Make a list of all the qualities wanted in a soul mate. Write them down on two pieces of paper. Burn one in a fire and tuck the other under the mattress.

Kate remembered reading about the power of the written word, the unconscious magic of dreams, and an empty craving squeezed her heart. God, she was so tired of being alone. What would it be like to meet someone who actually believed in love and commitment? A man to grow with in this lifetime and beyond? Someone who saw all of her faults and accepted who she was?

Kate sniffed and rubbed her eyes. Ridiculous. She was a big baby. Maybe she'd bring the book to Kennedy and see if one of her clients would believe in it. Sometimes a woman needed a placebo to fight for love. If she thought a love spell could work, she'd be more open to opportunities in the dating world. She closed the book, deciding to bring it to Kinnections in the morning, when the idea crystallized before her.

Complete the spell.

The voice whispered in her ear, a lilting pleasurable rumble that gave her shivers. She huddled under the crocheted blanket and looked around. Very weird. She didn't believe in that stuff. It would be ridiculous to try a love spell. Right?

She stared at the book and again the overwhelming urge to follow the instructions burned within. Kate hesitated, listening to Robert's snoring and the urging of the commercial to buy the latest ab equipment to get skinny and turn back the clock.

Complete the spell.

Loneliness swamped her. Maybe she needed her own placebo. Maybe if she did this silly spell, she'd believe in something she lost along the way. Her confidence and belief in true love. Somewhere. Someday.

She moved quickly before she could question her sanity. Kate ripped out two pieces of paper, grabbed a pen, and wrote down all the qualities she dreamed of in a man. Her man. She didn't think, just let the pen scratch across the paper in a fury, tapping into the well of her unconscious. She folded the papers, trudged to the bedroom, and shoved one under her queen-size mattress.

It took a while to find something that could contain a small fire, but she finally found a small metal bucket under the sink. She grabbed a lighter from the kitchen junk drawer, ripped up some papers, and lit the flame.

Kate held the list over the fire and shut her eyes. Chanted a few words to Earth Mother. Took a deep breath, cleansing her energy to send it into the universe. And dropped the list into the bucket.

She watched it shrivel and blacken. When it turned to ashes, she sprayed some water from the sink and doused the flames.

A looming sense of premonition swamped her, and a shiver raced down her spine. As if she had done something she could never take back, stepped down a side road that would bring her into a new pathway of life, a journey she would never have taken if thinking clearly.

Kate swallowed and pushed back the fear.

Silly. There was no such thing as love spells, of course. But maybe by clarifying what she needed, she'd open a portal that had been previously closed.

Damn, she was taking way too many yoga classes with Arilyn.

She cleaned up the mess, turned off all the lights, and went to bed.

ten

SLADE PUSHED A hand through his hair, straightened his tie, and guzzled a glass of water before his next client. He was exhausted, barely sleeping most nights, and his work schedule exploded with a rash of bad karma. It still amazed him how many wealthy couples never thought of a prenuptial, and how many more spent millions to try and break them.

He strode to the window and ignored his rumbling stomach. No lunch again. He liked the basic principles of helping others and loved the law. Fitting past cases together to complete a puzzle, the rich history of the American judicial system was something he was fiercely proud of—the cornerstone of equality and justice in rapidly declining institutions such as marriage.

But divorces were sometimes a real bitch.

Fog shrouded the skyline of Manhattan today, and the melting snow once blanketing everything in a sheen of white had turned dirty. Clumpy ice balls clogged the sidewalks and roads but didn't slow the frantic pace of the city. He gazed at where the beloved Twin Towers had reigned, a sadness always tingeing his heart at how the city landscape drastically changed after 9/11. The new memorial downtown held hope, though, and soothed some of the emptiness and grief of New Yorkers.

Slade finished his water, threw the cup in the wastebasket, and grabbed his notes. His office was fully equipped with a cherrywood desk taking up half the room, bookcases lining the wall, and burgundy matching chairs to inspire clients to tell all. Photos of George Washington, Abraham Lincoln, and the signing of the Declaration of Independence covered the walls and reminded people of justice. The thick burgundy rug was soft under the feet, and the smell of wood, lemon polish, and coffee hung in the air.

If he got partnership, they'd move him to the penthouse, with floor-to-ceiling windows, a wet bar, and a private bathroom/changing area. Slade thought the extras were nice, but he didn't want the promotion for the perks or even the money. He knew that as a full partner, he'd get to pick more of his own cases and take on a bit more pro bono work. He'd have the power needed to make more important decisions. The rest was all extra.

"Mr. Montgomery, your one o'clock has arrived."

He crossed to the desk and hit the intercom. "Send him in, please."

Slade took a deep breath for calm and to concentrate solely on his client. His schedule was overbooked, but when a friend from law school called to ask him for a favor,

Slade never hesitated. Pete Troy came through the doors. Immediately, Slade pegged him as the beta in his relationship. He stooped over, and combed his thinning hair to the side in a desperate attempt to stave off baldness. Reed thin and dressed in jeans, a slightly soiled sweatshirt, and comfortable sneakers, he introduced himself and took a seat. His hands twitched on his lap, and his face was all angular lines, giving him a kind look, yet a bit off-center. His brown eyes filled with intimidation and a bit of fear.

"Mr. Montgomery, I'm a bit out of sorts. I've never met with a lawyer before, but my friend Trent recommended you and said you could help."

"Call me Slade. Trent and I go way back to Harvard— he's a good guy. He told me a few things about your case, but I'd like to get a few more details. Everything we talk about is confidential; I'm here to help you."

Pete relaxed slightly. "My wife wants a divorce."

Slade nodded, his gold pen poised on the paper. He always preferred writing his own notes longhand rather than on the computer; it gave the meeting more intimacy. "Can you give me the facts leading up to her request for a divorce?"

He wiped his palms down his jeans and nodded. "She's a CEO of a major supply company, so she's the one who brings in all the money. Her job is really stressful, she does a lot of traveling, and I decided to stay home with the kids."

"How many children?"

"Three. My eight-year-old, five-year-old, and two-year-old. Two boys and finally the girl."

"Nice. Have you stayed home since your first son was born?"

"No, we had a nanny for the first few years, but I noticed too many problems. He'd complain about her, and finally I installed one of those cameras. Caught her drugging him with cough syrup to keep him quiet. I told my wife one of us had to stay home and agreed it would be me. My job was much less income, and with the savings from daycare, we came out ahead of the game."

Slade scribbled more notes. "Many families are making those hard decisions. So you remained home when your other two children were born?"

"Yes. My wife went back to work in four weeks because she was needed at the office. We've been drifting lately, I know we have, but I never realized how bad it was. She began staying later at the office, business trips on weekends. I felt like I was going crazy with no one for company but the kids, like my brain was getting fried. So I packed up the children and decided to surprise her in the Catskills. We rent a cabin there and she was staying to do some business in town."

Slade knew where the story was going as millions had before Pete's. He watched the man wipe his brow, his mouth curving down in a slight grimace. "I caught her with someone. Thank God, the children were still in the car."

"What happened?"

Pete blinked, seeming to concentrate fiercely on the lines in his hands. "Nothing. She didn't stop. She—she stayed with that man, and when she finished she came out and yelled at me. Told me to get the kids home and we'd talk about it on Sunday. You know the worst part? I listened to her. Just like I always do. I don't know how I became this type of person—this complete shell of a man. My wife was screwing another guy and I quietly left to wait for her at home."

Slade swallowed, his heart squeezing in pain for the man across his desk. He heard countless tales from women, but many fewer men admitted this type of pain. He carefully steered the topic back to the facts, knowing he wasn't a true counselor for grief. "I can't even imagine how painful that was. When she arrived Sunday, what did she say?"

Pete dragged in a breath. "She wanted a divorce. Told me to move out and that she'd hire a new nanny for the kids. Said I was useless, and she refused to have me taint the children with my unambitious and lazy demeanor."

"Hmm, interesting. I guess taking care of three children properly is lazy, huh?"

"To my wife it is." Bitterness leaked like acid through his words. "She's missed every important event of my kids' lives and now she wants them because they're a possession to her. She doesn't want her reputation ruined."

"What was your response?"

"I told her never. I will never give up the kids and refused to leave the house, afraid I'd never get back in."

"Excellent decision."

"She screamed and yelled and threatened. You see, she has all the money. The accounts are all in her name. I never even thought of it—she pays the bills, gives me an allowance for the kids, and I never need anything else. Now, I don't have a credit card, a job, or money. She closed the main account and moved all the money somewhere. I don't know what to do, Slade. I can't lose my kids."

His simple plea burned raw in Slade's gut. His fingers gripped the pen in a stranglehold. God, what people who supposedly loved each other do. And the kids were always the casualties in the ultimate battle of selfishness.

Slade knew there was no way he'd let Pete get bullied. He was the main caretaker and had done what countless mothers had done—put his children first. He'd pull out the big stuff for this case and not rest until he got him full custody. Fathers were still rarely given full custody, but this case could be a turning point. Worse scenario at this point—partial, but with the right tools and contacts, Slade knew he could win.

"Do you know who her lawyer is?"

"Bronte Edwards."

Slade winced. "Super hard-ass, but I've battled her in court many times before. She goes quickly for the jugular, but this is solid. I'm going to petition immediately for you to stay in the house. I'll need papers and proof on previous nannies, and anything you can get your hands on. I'll need to contact your previous employer also."

"Do we have a shot? I'm a father with no job. Is this even a possibility?"

Slade stared at the man, his stooped shoulders and tired face the symbols of broken relationships and lost hope. He carefully chose his words. "It's not going to be easy. Most judges still favor the mother, and if she presents a tearful, broken image in court, it may crucify us. I need to warn you, though. It's going to get nasty and hard. It's a marathon, not a sprint, and you'll need to dig deep and fight for those kids like you've never done before. If you commit, I promise to do everything in my power to get you custody. But there are no guarantees."

Pete hesitated, hung his head. Slade waited, knowing this was key to the case. Too many of his clients couldn't take the long-term emotional abuse and surrendered early. He didn't blame them—many could not care less about what they left behind and just wanted a clean slate.

"My kids are my life," he said simply. "I'm in."

Slade worked with him for the next half hour and gave him a list of tasks, some to help focus, some to help in court.

Pete stuffed his shaking hands into his pockets. "Thank you, I feel much more confident. Umm, I'm so embarrassed, I know about your standard fee, but do you know how much this will take? I don't—don't have anything to give you right now."

Slade shook his head. "If we win full custody and full alimony, my fee can be paid then. If not, this is pro bono."

Pete frowned. "I don't understand? You mean free? You don't even know me—why would you do that?"

Slade grinned. "Because you're a friend of Trent's. Because you're a man who's fighting for his family. Because you've been wronged. And I take a few of these cases on throughout the year, so I don't want you to feel guilty or like I'm doing it out of pity. I just want to make sure your kids are safe."

Pete gave a jerky nod and turned his head quickly. "Thank you. Thank you."

"I'll be in touch."

His client hurried out, leaving him in silence. The buzz of the phone and low murmuring from conversations drifted in the air. A heaviness tightened his chest and constricted his breath. This was going to be a long battle and a ton of money. He'd have to kick in some of his own or his boss would go ape shit. Still, he'd be damned if he let Pete hire an incompetent attorney who only cared about getting his fee. Those children needed him.

He groaned and rubbed his hands over his face. He craved his recliner, a cold beer, and his DVR. Instead, he had to go out on a date with Emma, a woman who might be perfect for him.

A woman who wasn't Kate.

Still, he swore he'd try. If someone else could dig Kate Seymour out from under his skin, he'd be eternally grateful. Stalking her in bars and stealing kisses wasn't his usual style. Of course, he'd never had to chase a woman this hard before either.

Slade glanced at his watch and went back to work.

TEN O'CLOCK.

Kate absently rubbed Robert's head and tried to concentrate on *Bridesmaids*. She usually laughed her ass off, but the image of Slade on his date kept ruining her concentration. So stupid. She was so stupid.

She pushed away the remnants of her homemade hot fudge sundae and patted her overfull stomach. If only she could relax and go to sleep. Did she still have that joint from her mother? Did she dare light up and sink into criminal activity?

Or . . . she could take out the neon pink vibrator. Of course, the thing looked like it could choke a horse. What was her mother thinking? The image hurt her brain, so she refocused on the movie and tried not to think of drugs and sex.

Her phone vibrated.

Heart pounding, she studied the number. Her finger paused on the Answer button for a moment. Then she hit it.

"Why are you calling me?"

His husky laugh curled her toes and stroked between her legs. Damn, the man was dangerous even over the phone. "Thought you'd want me to check in. See how my date went."

She swallowed and wondered why he had so much fun torturing her. Kate kept her voice cool and clipped. "Of course. I always encourage my clients to call and give us full feedback. Did you enjoy yourself?"

"I did. Wait till I tell you about this."

"You didn't sleep with her, did you? I gave you specific rules to follow, Slade, and I mean it."

"No sex, I promise. But it was pretty damn close."

She tried not to sway in the chair. "Oh. Well, I g-g-g-guess that's a good sign."

"Imagine this. Tender, fresh meat that melted in my mouth. Cooked medium rare, with just a slight seasoning of peppercorn for a bit of heat. The potatoes came with some crazy type of Gorgonzola cheese, which complemented the rib eye, and crisp asparagus in a lemon butter sauce. Do you believe it?"

Relief cut through her first, then pure aggravation. "Are you kidding me right now?"

"No, I swear. You have to check this place out, it's close to Tribeca, but I never had the opportunity to eat there. It's called Mums and they have the best steaks I've ever seen. It's making a big name for itself."

Her voice rose. "I don't care about the food! How was

Emma? Did you like her? Did you get along? Did she have a good time? Do you even know what she had for dinner?"

Silence fell over the line. "Of course I know what she had for dinner. Pity she didn't try the meat, she's sort of a vegetarian so they made her a platter of fresh vegetables. But even those were grilled and seasoned nicely. And she did share the wine. I went with a peppery, spicy Pinot Noir."

Kate squeezed her eyes shut. "What is wrong with you? I'm working very hard to match you correctly, and I think you're sabotaging the whole thing! How was the date without the food?"

"Geez, we went to dinner, I figured you'd want to know the details of the meal. Emma was great. Pretty, funny, we had a good conversation."

"Finally. That's a relief. When do you want to go out again?"

"Oh, I don't want to see her again."

She clenched the phone and dropped her voice to a whisper. "What?"

"You did a brilliant job, Kate. You're definitely very good at matching people. I'm starting to realize you're not as much of a con artist as you are misguided. Still, my sister can end up a casualty with all your good intentions, so I need to keep an eye on this whole process."

"I'm honored I've been promoted to crazy rather than

a criminal. Why don't you want to see Emma again? Are you really closed off to finding your mate? I told you this process can't work if you don't—"

"I know, I know, I'm open. I tried, and I pictured us together, and on paper it was perfect. But she's missing an unknown spark, something I can't put my finger on."

"Sexually?"

"Maybe. It's an unknown quality a woman has. I either feel it or I don't."

The realization slammed through her. All of the perfect characteristics Slade had recited were for paper purposes. To find his correct match, she needed to look deeper. Maybe a woman with more of an edge, a bit more assertive, more of a challenge. Yes, as a lawyer, he craved a bit of mental banter, physical sensuality, and kick.

Elena.

She was a bit of a wild card, but definitely worth a shot. Elena would surprise him on all levels. The only danger was Elena didn't like to play by the rules, and if she wanted him physically, she'd go after him. Kate teetered on her decision to send him to the arms of a woman who could claim him.

But that was her job.

"I know who I want you to date next."

"You?"

She flinched at the silky, caramel tone that wrapped her in goo. "No, we're not good for each other. Her name is Elena and I think you'll be perfect. She's different from the others. Are you willing to go out this week again? I can set it up quickly."

"You still want to play this game?"

His meaning throbbed in her veins and mocked her as a big fat liar. No, she wanted to rip off his clothes, climb on top of him, and ride him to oblivion. She wanted to claim him for her own. Kate imagined him home, sprawled on his couch, shirtless, all that rough toasty skin bare to her view. Imagined him hard and throbbing beneath her stroking hands. Imagined his head buried between her thighs and bringing her to pleasure over and over again. She had to fight the attraction and find his match. It was the only true way to free them both and prove her business a success.

"Yes. It's not a game to me, Slade."

His voice hardened. "Got it. I'm free tomorrow night. Set it up."

She opened her mouth to say something, but he clicked off the line.

Kate stared at her phone for a long while, wondering if this time she had finally pushed hard enough for him to go away. Robert whined, as if sensing her distress, and pushed his nose into her palm. She sank into the crocheted blanket, petting her dog and watching her movie and telling herself she was happy with her life.

KENNEDY POKED HER HEAD into the office. A huge grin flashed her gorgeous white teeth. "Guess what?"

Kate pushed the mounds of paperwork away from her, swiveled her chair around, and stretched her legs. "What?"

"Edward and Justine are getting married!"

Kate broke into delighted laughter. "I can't believe it. Yes, I do, I knew they were the perfect match from date one. How did you find out?"

"They're here in my office right now. Come and see them."

Kate got to her feet and followed Kennedy into the office. The couple sat on the white couch together, holding hands. Kate remembered the first time Justine had come in, unsure, shy, and inexperienced with dating. She'd held a small mixer to get an idea of her type and immediately sensed a connection with Edward. All it took was a simple nudge in his direction, and after the first date they'd become inseparable.

Justine caught sight of her and squealed, jumping from the couch to give her a big hug. "I'm engaged!" Laughing, she shoved the pristine round diamond out in the universal gesture of a new fiancée. Edward grinned and stood. He towered over six feet, and Justine barely topped five two, but together they fit perfectly, her reddish curly hair tucked neatly into the crook of his shoulder, his arm naturally resting at the small of her back.

"I'm so happy for you guys. The ring is gorgeous! When's the wedding?"

"Next May. And of course, the whole staff of Kinnections is invited. It wouldn't have happened without you."

Edward beamed. Kate's heart clutched with emotion, and once again she realized this was the reason it was all worth it. Bringing people together to start their lives was a heady power. Satisfaction rushed in a powerful flood. She prepared herself for the sting but moved forward to hug them both together, waiting for the release of energy to escape that always proved she'd made the perfect match.

But she felt nothing.

Kate held on a bit longer, desperate to experience the heady rush, but there wasn't even a rustle of recognition. Were they correctly matched? She stepped back, keeping her smile in place while her heart galloped like a mad pack of Thoroughbreds. Oh, God, what if she matched them wrong? She always confirmed the connection when her clients got engaged or married. Panic nipped at her nerves, but she kept calm and engaged in light chatter about the wedding and their future plans.

By the time they left, Kate was on the verge of a full panic attack. She dropped into the matching blindingly white chair by Kennedy's desk, mashing her knuckle against her mouth. Ken came back and dropped into the leather chair beside her. A frown marred her brow. "Are you okay? Did you get too much of a shock this time? I told you not to touch the newly engaged couples, Kate. What if you get some crazy electrocution thing that fries your brain?"

Kate lifted her gaze. "I didn't feel anything, Ken."

Her friend stared at her, dumbfounded. "What do you

mean? Oh, my God, are you telling me they're not a match?"

Kate dropped her face into her hands and groaned. "I d-d-d-don't know! I don't know what's going on. I lost the t-t-touch. Completely. I'm working blind, but I haven't told anyone because I keep thinking it'll come back. Now I'm terrified it's gone forever."

Her body shook. Funny, how many years had she prayed for the gift to go away? She craved normalcy and hated consistently knowing if two people were meant to be committed or not. It was too much pressure, so she decided to use her talent for good, to help bring people together rather than sit helplessly by and watch them either miss each other or marry the wrong partner.

Now, she got her wish. Emptiness pulsed in her gut, a lack of something inherent within her. What was she going to do?

"Don't panic, sweetie. We'll figure it out." Kate lifted her head and watched Ken turn to the cabinet behind her, take out a shot glass, and a tiny bottle of amber liquid. "Here, drink this." She pushed the shot across the desk.

Kate sputtered. "Are these the liquor bottles from hotel minibars?"

"Yeah, I have a collection. When I get bad news, sometimes I drink one to settle my nerves. It's good for you."

"God, first pot with my mother and now hard liquor with you on the job. My morals are slipping faster and faster."

"Shut up and drink." Kate obeyed. The sting of whiskey slid down her throat and she choked back a cough. Her eyes watered. Ken nodded with approval. "Better. Liquor is truth serum, kind of like PMS. It helps you not to lie to yourself anymore. Now, I want you to tell me everything. When did you lose it?"

"I can't remember exactly. I kept noticing I wasn't getting any reactions from being around couples. At first, I thought it was a temporary glitch, but I got nothing from Edward and Justine. I haven't experienced even a tingle, no matter who I come in contact with. It's gone."

"Probably temporarily in hiding. Have you done anything different lately? Involved with someone I don't know about?"

"No."

Kennedy pursed her lips in thought. "What about Slade? He came into Mugs the other night for a few. Hung out with Jane, but then he disappeared. Funny, I didn't see you after either. Unless . . ." Her eyes widened. "Holy shit, you're screwing around with him, aren't you?"

Kate wrapped her arms around her chest. "No. Not really. Oh, God, I don't want to! I mean, I want to, but he's completely wrong for me, and he's a client. I just want him to go away, get out of my life. The only way I can accomplish it is if I set him up with the right woman."

Ken narrowed her gaze. "What if you're the right woman?"

"I'm not, I swear. He only wants to sleep together and wring it out of our systems so I can then match him properly. I'd never do a one-night stand."

She ducked her head to avoid Ken's knowing look. "Okay, I have a few things to say to you but I need Arilyn in here. Time for an intervention." Ken pressed the intercom button on the phone. "Hey, can you come into my office for a sec? I'm with Kate."

"You won't get Arilyn to bully me," Kate said. "She's on my side."

"Not this time, babe."

Arilyn floated into the room, clad in a long silvery skirt, white T-shirt, and sandals. Her hip-length hair shimmered in red gold, and she took the third seat with her usual feminine grace. "What's the problem?"

Kennedy slid over a shot glass to Arilyn filled to the top. "Kate lost the touch. She wants to have sex with Slade, but she's too afraid. He wants her for one night in a thwarted attempt to get over their chemistry, and she just wants to match him with another woman, thinking the whole thing will go away."

Arilyn processed the information. Reached out and tipped the glass back, swallowing the slide of whiskey in one perfect gulp. Set the glass back down without a hitch and faced her. "You have to sleep with him, Kate."

Kate gasped. Her calm serenity billowed around the shocking words. "What? N-n-n-no! Sleeping with him will be disastrous. If I match him, I'll get the touch back, I know it."

Arilyn clucked with sympathy. "Darling, I think we misinterpreted your connection with Slade. At first, I thought you were meant to find his match. But if you lost your abilities and still feel a connection to Slade, the only way to get the touch back is to sleep with Slade. Giving your body over and taking a chance. You're fighting your natural attraction, and that's not a good thing. Especially if it's only about fear."

Her mouth opened and closed. She never imagined Arilyn would agree to help her lose her virginity, but her words brought a strange sense of clarity. Could that be the solution? Her body quaked with terror and something else. Something she hated to define, but it was more like . . . excitement.

Kennedy jumped in. "You're blocked. Open yourself up to a sexual experience with Slade, and I bet your abilities will come rushing back."

"What are you so afraid of?" Arilyn asked gently. "Slade? Losing your virginity? Or losing your control?"

Kate shuddered. "All of it."

"Then it's time to find out what will happen if you give up that control. Remember the yoga classes we take? Control is only an illusion to calm yourself into believing things will go a certain way. Give up the control, let life lead, and you will find a rich discovery."

"And endless orgasms," Kennedy piped up.

Kate smothered a laugh. "God, I can't believe I'm seriously considering this. I set him up with another date tonight. Things with Hannah didn't go well. He said she's too perfect. Then he went out with Emma and said he was missing some spark he couldn't name."

"Hmm, interesting. Who's the new date with?" Ken asked.

Kate winced. "Elena."

Arilyn shook her head. "Oh, this is bad. She's pretty assertive with men she finds a connection with. The complete opposite of Hannah and Emma. If you were looking to push him into bed with someone else, you found your girl."

She swallowed past the lump in her throat. Elena was known to make men crazy with lust and lead them on a chase. In a way, she was perfect for igniting Slade's love of the hunt. The idea of Elena touching him with her hungry gaze made her nauseous. But in a way, wasn't she throwing him a test? If he buckled to Elena's sexuality, he'd prove two things. Breaking the rule of sex before monogamous dating. And confirming he only sought the challenge of a chase.

If he failed, she'd prove he wasn't the one.

If he passed, she may not have any other barriers to hide.

"You can still call him, you know," Kennedy offered. "Tell him you want him. Bet he'd cancel the date with Elena."

Kate dragged in a deep breath. "No, this needs to be played out. Maybe Elena and he will be better suited for each other. She calls to his primitive side, but she's super smart. She's also a career woman, and Slade enjoys battling wit to wit. Maybe I'll have my answer tonight."

Arilyn and Kennedy shared a look. "Or maybe you won't have anywhere else to run."

The statement echoed her own thoughts.

As she thanked her friends and walked out of the room, Kate wondered if it was already too late.

SLADE CLOSED THE DOOR behind him. The silence of his home descended in a deafening air that mocked his decision to send Elena away. He turned and studied the empty rooms.

When he left his marriage behind him, he longed for peace. Stability. His failure in the institution mocked him, so he focused his energies on helping others who were betrayed and had no advocates. When he lost his parents, Jane became his sole responsibility. He tried to care for her but also failed to protect her from the heartbreak the world cruelly threw out.

The lesson was clear. Nothing lasted, and one needed to prepare for the eventual pain of a broken relationship. He figured letting Kinnections try to set him up with a companion who could fit seamlessly into his life and share his company took most of the messiness away. He didn't believe it would actually work, but at least the goal was clear. Until one woman wrecked all of his expectations.

Kate.

She ignited all the hidden instincts long buried. When was the last time he dragged a woman into a corner with the purpose of kissing her senseless? Her constant insistence he belonged with another pissed him off and caused a hurt he didn't want to examine. As soon as Elena climbed off her Harley, shook out her hair, and gave him a knowing grin, he'd known where the night headed. Sure, Kate warned him he needed to actually enjoy a woman's company on a few dates before jumping into bed. But Elena was different. She exuded a sensual vibe that said they were two grown adults and could do what they wanted. On their terms.

She was also interested.

His body mildly reacted, but within a few minutes he'd remained cold. He was terrified no one would ever be able to match the electric chemistry he shared with the woman who didn't want him. Slade wined and dined her, surprised at her engaging conversation and wicked sense of humor. Once again, he admitted that Kate got him right. He did need someone less than perfect, and the layers Elena offered intrigued him even more than Hannah. More than Emma.

But she wasn't Kate.

When Elena refused to wait and kissed him, he'd kissed her back. Tried desperately to work up enough interest to take her to bed. It would be good for both of them and finally show Kate that he was done playing games.

Until he realized Elena was just a poor imitation of the only woman he wanted.

He pushed her away with regret. She studied his face, understood, and left in a roar on her badass Harley bike. Like a chump, he watched her leave and now stood alone in his magnificent home, with no wife, no dog, no lover, and an endless mocking silence.

No more.

The rage and frustration took root and flowered. He was done sitting around and waiting for something that wasn't coming. He'd told her she needed to come to him, on her terms, but if he didn't take what he wanted—what they both wanted—he'd continue on an endless path of dates that had no meaning and implode from frustration.

Slade grabbed his keys and went to claim her.

KATE ROLLED OVER FOR the hundredth time and shoved the sheets back. Sweat beaded her body, and her skin was oversensitive to any fabric, even the soft cotton of her T-shirt. Her core throbbed and wept for relief that no hot pink ginormous vibrator could ever satisfy. Images of Slade and Elena making love in his bed tortured her vision. She anticipated his call, detailing his meal and telling her to try again.

Tonight, the phone remained silent.

With a low curse, she sat up and ripped off her shirt, hating even the slight brush of contact against her swollen breasts. She was being punished and it was a doozy. She'd pushed him into the arms of another woman, afraid to claim him for herself, and now it was too late.

The clock digits shone in neon green. Midnight. Robert whimpered from his spot in his orthopedic bed. As if he was also disturbed by her inability to sleep, he shifted fitfully in a drive to get comfortable. Kate sighed and sat up. Maybe she'd put on a movie. Or fire up her iPad and read. Anything but keep thinking about Slade naked with someone other than her.

Loser.

She kicked off the covers and trudged topless into the living room. She grabbed a bottle of water, turned on the reading lamp, and heard the noise.

Kate froze. What the hell? Adrenaline rushed through her and she jumped for the phone to call 911 when the doorbell rang.

Tiptoeing to the door, she peered out the sidelights.

Slade stared back at her.

Kate jerked back with a gasp. What was she going to do?

"I saw you, Kate. Let me in. Now."

She bit her lip and pondered. This was not a good idea. "It's midnight," she hissed through the door.

"I know what time it is. I'm freezing, open the frickin' door."

Crap, she was naked! She grabbed the afghan from the chair, wrapped it around her like a toga, and slid open the lock.

He walked in like he owned the place and her. His gaze took in her makeshift outfit, probing the loose holes of the blanket and uncovering the skin beneath. Her nipples hardened instantly. A dangerous air of masculine temper sparked the air, the surge of testosterone wrapping her in a spell that dragged her back to basic instincts desperate to escape years of civility. To mate. To give.

To surrender.

Kate shivered. "What are you doing here?"

"It was a test, wasn't it?"

She didn't pretend to misunderstand. The knowledge she'd run out of options squeezed her like an insect wrapped tight in the silky rope of a spider's web. Kate lifted her chin.

"Yes."

He growled and took a step forward.

One sharp bark jerked her head around. Robert paused in the doorway of the bedroom, watching the scene. He dragged his body down the hall at rapid speed, placing himself in front of her like he was a fully trained guard dog ready to take down an assailant. Love and pride surged for the unbreakable bond of his protection. Kate opened her mouth to calm him, but Slade had already moved.

With a humble grace that left her speechless, Slade knelt before Robert in supplication. He offered his hands slowly out in the universal gesture of surrender. "Thank you for taking care of her," he said gently. "But I would never hurt her. I swear to you on all I hold dear in this lifetime, I will never hurt your mistress."

She held her breath as he leaned forward until he was nose to nose with the pit bull. Moments passed. A look of shared understanding and something deeper passed between them. Slowly, Robert relaxed his rigid stance, bowed his head, and licked Slade's palm softly. Then he dragged himself back into the bedroom.

The last of her defenses shattered. Kate stared at the man who had humbled himself before her dog, honoring Robert's emotions as if he were human. Slade rose to his feet, stripped off his jacket, rolled up his shirtsleeves, and met her gaze head on.

Raw, hot sexual energy buzzed around them. Her mouth watered at the sight of his half-unbuttoned shirt, the long, tanned column of his neck, and the locked tension of his jaw. His gaze pinned her without mercy, letting her know this was her last chance to run.

"So, you admit you put me to a test." His words came out lazy, as if he had all the time in the world, but his body tensed like a predator ready to pounce if provoked. "Did you want me to sleep with Elena? Let you off the proverbial hook?"

"No." She pressed the blanket tighter to her body. "Half of me wanted you to fall for her so I'd be free. I could hate you, remind myself you weren't meant to be mine. But the thought of you touching her made me crazy."

He lifted a brow. "A little honesty, Kate? Good. Since this seems like a good night for clichés, let's put all our cards on the table. I wanted to sleep with her." He ignored her wince and kept speaking, refusing to let her break the stare. "I was pissed off by your games and ready to end it. I kissed her."

Hurt lanced deeply, but she struggled to keep her composure. How could she be betrayed when he only did what she wanted? "I understand," she choked out.

His face tightened. "No, you don't understand. That's the problem. I kissed her, tried to work up a physical reaction, and got nothing. I want you. Only you. The real question is, why won't you admit you want me just as much?"

The looming confrontation crashed over her and left her nowhere to run. Is this the type of woman she'd become? So scared of being hurt or dragged into a situation she couldn't control, she quaked with fear? Shame made her lift her chin high in the air. He offered one night of pleasure. She tried to mock his offer by stripping it down to just sex, but they'd already shared much more. Secrets, intimacy, honesty. Isn't that what she was running from? The knowledge that once he pushed deep inside her, he'd be buried in both her body and soul permanently?

Time to put on her big-girl panties and follow Frost's less-traveled road. "I'm scared."

He cocked his head. "About?"

She shifted her weight and forced herself to confront the truth. When was the last time a male stripped her bare? Dared to want more than a fleeting physical encounter that barely skimmed the surface, refusing to dive deep enough to feel anything real?

Never.

She waited for guarantees in a world with none. She hid behind her company and put everyone ahead of her, urging them to let go and allow love into their lives. Yet she kept herself isolated and alone, with only Robert for company, on a hypocritical throne above the rest of the world. Dear God, wasn't it time to let go? Take a chance with no thought to an agenda or plan or list she could calmly check off?

Kate refused to cower beneath the blistering doubt in his gaze. "Because I've never felt this way before," she whispered.

He paused a beat and let her wait in miserable silence. "Better. I swore you'd have to come to me, but I couldn't wait. I passed your test and now you owe me. What are you going to do about it?"

Her throat closed up in pure nerves, and she clutched the blanket as if the soft yarn could save her. But there was only one thing that could save her at this point. Complete surrender.

The man before her would demand no less. Arilyn's words drifted past in a gentle reminder.

The only way to true happiness is by letting go of control. The rest is just an illusion.

Kate squeezed her eyes shut and reached for courage.

Then let the blanket drop.

Cool air rushed over her flesh, pebbling her nipples. She opened her eyes and waited.

He drank her in with a hunger that stripped away all civility and left her raw and vulnerable. His gaze roved over every trembling inch, lingering on the thrust of her breasts, the drenched core of her sex hidden by a scrap of lace, the length of her bare legs. Kate fought the instinct to cover herself with her hands, knowing he'd never allow her to hide from him again. She straightened to full height, proud in her nakedness, daring him to take what she finally offered.

He didn't move. Didn't speak. The air in the room charged and jumped like a live fuse. "If I cross this room, there's no more running away. I'm going to fuck you until there's nothing left. I won't be gentle. Think carefully, Kate. I'm not playing games with you anymore."

She trembled from the dark threat, but her body

begged him for more, to show her everything he had and not hold back. This was what she'd been waiting for—a man to want her with the passion that wasn't quite civil or proper. His erection pushed against the fabric of his pants, his muscles locked and poised for his leap once she gave him the words.

Her voice shook. "I don't want to run anymore. I don't care about the future, or what's right or wrong. I'm yours, Slade. Tonight, I belong to you."

He ripped out a curse and crossed the room.

His mouth took hers in a hard, brutal kiss, his tongue pushing between her lips to set the tone of his dominance. She whimpered in sheer pleasure, opening and taking each thrust deep, drunk on his taste and his smell and the blistering heat of his skin.

Slade wasted no time on preliminaries. He reached down and lifted her, and she wrapped her legs tight around his hips as he walked toward the bedroom, his mouth never breaking contact. She floated in a crazed sea of sensation, her flesh quivering for more, and he placed her on the bed while his hands ripped the fragile silk from her body.

"I can't slow down. I had plans to torture you until you begged for me, to make you come a thousand times before I even entered your body. But I need to be inside you. You drive me crazy, Kate. Spread your legs. Let me look at you."

With a wanton openness she never experienced before, she spread her thighs wide. Her arousal leaked over her thighs, her pussy splayed open and bare for his hot gaze. Slade ripped off his shirt in record time, visually feasting on her throbbing clit as he unbuckled his pants, kicked off his shoes, and removed his briefs. "You're so gorgeous. I've been dying to know your taste, baby. I want to lick you for hours and play with that delicious pussy. But I don't know how much longer I can wait."

Kate moaned at his dirty words, her nipples stabbing for the relief of his tongue and fingers. She writhed on the bed while he ripped open the condom wrapper, slipped it on himself, and climbed on the mattress.

Slade knelt between her legs and ran one finger down her drenched slit. She cried out as her swollen flesh begged for more. With a low growl, he dipped his head and dropped gentle, teasing kisses over her drenched core. The whisper softness of his lips, the hot lash of wet tongue, all swirled together and cranked the tension in her belly so tight she thought she'd shatter with one more touch. Her clit hardened and demanded relief, but he ignored it, sliding his tongue over the sides and pulsing his fingers in tiny increments into her channel. She wriggled for freedom, but he kept her held tight, stabbing his tongue around her pulsing clit. Then slipped two fingers deep inside.

She cried out in delicious agony. Breath strangled in her lungs so she was only able to emit tiny pants as those talented fingers rubbed and plunged in a rocking rhythm that drove her right to the edge.

Kate arched, ready to explode, but he gave a sexy laugh and removed his fingers. "Not yet, baby. Not until I'm deep inside you." He lifted her ankles, placed them on his shoulders, and looked up her body.

Kate shook at the seething, sexual energy crackling between them, soaking into her skin until every pore and cell wept for him to take her. His massive erection poised at her entrance. She fisted her hands in the sheets and wondered if she'd splinter into a thousand pieces once he slid inside.

His eyes blazed. "Give me everything. I won't settle for anything else."

She sucked in her breath, suddenly terrified at her vulnerability. What was she doing? Giving her virginity over to a man who believed in nothing but the moment? He'd destroy her, take everything she had, and leave her with nothing. Panic reared. With a cry, she opened her mouth to stop him, but it was too late. He surged inside with one long slide and claimed her.

A sharp pain seized her. She grabbed for breath, dug her nails into his back, and tried to process the swirling sensations ripping her body and mind. Slowly, the burn faded into a sense of overfullness. Her body adjusted, squeezing his cock, her wet channel snugly accepting his length even as her brain fought the final battle. "N-n-no, don't, I can't, oh, God, it's too much."

His powerful muscles drove her deep into the mattress, and Kate pushed at his shoulders, half aware she didn't know if she should push him away or pull him closer. His skin was hot and slightly damp. An instinct to surrender to everything he wanted shimmered through her, but she fought the claim, afraid he'd take every piece of her body and mind and soul. "Look at me, baby. Open your eyes."

Kate half sobbed and obeyed. His warm palms cupped her face, and he held completely still, his cock pulsing deep inside until she didn't know where she ended and he began. A rocket of sensations exploded inside, which her brain desperately tried to make sense of—stretched, achy, wet, hot. As if he realized her barriers, a low growl emanated from his chest.

"No, you will not hide from this. Let go, Kate. No more hiding."

He rocked his hips in a delicious friction that slid over her clit and eased himself deeper. His mouth took hers, his tongue diving in with firm strokes, penetrating her in every way until she surrendered to his command.

The heat intensified, and now there was no pain, just a gorgeous growing pleasure that bloomed in her gut and spread out to every inch of her body. He increased the pace little by little, taking her higher, until she begged for more. She dug her nails into the mattress, lifted her hips, and let him ride her hard, fast, demanding every inch be opened and vulnerable to him.

Kate bit her lower lip as the tension twisted so tight it became excruciating. "Please, oh, please. Slade, I need—"

"That's it, baby, all of it, more." He groaned, rolling his hips and hitting a spot deep inside that shimmered with vibrations. Kate hovered on the brink of release, and he kept her there, drinking in every facial expression, not allowing her to conceal anything else.

His finger reached between them and slid over her clit. The orgasm took hold and shattered. Kate screamed as her channel milked him, and he rode out every last shudder, lengthening pleasure until convulsions racked her and wrung her dry. He gritted his teeth and groaned with satisfaction, letting himself go. His body tightened and he shuddered above her, the shock of pleasure too intense for any words. He slumped, tucked her neatly into his body and rolled so her head lay on his chest. Limp, sated, wrecked, Kate melted into him, closed her eyes, and rested.

"WOW."

Slade grinned and looked down. Her pin-straight hair was tangled and had that tumbled-after-sex quality. Sweat glistened on her skin, and the delicious scent of female arousal drifted to his nostrils. Her lips were parted and slightly swollen. Her muscles melted into him as if she was a natural extension of his body, her ankle hooked over his thigh, her hip a gleaming expanse of curve and pale white flesh that contrasted with his own olive skin.

"That's all you got?"

She blinked and stretched with a lazy grace that stiffened him to full staff. He was crazy to think one night with her would wring her out of his system. He'd never thought about the full danger of snagging a taste, then getting hooked. Slade pushed down the niggling worry that told him laying the trap to catch her had backfired. She'd trapped him just as well.

"Thought you'd be happy. I'm beyond words."

He chuckled and smoothed back her tangled hair. "True. That's probably a miracle."

She lifted a hand to try and punch him, but it fell helplessly to her side. "I'll make you pay later."

"I'm sure you will." He cupped her bare breast, playing with her nipple. The nub hardened instantly under his teasing thumb. "But not until I wreak my own revenge."

She arched into his touch. Power rushed through him at her raw response. The inner caveman he always beat back roared to life and shattered his civilized veneer. God, how long had he fought this only to be overwhelmed the moment they touched? Still, he needed to keep it strictly to the bedroom. Already, Kate pushed buttons he never knew he had, making him long for the unthinkable.

More.

"If it contains any of the moves you did before, bring it."

"Baby, I almost spilled my seed before I got inside of you. You've got a hell of a lot more coming."

He squeezed her breasts, tightening on her nipple, and she gasped. He watched her carefully and caught the tiny thrust of her hips, the tripping of her pulse in her neck. Oh, yeah. His Kate liked to play a bit on the wild side. He couldn't wait to explore every one of her limits and beyond.

Curiosity burned to know more. She hid so many layers behind her composed businesswoman persona. Each time she revealed more, his fascination intensified. Slade kept up the caress, lulling her into a state of relaxed arousal. "When I first met Robert, you said something that stayed with me. Just because someone was broken doesn't mean they should be thrown away."

"Yes."

"You were talking about more than Robert, weren't you?"

She took a few moments before answering. He stroked and tweaked her nipple to urge her on. "I stutter."

The simple admission tore through the room like a misfired champagne cork. "What do you mean, baby? You had a stuttering problem?"

"I still do. When I get nervous or stressed, I lapse back. I've gotten it under control in my adulthood, but I had a hard time."

He continued his gentle massage of her breasts. Remembered the few times she seemed to trip over her tongue. He'd assumed it was because she was overwhelmed by his pushiness to get her to confront their attraction. "Don't schools do therapy for that?"

She didn't speak for a while, as if wondering how much to tell him, but he kept his touch soothing. The connection of skin on skin guided her into a deeper state of intimacy, where sharing secrets in the dark blocked out the reality of the day-to-day world. "I started when I was eight. Usually children who stutter get help and outgrow it. At first, everyone thought I was just shy or nervous. I began to shut down more and more in order to stop it. I had all these thoughts and things I wanted to say, but when I opened my mouth, everything got tangled up. It was like a crazy cycle I couldn't break. I had decided to ask for help when my dad got transferred to upstate New York for his job. I had to move, and meet new people, and it started all over."

Slade frowned. "What about your parents? Didn't they try to help?"

"They seemed to think I'd outgrow it, but the school finally convinced them to send me to a regular therapist. My mother believed I was fine the way I was, that I was nervous and trying too hard to express myself. She enrolled me in yoga classes and music, believing I needed to let go and accept who I was. Dad backed her and they'd just confirm they loved me exactly the way I was. That in their eyes, I was already perfect. You see, my mom lost two children before she was able to carry me to term. They called me their miracle baby."

Slade analyzed her words. On the surface that type of love was hard to fight, the natural acceptance of parents who loved their child. The burn of perfection a mother's gaze saw in the baby she'd always wanted. But what was the price for Kate? How would it feel to be so frustrated with speaking? To want her parents to say it was a problem and get her the help she needed, but too afraid to confess she failed them? "Was school hard?"

She stiffened beneath him. Raw pain slammed into his gut at the idea of her being hurt by others. Like his sister. How many times had he found Jane crying, broken, trying to make it in a world where cruelty was flaunted and sensitivity was demolished? She never fit in with the right crowd, so she was consistently punished. "Yeah. I got bullied, of course. Some teachers tried to help; others ignored it. I kept to myself, and since I transferred late in the game, I barely made friends. For years, I felt so isolated and stupid. Why couldn't I speak normally like everyone else? Kids used to finish my sentences for me or imitate me. It got so bad I decided never to open my mouth, even to answer my teacher. My grades plummeted. But it taught me some hard lessons. Even things that are terrible finally end. If you lock down and fight through it, eventually the bad stuff is over."

Pride surged. Damn, she was strong. How many people

bitched and whined about their upbringing? Blaming others for bad choices and never looking inward? "I graduated and got into NYU. I met Arilyn and Kennedy in my first semester, and we bonded immediately. Manhattan was a big city, full of people who were too busy to care if I didn't speak perfectly. I found a great therapist and finally learned techniques to control my speech."

"But you finally got your happy ever after with Kinnections."

"Yes. Our famous drunken idea became a reality because we fought hard for it. My therapist really helped with my growing confidence, and I realized just because my speech would never be perfect, it didn't mean I couldn't own my business and make it a huge success."

"You amaze me." She shook her head in denial, but he forced her chin up. "You're an intelligent, capable, well-spoken woman, and I would've never known you had such a struggle."

"We all did. Kennedy battled a weight problem and then struggled with anorexia. Arilyn was a real geek and a complete outcast. We made it. I didn't tell you this for pity, Slade. I just wanted you to know . . . more."

Her confession shattered him, along with her inner strength. All the ridiculous assumptions he made about her and her crew haunted him. The idea of such vibrant, passionate women battling peer pressure and inner demons reminded him he had forgotten an important lesson. One shouldn't judge the surface before knowing the truth. Shame filled him. Isn't that what others consistently did to his sister? Assumed she was an overemotional geek who spurned others because she thought she was better than everyone?

"Thank you for giving me that gift."

"Slade?"

"Yes, baby?"

"Will you tell me something? Something you haven't told anyone else?"

He jerked back and studied her face. Curiosity gleamed in her eyes, but there was more. A vulnerability and longing to connect, to share an intimacy beyond their lovemaking and transcend the physical. The sexual pull between them was so strong it shimmered around them in a visible aura, but Slade realized in that moment she wanted to hold something more from this encounter. Something to remember in the harsh light of morning that wouldn't drift away in a wisp of smoke.

His heart lurched in his chest. From fear. From the bonds of confessing his own secrets to this woman who held more power than she knew. But he couldn't deny her, not tonight.

"I met my ex-wife in high school. I was young, full of angst, and too many hormones. I was at the top of my class, driven to succeed, and she was the bad girl on campus. I had been accepted to Harvard, and she decided to go with me, so we eloped at graduation." The image shimmered before his vision in all its taunting mockery, but he pushed on, determined to give her the story. "God, we were doomed from day one. I wanted to be a lawyer more than anything. She wanted to be my wife and thought marriage would be fun. Like high school. Needless to say, it wasn't, and things turned into a mess."

"Did she go to college, too? Want a career for herself?"

"Tracey wasn't ambitious. She wanted to party, have fun, and be a lawyer's wife. She craved excitement like a junkie, loved living on the edge." A humorless laugh escaped his lips. "School took everything I had. I rarely saw her, and when I did we'd fight, and she'd threaten me with cheating. We held on until I graduated, interned at a firm, and finally scored a job. We moved to New York together, but by then, we barely had a marriage. I came home one day early and caught her with another guy. Sad part was, I didn't even blame her. She was lonely, and I couldn't give her what she wanted. We divorced and moved on."

He fell silent. Kate rolled over and propped her chin in her hands. White-blond hair slid over one eye. Those lush lips pursed as if she were thinking and sorting over his story. "Do you still blame yourself?" she asked softly.

He almost jerked at the direct question but managed to hold her gaze. "Sometimes. I was selfish, and concentrated on my future rather than on us as a couple. I wasn't suited for marriage."

"You were young. Raw. Our first loves are the ones who define us, who teach us lessons and make us stronger. You've grown and know who you are. Look at the way you protect your sister and look out for her. You take care of the ones you love."

The breath whooshed from his lungs. The simplicity of her words rocked his core, the understanding on her face without pity or judgment, just acceptance. Of him. A surge of heat took hold, stiffening his dick, and her eyes widened as she reacted immediately to the lust that pulsed in every pore and demanded he sate his hunger. There was only one way to express himself and dump the whirling emotions needing outlet.

"Slade—"

"I want you. Again."

He gripped her arms and flipped her on her back, climbing on top to straddle her. The gorgeous bared curves of her body lured him to taste and touch every inch, until she wiggled and begged for mercy. With a growl, he lowered his head to rub his stubbled jaw against the softness of her breasts, his hands urging her thighs wide apart. She moaned and allowed him full access. Her nipples stood tight and hard, and he licked them, nibbling and teasing until her skin quivered and her breasts were swollen. "I love your breasts. One day, I intend on making you come just by licking them. I wonder how long it will take before you beg for mercy?"

She shuddered, and he laughed low in satisfaction.

Using his thumbs to pull her engorged lips apart, he slid his fingers back and forth over her wet, pink folds. Teased her clit to a hard nub. Then delved into her channel. She sucked him in with pure greed, and her fists beat the mattress in agony, held on the verge of an orgasm without a way to get there. A violent rush of possessiveness claimed him, making him want to give this woman excruciating pleasure, to give her a memory she'd never forget, to demand her complete surrender of everything she was, good and bad, light and dark, inside and outside until there was nothing left he didn't own.

He curled his fingers and dove deep, hitting the sweet spot as she screamed. "How bad do you want me?" he asked, loving her fierce reaction and the way she demanded her pleasure.

"I can't take any more, please, let me come."

"You can take more. Give me more." He kept up the rotating thrusts, while he nibbled on the sensitive flesh of her belly, then back up to her breasts to suck hard on the strawberry tips. Her heels dug into the mattress, her panting breaths filling the room.

"I'll do anything, Slade, anything, please."

Her pretty begging made the skin on his cock pull and tighten. He wasn't going to last long, the driving need to be inside of her fogged his mind and intentions to sexually tease and torture her. But he'd have his revenge. Now.

"Beg me again, Kate. But call me counselor."

She gasped, but was too far gone to deny him. Her pussy clamped down and drenched his fingers, his teeth poised on the hard nub of her nipple, waiting for the final break.

"Counselor! Please make me come!"

The sweet words hit his ears the same time he drove three fingers hard into her tight, soaked channel.

She clenched and shattered around him. Her muscles gave up the fight and her whole body shuddered, while he kissed her deep, drunk on the taste of her honey, which was sweeter than cotton candy. She'd barely stopped convulsing when he ripped open the condom, covered himself, and drove home.

His.

The mantra echoed in his brain as his dick pounded her hard, taking her back up with raw, controlled motions. She fell into the second orgasm easily, with his name on her lips. He followed her over the edge and took a leap he'd been denying himself for years, giving himself up completely to this moment, the orgasm not only seizing his body but going much deeper, until there was nothing left of him.

Slade kissed her cheeks and smoothed back her hair. She was already falling into a half sleep, and he quickly disposed of the condom, joining her back in bed and holding her tight. He allowed himself to tumble into slumber with a final thought flickering through his mind.

What had she done to him?

Slade slept.

eleven

KATE GROANED AND shoved her face into the pillow. She surfaced from the hazy world of sleep and noticed a few details. She clung to the side of her bed when she normally slept right in the middle. A heavy scent hung in the air, deliciously musky and sinful. And why did her thighs and legs feel like they were on fire? She ached deep in her muscles, especially between her legs. Fragments of memory shifted past her.

Kate jerked up, eyes bugging out of her head.

Oh. My. God.

She'd slept with Slade Montgomery.

Kate squeezed her eyes shut as images of last night hit her full force. Begging him to do bad things to her. His mouth between her legs while she called him counselor. His wicked growl when he told her to give it up. All of it.

And she had.

"Wanna go for round twenty-four?"

Her eyes flew open. She gazed open-mouthed at the vision before her. Jeans riding low on hips. Bare-chested and revealing an endless expanse of toasty brown skin. Golden hair tousled and falling seductively over his forehead. Dark stubble darkening his jaw and framing those lush, full lips that were made for sin and teased endless orgasms from her throughout the night. Oh, God, was that an erection? His jeans clearly showed a massive shape pushing out from the fabric. Kate gulped. Why wasn't she experienced with this stuff? She wished she were cool like Kennedy. No way was she walking around without clothes either, especially in the harsh morning light. That mole on her ass was definitely not her strong suit. She pushed back her hair, wondered how bad she looked, and tried to gather some composure. "Umm, I d-d-don't think so. I need t-t-to walk Robert."

"Already done."

She frowned. "What do you mean? He never goes out with anyone but me and Gen."

Those broad shoulders lifted. "Went with me. I watched you work the cart before, so I figured it out quick. He peed and pooped. I found the kibble in the cupboard and gave him fresh water."

Irritation buzzed through her. What was he doing taking over her routine? This was her house. Her life. Feeling ridiculous and grumpy, she held the sheet tight to her breasts. "Oh. Well, thank you. I need to make the coffee."

"It's brewing now."

She stuck out her chin. "My pot is old as dirt and barely works. I better help."

His lip quirked. "Haven't met a coffeemaker I couldn't

tame in this century. Why don't you take a moment and relax? I'll bring you a cup."

He strode from the doorway and disappeared.

Why was she so angry? Maybe it was the casual expertise and good humor he revealed in the morning after. How many had he experienced? Dozens? Hundreds?

The scurry of paws on the floor broke her depressing thoughts. Robert raced into her room and paused beside her. Kate grinned. "Bedtime?"

Two barks.

She reached down and lifted him onto the bed. Robert loved snuggle time after his morning walk. He smelled fresh and doggy at the same time, and she pressed her forehead against his and enjoyed the comfort of his love, no questions asked, no fear, and no holding back.

God, she loved him.

She lay back on the pillows and stroked his belly. What did she do now? Wait for coffee and then have the "talk"? At least she would get her touch back. She had satisfied every dark desire and given him everything. If that didn't do it, she'd face the knowledge her gift was gone forever.

The idea of acknowledging a perfect night and watching him go on other dates she set up made her belly lurch. Could she continue trying to match him? She still hadn't proven her talent and confirmed his sister was safe. But there was only one thought that kept echoing in her head.

He was hers.

Crazy, yes. But she didn't want to be cool and pretend she didn't have deeper feelings than she did. Maybe she'd break her cardinal rule and take him off the Kinnections list so he could be hers? After all, he'd mentioned before that it was silly to keep fighting their attraction. If she opened herself up, they had the potential of having a real relationship. Exploring each other to see if they fit in other ways than in bed.

Her phone vibrated from the nightstand. She checked the text that had streamed in. From Hannah.

> Hi Kate! Really enjoyed my date with Slade. I think he's the one! Hasn't called back yet though. Have you heard any feedback from our meeting? Hate being stalker type so figured I'd check with my fave matchmaker first. Thanks, as always for everything. ☺

Crapola.

Kate stared at the smiley face at the end of Hannah's text and got sicker. Somehow, she had stolen Hannah's man. In a twisted way, of course. Not on purpose, of course. Emma's text had streamed in the other day, glee-fully informing her they had a great date and she was waiting for his call. While her clients waited, she was in bed with him.

Bad karma.

She groaned. Get it together. Slade hadn't connected

with Hannah or Emma, and there was nothing to do about it. She'd call them as soon as she got into the office and break it to them gently. Kate had been the bad news breaker many times. In this business, breakups and non-connections were job hazards but part of the journey. She always hated when one client liked another more, but had nailed that speech down like a pro.

She just needed to make sure they didn't know the real truth.

Slade came in with two steaming mugs. Kate cleared her throat. "My mouth's watering."

He handed her a mug and arched a brow. "For me or the coffee?"

She gurgled a laugh. He was so damn arrogant and sexy. "Coffee."

"Bummer."

She sipped the hot brew, then looked up. "How'd you know I like it black?"

"No cream or half-and-half in the refrigerator. Sugar bowl is hidden. I took a chance."

"Very nice, counselor."

Green eyes blazed with stinging heat. "I don't think I'll ever hear that term and not think about your face when I made you come."

Her cheeks pinkened and she buried her nose in her coffee. Robert gave a doggy moan and sank into the fluffy goose down comforter. Slade's low laugh drifted across the room. "God, you're sexy when you blush. All fire and brimstone one moment, all shy virgin the next."

Boy. If he only knew.

At least his words caught her sense of challenge. She kept her voice measured. "Have you been using that famous charm to manipulate others your whole life? Just remember you didn't make me do anything I didn't want."

His intimate gaze dropped to the sheet she held tight against her chest. Her nipples poked through the satin in an effort to come out and play. "That's what made it sweeter," he growled. "Knowing you liked begging."

Wetness leaked from her thighs. Kate realized she was already too far gone. She'd never get enough of him. She ached for him to take her again, though she was sore. His cock responded to the unspoken need of her body and sprang to life. Her mouth watered to taste him, feel his hot, full length stretching her lips wide and controlling his pleasure. Slade muttered a curse, put his mug down on the table, and walked toward her. With gentle motions, he lifted Robert from the bed and placed him back on the floor. Transfixed, she allowed him to take her own cup and rip back the sheet.

A thrill coursed through her at his open, hot stare, taking in every inch of her nakedness, scenting her arousal. He pressed one knee down on the bed and her eyes half closed, waiting for him to take her on another wild ride.

"God, Kate, did I hurt you?"

His sudden question ripped through the pulsating silence. Her eyes flew open and followed his gaze. Blood smeared the sheets and stained her inner thighs. Slade sucked in his breath as the evidence of her virginity flashed in vivid neon.

Crap. It hardly hurt, so she didn't expect any blood. Kate sat up and pulled the covers tight against her chest. "N-n-no, of course you didn't hurt me."

His fingers twisted in the sheets and he yanked them back. Seconds ticked by. His erection withered away and when he finally looked up, her lover was gone. The man who replaced him was steeped in ice, his lips turned downward in a half sneer. Kate shivered. She prayed for strength to hide her vulnerability and her rapidly plummeting confidence.

"You were a virgin."

The hard words assaulted her ears. She sprang from the bed and grabbed her terry robe, belting it firmly around her and escaping his accusing gaze. "So? It's no big deal."

"Holy shit. I don't believe this." His jaw clenched and fury emanated from his pores. Robert lifted his head and gave him a wary look. "Why didn't you tell me?"

She shrugged and ignored the ball of ice in her gut. "Because it means nothing and I wanted to escape an unpleasant scene such as this. It was just a technicality, Slade. Nothing to worry about."

"I was your first lover. You waited this long for a reason. Why me?"

She prayed for the floor to swallow her up whole but knew she was stuck. Hmm, was this the time to tell him she had a special touch and never felt a connection with another man? Or should she confess her witchlike gene's disappearance and her plan to sleep with him to gain it back? Somehow, neither option seemed viable, so she cocked her head and lied again. "I've been busy. Never got around to it."

He emitted a vicious curse. "I hurt you. If I had known, I would've been gentler, more considerate. I would've seduced you and made sure you were ready. Did I bruise you, too?"

Kate let out a laugh. "You gave me multiple orgasms and never hurt me. Honestly, this whole martyr routine is embarrassing. Can we drop the subject, please? I'll make us some breakfast."

She tried to move past him, but his arm snaked out and gripped her upper arm. Tingles immediately crackled to life, and he stared at their joined flesh as if just figuring something out. "Have you ever felt this electricity before, Kate? To another man other than me?"

She stuck up her chin and hit him with her best shot. Screw this. Truth would be better and knock him back on his ass. "No. Maybe that's why I finally decided to do it with you. I have no regrets about what happened last night. Do you?"

He jerked back and nausea hit. Dear God, he regretted it. In the harsh morning light, knowing she was a virgin, he actually felt guilty. What was he so afraid of? Expectations of their relationship? Knowing he would always be her first? Or that he might actually feel something for her? Panic lit his eyes, and he suddenly looked at her not as a lover, but as more of a woman spinning her web to trap him. Kate fought the impulse to laugh in his face. Who would've thought an innocent virgin could scare the big bad wolf?

"No. But we didn't talk about what last night was about. I don't know if—if you have ideas about us. What do you want?"

The joy from last night drained out of her. Kate stared at the man she'd given everything to, who now resembled a stranger, hopping from foot to foot in an effort not to shoot out the door. "I want nothing," she said woodenly. "Last night I wanted sex. With you. This morning, I want to get back to our original agreement and business relationship."

"Forget we slept together? You give me your virginity and now want to pretend it never happened?"

Kate forced herself to shrug. "It wasn't a gift, Slade, it just was. We've already agreed that a long-term relationship won't work for us. We got it out of our system, so let's move on."

Relief carved out the lines of his face. Her heart shattered into tiny pieces and it hurt to breathe, but damned if she'd let him see an ounce of her pain. Slade Montgomery didn't believe in anything she needed, and pretending they could be something more than one night would only prolong the torture. She reached deep for calm, knowing it was the only way to end this now.

"I don't want to hurt you," he gritted out. His hands trembled as he pushed his fingers through his hair, looking like he'd rather be anywhere else. "I'm not built for forever. At least, not with someone who thinks love is a fairy tale and we'll live happily ever after. You haven't seen the things I have, the truth of what so-called love does to people. There is no forever!"

The hurt rose up in waves and drowned her. Kate dug her nails in her palms and took it all. How stupid. He'd stated his openness toward love, but he was only playing a game. Thinking he could find a woman who believed in companionship, a woman with no expectations or silly ideas. A woman who would never be her.

"You're wrong, counselor," she said softly. "I'm not looking for forever. But I am looking for someday. I think I deserve that."

He flinched. "I'm sorry. I'm—"

"No. Right now, I think it's better if you leave. And no worries. If I believe there was anything more than great sex, I'll remember the advice a very smart man once told me." Her eyes burned bright and hard. "It's just the oxytocin. Nothing more. Nothing less."

This time when she passed, he let her go. She busied

herself in the kitchen and ignored him when he stopped at the counter. Kate concentrated on whipping eggs and preparing French toast, praying he wouldn't test her or touch her. After a few moments, the door closed behind her without a word.

She surrendered the spoon, slumped against the granite island, and allowed herself to mourn something she never had in the first place.

KATE LOOKED AT THE mansion in front of her as Genevieve drove up the winding driveway. She almost canceled the outing, but guilt over missing out on Gen's family party drove her to try to be social. Besides, she barely saw her best friend anymore and was looking forward to an afternoon of fun.

"I never thought I'd be so depressed after sex."

Gen cut the engine and shook her head. "Let's look on the bright side. You had plenty of orgasms, and usually the first time you get a big fat zero. You found out his true character before you can get more involved. And you probably got your touch back, which is a boon for business."

Kate laughed. "Leave it to you to look on the bright side. I guess you're right. I'm giving him over to Kennedy for future dates so I won't have to really see him anymore. I'll get over it."

"You know what Ken says. The fastest way over a man is under a new one."

Kate rolled her eyes and opened the door. "No thanks. I think my remote and Robert are enough for me for a while."

They made their way up to the sprawling villa, a mass of brick and stone rising three stories in the air. Multiple balconies looked out over lush gardens and wooded paths, and shouts of laughter echoed in the air. When Kate met Gen at college, she'd immediately been welcomed into the family fold—a close-knit Italian group who hosted Friday and Sunday dinners and fed their guests heartily while they were on a shoestring budget.

"How old are the twins now?" Kate asked, hoisting up the big racetrack gaily wrapped with dinosaur paper.

"Six. Everyone should be there. Maggie and Michael said they wanted a jungle party, so who knows what to expect. Uh-oh, here comes Lily."

Kate laughed as Gen's niece caught sight of them, squealed, and tore down the gleaming parquet floors and into her aunt's arms.

"You look so beautiful! Did Aunt Maggie give you that outfit?" Maggie was Gen's older sister Alexa's longtime best friend, and had taken it upon herself to make Lily the trendiest youngster around. Lily hugged her tight, grinned with pride, and gave a full twirl in her chic denim dress with hot pink ankle boots. "Daddy said the other dress was too weird." Lily wrinkled her pert nose, her corkscrew inky curls so like her mother's own unruly hair. "He told Maggie to take it down a notch. Then Maggie stuck her tongue out at him when he left and Mommy told them to stop acting like babies because there were already too many children to begin with."

Gen laughed and tugged on a wayward curl. "Where's your sister?"

"Maria is following Luke and Ethan around. I think she wants to marry Luke."

"Cousins don't marry, honey, but that's okay for now. Let her torture him a bit. Luke needs a bit of his own medicine."

"Yeah, Luke already spilled the punch when he climbed the tree and tried to see if he can jump into the bowl like he saw on the cartoons. Uncle Michael put him in time-out, and Maria said she'd sit with him and keep him company."

Kate bit her lip at the image. "We'll be right out, honey, we're just going to say hi to everyone first."

"K!"

Lily ran out, and they weaved their way through the elaborate rooms, decorated in bright blues and greens. The jungle theme showed the boys' obsession with animals, and a variety of stuffed monkeys, tigers, and zebras jumped from corners amid piles of wrapped presents with brightly colored bows. They stopped and chatted with guests along the way and finally hit the main destination.

The bar.

"Ah, my favorite girls are finally here! Surgeon in training and matchmaker extraordinaire." Kate grinned. Nick, Alexa's husband, stood behind the bar and seemed pretty happy to be out of the backyard where all the action was occurring.

"Right now I think we're dying for a cosmo," Gen said. "Know how to make one?"

"The *Sex and the City* drink, right?"

Gen laughed. "Well, that's been off the air for a while, but we'll take it. Is everyone outside?"

"Yeah, it's a jungle out there. Literally. Michael and I fought over who would tend bar, but I won so I'm staying put. Where's David?"

"Coming later."

"Good." He winked at Kate. "How about you? Where's Robert? You could have brought him."

Kate wondered how her date always became her dog, but it was too sad to analyze. Especially after her night with Slade. "Shelly's taking him to the dog park today. I figured I'd be footloose and fancy-free."

"Sounds dangerous." He handed her a perfect pink drink and stuck in a yellow umbrella. "There you go, honey. Enjoy. Izzy's not here yet, hopefully later."

Gen's twin sister, Isabella, seemed to be going through a hard time. Gen used to be close to her, but lately Izzy's edgy temper and almost cruel sarcasm put a wedge between them. Sad, since Kate always wished to have a sister of her own. She knew it bothered Gen a lot, and she hoped time would soften some of the wounds that opened between them.

They threaded their way to the back deck and stopped cold. "Wow, Gen. Now this is what I call a kids' party."

Tables and chairs were laid out among dozens of play stations, small fenced-in areas with different activities for the kids. Puzzles, toys, and a small petting zoo boasting furry animals to be fed with baby bottles. An elaborate vine was tied between two trees to give a mini zip line effect, and a worker helped kids take turns getting strapped into the seat and taking a slide from one trunk to another. A huge pushcart with peanuts, popcorn, and cotton candy served swarming children, and a giant circus truck was parked a mile away on the lawn. Kate squinted and peered across the lawn. Was that an elephant?

"You're here!"

Alexa enveloped them in a warm hug. Gen's older sister was beautiful, with her black corkscrew curls, bright blue eyes, and curvy figure. Her kindness and humor radiated in waves, and Kate loved being around her. "Umm, Al, is that an elephant?" Gen asked.

Alexa gave a deep sigh. "Yep. But don't worry, there's no abuse going on. I investigated this before I let Maggie go with the idea. His name is Sam and he's from a rescue camp for elephants retired from the circus. It's only for two hours, and he's well taken care of. The petting zoo is fine, too. I thoroughly checked out the owner and she's from an organic farm in Wallkill that educates children on the proper way to treat animals."

Kate laughed. Alexa was a fierce animal advocate and spent some of her free time volunteering for shelters. "Got it. Glad you set me straight. This is some setup."

"Yeah, what would you expect from Maggie?"

"I heard that."

The husky voice came from behind. Gen gave her a hug while Kate admired her designer jeans, three-inch platform boots, and trendy leather jacket. She looked like she was slumming in Beverly Hills rather than at a children's party. "Gen, is your hunky doctor coming today?"

"He's popping in later, he's at the hospital."

"Kate, darling, where's Robert?"

"Dog park."

Maggie lifted a brow. "Dateless, huh? I have a yummy male model I'd love to set you up with."

Kate laughed. "Don't know if I'm the model type, Maggie."

"Nonsense, they're everyone's type."

Gen shook her head. "Where are those gorgeous birthday boys?"

Maggie blew out a long breath. "Luke's in time-out again. Ethan is running around like a nut on crack, so I know he stole some birthday cake. I blamed Michael by mistake because it's his favorite dessert from La Dolce Maggie."

Gen grinned. "Picking your son over your hubby, Maggie?"

"Darlin', I'm just trying to keep him on his toes."

As if his ears were burning, Michael paused behind her, his finger over his lips to keep them quiet. Gen pressed her lips together to keep from giving him away. "Interesting. What's the best way to keep your man in line, Maggie?"

She cocked a hip and winked. "Sex, of course. I'd say sex and food, but since I can't accomplish the latter, I excel at the former."

Alexa caught on to the joke and rolled her eyes. "Oh, please. I've seen who wears the so-called pants in your family, and it's not those stylish Pradas you favor. Your husband crooks his finger and you melt into a pile of goo."

Her green eyes snapped with annoyance. "That's libel. Or slander. And untrue. All I have to do is snap my fingers and my man obeys."

The words escaped her mouth the moment her husband's arms grabbed her waist. Maggie gave a small screech and jerked around, but Michael held her against him with ease, refusing to let her move. "Mouthing off again, *cara*?" he drawled, his hands familiarly stroking her into instant submission. Kate watched in fascination as Maggie relaxed against him, her eyes sparking with a heat that hadn't dimmed in almost eight years of marriage. Raw need clawed at her throat. God, how she wanted to feel like that. Completely possessed and entranced by a man. An image of Slade rocketed past her vision. Poised at her entrance, jade-green eyes burning with hunger, fingers intertwined while he pushed deep inside and claimed her, body . . . soul . . . heart.

Tears pricked her lids. Damn, she must be hormonal. One lousy night and she had surrendered not only her virginity but her emotions.

"Oops, sorry babe. Just girl talk."

Michael lowered his head and growled loud enough for everyone to hear. "Perhaps I'll wrest a heartfelt apology from those lips tonight. Or other things."

The dark promise caused Maggie to shudder, and Kate swallowed hard at the sexual power before her.

Alexa waved her hand in the air, more used to her best friend's ways. "Cut it out, guys. This isn't a BDSM outing, it's a kids' party. And no more talking about sex, Carina's here."

On cue, Michael's younger sister waddled up to the deck. Misery carved out her features, though she looked adorable in a cute maternity T-shirt, jeans, and pink canvas sneakers. Her thick hair was tied back, and her cheeks were flushed and full. "Ugh. I don't want to hear a thing about sex. That's how I got in this miserable condition."

Michael groaned. "TMI, dear sister."

Max followed his wife, supporting her by the elbow. "I'll get you some seltzer, babe."

Carina groaned and placed her hands on her massive belly. "I miss alcohol. I miss seeing my toes. I miss sleeping."

Alexa and Maggie shared a look and patted her shoulder. "I know," Alexa said. "But in a few weeks you'll have all the joy and happiness you can imagine. Motherhood is an amazing, perfect gift that makes all of this discomfort well worth it."

Luke streaked across the lawn, naked. His crazy spiked hair and manic laugh reminded her of a comic book figure. His bare buttocks winked in the sun and groups of children hooted and hollered, pointing and jumping up and down with glee.

Maria followed. Her princess dress was covered in mud and she raced after him with one shoe on, one shoe off, screaming his name into the wind.

Carina lifted her brow. "You were saying?"

Maggie sighed. "Never mind. Labor will hurt. Motherhood will make you a slave. You'll be sleep-deprived, mean, crazed, and the happiest you've ever been in your life."

Alexa nodded. "Yeah. What she said."

Gen smashed a knuckle against her mouth and tried to keep a straight face. "Umm, I'll go check on them. And, umm, find Luke's clothes. Kate?"

"I'll help."

"Thanks, guys," Maggie said.

They trudged across the lawn after the nephews and nieces, drinks in hand. Kate smothered a giggle. "Your family is a trip."

"Yeah, but your mom smokes pot. That's pretty damn cool."

The next few hours whizzed by in a dizzying rush of children, sugar, screaming, playing, and drinking by the adults. They sang "Happy Birthday," cut the cake, and lounged around the massive kitchen, sipping cappuccino and espresso. David finally showed up, and Kate watched as her friend relaxed into David's embrace, seemingly comfortable and at ease. That same odd warning voice flashed within, and Kate casually brushed both of their arms to see if she caught any type of sensation between them.

Nothing.

She frowned. Were they not suited? Or was her gift still missing? Surrounded by happy couples, Kate made her way back to the bar, where Alexa and Nick held hands and spoke in low voices. She edged in, determined to prove once and for all if her gift lingered. The couple usually gave her quite a jolt when touched, a strong sign of a soul match. Kate reached for a glass, murmuring an apology, and managed to graze both their wrists.

Nothing.

Her hope plummeted. The touch hadn't returned. What if she'd lost it permanently? Kate pressed her back against the wall for support and tried not to panic. If sex hadn't worked, what was she missing? All the time she cursed her gift, she realized it was also a part of her. She'd built Kinnections on the knowledge she'd be able to confirm a good match, weaving a solid foundation so clients were well taken care of. What now? What was her role if she had no touch?

A voice distracted her from a total freak-out.

"Well, isn't this cozy? The power couple ready to take on the world. Surgeons unite and all that jazz."

Silence fell over the kitchen. Gen's twin sister, Izzy, stood framed in the doorway. Leather pants that hugged every ripe curve, thigh-high boots with wicked spikes and silver studs, and a black tank dipping way too low in the front to display the thorned rose tattooed on the curve of her breast. Numerous silver chains tinkled around her neck, and her diamond nose ring flashed in the light. Gen's voice broke the tension. "We missed you, Iz. The boys were asking about you. How are you?"

Izzy shrugged. "Good to know someone noticed. I'm fine."

Alexa stepped in, her gaze registering disapproval over her sister's outfit. Her hug was barely returned. "Hot date tonight?" Alexa teased. "I know you didn't dress up like this for us."

Isabella's head whipped around. "Why do you assume I'm giving it up to some guy? I dress like this to please one person. Myself."

Nick's voice slashed across the room. "Enough. You know Alexa was only joking. Take it down a notch."

A mutinous expression crossed her face. Kate caught a glimpse of raw longing like she regretted her remark but had gone too far to back down. "Whatever." She clicked away on her high heels.

David shook his head. "Unacceptable behavior. She shouldn't have come."

"She's family," Gen said.

David frowned. "That girl is heading toward destruction, and I'm not letting her take you with her. You shouldn't be involved with anyone doing drugs. It could ruin your career."

Kate was about to speak up for her friend when she was interrupted. Gen's best friend, Wolfe, stood framed in the kitchen, his massive height dwarfing the rest of the room. His shaved head, sizzling blue eyes, and powerful body gave the impression of hot and bad boy in one firm twist. A wicked serpent tattoo curled up his shoulder and the side of his neck, and a diamond winked in his left ear. His brow was also pierced, and he wore leather wristbands with a long-sleeved black shirt, giving him an edgy look that usually made women drop their panties.

Somehow, Kate had never been affected, maybe because of his long-term friendship with Gen. She always wondered if there was something more between them, especially since Wolfe seemed to loathe David, but her best friend always insisted there was no sparks between them and they were only friends.

"She's not on drugs," Wolfe declared in his deep, husky voice. "She's in pain," he said simply.

Gen bit her lip. "I can't reach her," she said. "I've tried, but she wants nothing to do with me. She acts like she hates me."

"Be patient. Eventually, she'll need you."

David let out a breath. "She's jealous of Gen's success. Better to give her space and let her be."

Wolfe studied David for a while. Then shook his head and walked away.

"They'd be perfect together," David muttered. "Surprised they never hooked up. Or maybe they did."

Kate tapped her lower lip. Hmm, Izzy and Wolfe? That was a match made in explosive heaven. They both seemed to seethe with some underlying pain, but Wolfe had a much tighter hold on his emotions than Izzy did on hers.

Kate glanced at her watch. Time to get back to Robert. "I gotta go soon, Gen. I'm going to hit the bathroom."

Her friend nodded.

Kate put down her mug and headed upstairs. She climbed the sprawling staircase, her fingers skimming the smooth mahogany banister. Past the dripping Swarovski crystal chandelier, down the hallway, until she heard voices. Uh-oh, intimate conversation ahead. She turned on her heel to retreat and then recognized Wolfe's tone. Then Izzy's voice rang clearly through the air. Kate froze.

"Why do you torture yourself? I see the way you look at her. She can't give you what you need, babe, but I can."

Kate battled the awful need to see what was going on

against her respect for privacy. Her bad side won, and she stood silent, listening to the unfolding conversation.

"Don't."

The low warning was ignored. A husky laugh and the sound of heels on wood. "You say no, but your body says yes. What are you fighting so hard for? Gen's with David and she'll never look at you the way you need. Besides, she's like a timid little virgin in the bedroom. I can satisfy you the way you need."

Kate craned her neck to peep through the doorway. Izzy posed before Wolfe, one hip cocked, her breasts thrust out so he got a perfect view of her impressive cleavage. He stood still, the lines of his face carved in anger, arms crossed in front of his chest as if he had no interest in her seduction attempts.

"I'm not stupid, Izzy. You're going through a bad time right now and just want to be distracted. But sex doesn't do it. Neither does hate. You have an incredible family ready to support you. Why are you fighting so hard to drive them away?"

Isabella shimmered with fury and practically spit in his face. "Don't play the therapist role with me. You know shit about my family or the way they treat me like dirt. Believe I'm less than my perfect twin sister. Refuse to accept who I am because it doesn't fit in with their idealistic view of their children. I'm sick of them and their expectations. Even you got conned."

She closed the distance and pressed her body against

his. Wolfe hissed in reaction but didn't move. With a preda-
tory smile, she rose on her toes and stopped inches from
his mouth. "You're just like me, you know. You think Gen
will bring something good and right into your life. But
you're not meant to be that man, Wolfe. You live in the
dark. You like dirty sex, and a bit of pain, and see the reality in life. Not like my silly, sheltered sister. Why don't you
just be the man you are and take me? I'll give you everything you ever wanted." She licked her lips and ran a finger
down his cheek. He stiffened, his gaze locked on hers. "I'll
even let you pretend you're fucking her if you want. Won't
that make it even better?"

The air sparked with tension. Kate waited for Wolfe's
reaction.

He pushed her gently away and stood back. His face
reflected a mix of regret, lust, and pity. "It doesn't work like
that, Izzy. I don't know what happened, but it's tearing you
up inside. You can talk to me, you know. I'll listen."

Izzy pushed him hard, snarling like a pissed-off cat.
"Fuck you, Wolfe. I hope you're happy in your ridiculous
fantasy that my sister will notice you one day. You're way
below her standards for a lover. I feel sorry for you."

Kate couldn't hear anymore. She slowly backed up and
headed toward the other bathroom. Whoa, that was heavy
stuff. Was Wolfe in love with Gen? Did Gen suspect? Or
was that just Izzy's crazy assumption in order to cause
drama? It was like *General Hospital* on steroids.

Kate finished up, washed her hands, and headed back

to the kitchen. David gave her an uneasy feeling, but she never interfered with her friend's love life. Gen seemed happy with the surgeon, but maybe Kate should tell her what she overheard. She rarely kept secrets from her best friend.

She was about to get her coat and begin her good-byes when David snagged Gen's hand and pulled her to the center of the living room. Foreboding washed over her as David raised his voice for everyone's attention. Guests milled in groups and lounged on the coffee-colored sofa and chairs, huddled by the bar, and sat cross-legged on the Persian carpet. "Excuse me, everyone. I'd like to say a few words."

Yep, this whole day was jacked up, beginning with Slade walking out the door.

"When I first met Genevieve, she turned my world upside down. She's a stubborn, brilliant, beautiful woman who turned my life from black and gray to color. I never want to go back to the person I was. And being here with everyone tonight, in the warm clasp of family, made me realize I don't want to waste another second."

David dropped to one knee. Removed a small box. And snapped open the lid.

Gasps of pleasure surrounded her. "Genevieve Mac-Kenzie, you are the woman of my dreams. I love you with my heart and my soul, and want to spend the rest of my life with you. Will you marry me?"

Kate watched a dozen expressions cross her friend's face. Shock. Confusion. Happiness.

And fear.

What was that about? Gen's gaze wavered, then shifted across the room. As if seeking someone out. Kate glanced over and caught Wolfe staring at the couple. His face like carved stone, no emotion was evident in his features.

Kate held her breath, wondering what was really going on. Then her friend's answer echoed through the room.

"Yes, David. I will marry you."

When Kate looked back, Wolfe was gone.

And she wondered if Gen was keeping her own secrets.

twelve

*H*E WAS A dickhead.

Slade stared at his computer and tried to make sense of the endless notes for his next client. Sunday was a complete blur, with moments of clarity where he fought the need to show up at Kate's door and beg her forgiveness. He'd certainly won the Prick of the Year award. After trying to seduce her in every way possible, he finally got her in bed, spent hours in orgasmic ecstasy, and treated her like some freak because she was a virgin. He belonged in one of those bad eighties flicks and he wasn't even in high school.

Shame beat through him. The truth taunted and kept him from calling her. One night with Kate Seymour would never be enough. He craved more, wanted to spend hours in her company, learn all her secrets, and go over every inch of her delectable body. He wanted to hang out with Robert and watch movies. He wanted to cook for her, bring her coffee, and read the paper in bed.

The images streamed in a long vision that scared the living hell out of him.

It was more than sex, but he couldn't handle it. Knowing he was the one who finally claimed her virginity made him want to roar with satisfaction like the primate he fought not to be. Slade also realized it strengthened the bond between them like an invisible, unbreakable string. He'd always be her first, and in some way, special. Too bad he had jacked up that good memory for her.

Slade pushed away from the desk with a groan and wished for that minibar. Instead, he grabbed a chilled bottle of water and wondered what his next move would be. He doubted she'd want to match him with anyone else, and honestly, he had no desire to go out on any dates when he wanted only one woman. A woman he should stay away from since he couldn't offer her what she wanted, needed, and deserved.

Even though it didn't exist.

His original plan to debunk the company had fizzled. Yes, he'd keep an eye on Jane, but Kinnections wasn't looking to do anything illegal or immoral. In fact, the women who ran it did so with pure hearts and an intention he admired. There was nothing left keeping them together.

Slade ignored the twinge of pain in his gut and reached for the phone. Enough. He'd call her, apologize for his rotten behavior, and formally withdraw his name from her list. He'd hoped for an engaging affair with a woman who enchanted him, but he had no right mucking around in her life. She was a woman who didn't screw around—for God's sake, she was almost thirty and still a virgin. And that meant the man she let in her life would be important.

Sweat pricked his skin at the idea of being counted on to provide a happy ending. God knows, his last client had proven the truth. The poor woman was left alone with two kids while her husband moved in with his latest fling, twenty years younger and blowing through the kids' college fund faster than he could make it back.

Slade punched out the number.

"Kinnections, may I help you?"

He dragged in a breath. "Hi, Kennedy, it's Slade Montgomery. Can I speak with Kate, please?"

An awkward pause. Crap, how much did she know? Did Kate tell her everything? "Kate's not here. Can I take a message?"

"Is she in a meeting? It's important, I really need to know."

Another pause. "Actually, she's at the vet now. Robert got sick. I doubt she'll be back, but maybe you can try her on her cell tonight?"

He tried to calm his racing heart. "Do you know what's wrong with him?"

"Some type of infection. Look, I'd give her some time and—"

"Which vet?"

"The Animal Menagerie Hospital. Umm, Slade, I don't think you should—"

He hung up. Stuffed the folders in his briefcase, grabbed his suit jacket, and headed out. He stopped at his secretary's desk to forward his calls, cancel some meetings, and whizzed past his boss's office, ignoring his pleas to pause for a chat.

Slade knew that dog meant the world to Kate. He also figured she was there alone, handling things in her life like she always did, with a poised control and fierce independence that never allowed her to show weakness. She wouldn't bother anyone else for support because she was the one who tried to take care of others.

Not today. Just once, he wanted to take care of her.

Slade refused to question his intentions as he got into his Jag and headed toward Verily.

"WILL HE BE OKAY?" Kate asked the question calmly, but her lower lip trembled. Something had been wrong with Robert, but she hated dragging him to the vet each time she suspected a problem. She'd learned to wait it out a bit, and many times it was a brief bladder problem or a minor skin infection she was able to cure by bathing him and slathering him with the special medicine the doctor had provided.

This morning, she'd had to express his bladder manually and knew he was in pain. Every time she went through the vet's doors, she wondered if she'd come back out. She was warned early that paraplegic dogs sometimes had many health issues along the way, but she swore to do everything possible to avoid them.

"This infection definitely spread out of control," Dr. Burke informed her. He stroked Robert's head with the kind affection from years of treatment and friendship. "I'm going to put him on strong antibiotics and wait on the results from the lab. Lots of water, and add a splash of cranberry juice for some acid. Keep an eye on him and give him some extra bathing time."

Relief loosened her chest. They'd gotten through some bad infections before, and usually Robert fought them off like a champ. His big brown eyes studied the doctor with serious intent, as if waiting for the final diagnosis.

Kate pressed a kiss to the top of his head, held up his chin, and looked him straight in the eye. "It's just a bad bladder infection, baby," she said. "Meds and baths. Not so bad. And more time with Mommy."

One lick. And as if he understood, he flopped his head back down on the table, totally chill that he knew it wasn't serious. Kate smiled and quickly analyzed the next two days. She'd stay home today, but tomorrow was the big expo in Manhattan. It had taken two years to get Kinnections into the lineup, so she had to go. Her mom could probably stay with Robert all day and then—

The door flung open. Slade walked in, his suit a bit rumpled, his gorgeous surfer hair mussed. "How is he?" he demanded, making his way across the small exam room and toward Robert.

Kate's mouth fell open. "W-w-what are you doing here?"

Dr. Burke frowned. "Excuse me, this is a private room for owners only."

"I'm a friend." His presence pumped up the room and took over. Kate let out another squeak, but he ignored her, bending down to look Robert in the face. "How ya doing, buddy?" The dog's tail thumped and his expression lit up. Shock billowed through Kate as Slade stroked him, glancing from her to the doctor with a worried light in his eyes. "Is he going to be okay?"

Dr. Burke cleared his throat. "Kate? Is this man a friend of yours?"

The question threw her off, but the word stumbled from her mouth without thought. "Yes."

"Sorry, doc. Slade Montgomery. Nice to meet you."

Slade shook his hand and Dr. Burke relaxed. "Likewise. As I was just telling Kate, Robert has a bladder infection. Antibiotics should work. He needs to be watched, bathed, drink lots of water. Manual expression of his bladder if he backs up. I'll call when the lab results come in."

"Good."

"Kate, why don't you wait outside and I'll bring him out shortly."

Slade rubbed Robert's ear and followed her out. She

eased into the waiting room where the Animal Planet network chirped merrily behind her on the small-screen TV and a golden Lab waited patiently with his owner.

She lowered her voice. "What's going on? Why are you here?"

Was that a glimmer of regret that flashed on his face or just the light? "I called to speak with you, and Ken told me you were at the vet. I thought you'd need help. I was worried."

The ridiculousness of the conversation hit her hard. He'd walked out the other morning after taking her virginity. And now he left work in the middle of the day to drive up to Verily because he was concerned about her dog? "Robert's fine, I've been taking care of him for years alone and don't need any help now."

"Who's been taking care of you, Kate?"

She stumbled back. Hurt sliced like a hundred paper cuts on her skin. No, she couldn't do this now. Not with him. "I take care of myself," she said stiffly. "You made it quite clear this is not a job you want anyway, so why are you here?"

"I don't know why I'm here. I'm a mess. I wanted to walk away, do the right thing by not screwing up your life. But the thought of you alone here, with Robert in trouble, I don't know." He blew out a breath. "I just thought I should come."

She stared up at him, shock keeping her immobile. The

truth of his words slammed her full force. What kind of game was he playing? Yet, he seemed just as confused, as if he wasn't used to letting his heart lead. As if she meant something more to him than he wanted. The bees' nest of emotion was a dangerous thing to touch, let alone explore, and Kate hated getting stung. Before she had time to make sense out of his impromptu speech, Dr. Burke came out with Robert in his arms.

"Here's our patient. I'll call you as soon as the results get back. Let me know if there's any trouble."

"Thanks, doctor."

She settled the bill and scooped up Robert, then headed toward her car. Slade stayed close behind, helping her with the door and settling him carefully in the back. "Are you taking the day off?" Slade asked.

Kate pushed her hair back and blinked in the sun. "Yeah, I'll stay home today. Tomorrow I have a big expo in the city, so my mom can stay with him—oh, crap."

"What?"

She leaned against the car and nibbled on her lip. "Mom's at a sex conference."

One golden brow shot up. "Sex what?"

"Never mind, you so don't want me to go there. Shelly can only stop in for a few hours on a weekday. I better cancel the expo. Ken and Arilyn will have to cover."

"I'll do it."

She cocked her head. "Do what?"

The determined look on his face gave her a glimpse of what jurors saw when he wanted something. A force of nature. "I'll watch Robert. Since the expo is in Manhattan, you can drop him off at my home for the day and I'll take care of him."

Kate sputtered out a laugh. "What? Absolutely not. You've never taken care of a dog before. Besides, you work."

"I can do my work at home. I'm perfectly capable of watching Robert and giving him whatever he needs."

"No, I'll stay home."

"And miss out on this type of opportunity for Kinnections? Bad business if you ask me. As the owner, you need to be there."

She glared. Unfortunately, he was right. Everyone worked, and she had no one to watch Robert. And missing out on the expo would set Kinnections back. She'd already made her contacts and they expected her to show. Kate shifted her weight and looked for any possible outs.

There wasn't one.

Slade grinned. "Glad you see it my way. I'll expect you around seven in the morning?"

She must be nuts. "Fine. If you think you can handle it, I appreciate you helping me out."

His features softened. Slade reached out and ran a finger down the curve of her cheek, leaving a trail of fire. "Thanks for letting me," he murmured.

He left her standing on the sidewalk, watching him walk away and wondering what she had just set back in motion.

THE NEXT MORNING, KATE walked into Slade's apartment and tried to calm her nerves. Bringing Robert into Slade's personal space screamed intimacy, which was the exact opposite of what they both decided they needed. Still, perhaps it was Slade's way of apologizing for his awful behavior. Kind of like a peace offering before they officially called it splitsville. Even though they had no real relationship to split up, just one night.

Her thoughts hurt her head, so she concentrated on her nosiness and gathering information. The high ceilings and loftlike atmosphere pegged the trendy Tribeca area, but Slade kept it simple and masculine. The circular glass staircase was fresh and fun, and the edgy lines of furniture, glass tables, and strong blue walls bespoke a man who knew what he liked. The living room was a man cave made in heaven.

Her heels clicked on the bamboo floors as she paused in front of the huge leather recliner. She stroked the soft material and almost groaned in appreciation.

"You like?"

Slade cocked his hip, his jeans falling low on his hips and accenting his washboard stomach and long legs. Seemed he favored jeans now. The man was sheer perfection, but even hotter in his own environment. The plain black T-shirt was faded and soft, and his bare feet gave off an intimacy she really didn't want to linger on.

"How could I not? I'm saving up for a new one. God, is that a remote?"

He laughed and handed it to her. "Yeah, full reclining position, seat warmer, and back massager."

Kate shuddered. "I'd never leave the house."

"You don't need to with one of these chairs." Green eyes lit with a lazy arousal, and she was dragged back to the night they spent together, feasting on each other until their bodies collapsed in exhaustion.

She took a step back. Wet her lips. "Maybe it's good I don't have one, then."

"Maybe."

They stared at each other. Energy crackled with a mad glee and tempted them closer. She broke the spell with deliberate precision, walking over to Robert and kneeling down. Kate pressed her forehead to his and spoke. "Slade will take care of you today. Be good, baby. Mommy will be home later."

"I got him peanut butter and bacon treats. How many barks?"

Kate stood and smiled. "One for bacon, two for peanut butter. I brought cranberry juice in case you didn't have any, just a splash in his water bowl. I'll give him a bath when I take him home tonight."

"No need, I've got a huge tub and you'll be home late. I'll get it done."

She hesitated, then gave a jerky nod. "Okay. Thanks. I'll call later."

"You look nice."

Her black suit was chic and fitted, and the new boots flashed a bright, shiny four-inch stacked heel. "Thanks." Did her voice crack? God, she had to get out of here. "See ya."

She hurried out of the house like her ass was on fire. When was the last time a man wanted to help her out, especially with her dog? He'd taken off work and seemed sincere. Yesterday, she'd picked up the phone to cancel, positive there was some type of ulterior motive to his madness. But she couldn't come up with a thing. He'd already seduced her, so that was off the list. He was already keeping a close eye on Jane and seemed satisfied with her treatment. He could've easily apologized for his statements that morning and been done with her. Yet her heart told her there was something bigger in his actions.

She thought about him all day at the Javits Center. Amidst conversations with potential clients, Kate networked hard, made a solid impression on a variety of business associates who thought Kinnections was the next big thing, and laughed with Ken and Arilyn. By the time they'd finished dinner with another matchmaking agency looking to merge and grow client databases, Kate drove back to Tribeca, exhausted but triumphant. Her company was finally getting noticed, and the future looked bright. Even without her gift, she believed in the skills of the team and again counted herself lucky that she could make her dream job a reality that paid the bills. The only thing that would bring it to a higher level would be sharing her happiness with a man she loved.

Who was not Slade Montgomery.

Yes, he'd wriggled himself into the seams of her life, but after tonight, she'd pull way back. No reason to torture herself with a man who wasn't meant to be with her. He may have had some second thoughts and tried to help her out, but continuing on this path would only hurt them both. Well, at least her.

She was buzzed into his apartment and tried not to limp as she crossed the threshold. Damn boots were a killer. Kate tried not to think of the long drive ahead and tempted herself with the image of her butt in the recliner, her sweats, and a good night's sleep.

"Hey." Her heart leaped at the wide grin on his face. The dragging of paws over the floors echoed and she opened her arms to welcome her companion. Face bright with expectation, Robert licked her and they snuggled for a few minutes. "He did great. I bathed him, then put the salve on his sores. He peed all day and drank lots of water. We had a good time, didn't we, buddy?"

Robert cocked his head and gave a half nod of agreement.

"Why don't you show Mommy what you got today? Robert, go get your bunny."

The dog turned, disappeared briefly, and returned with a fluffy stuffed bunny clasped between his teeth. Kate gasped. "What do you have, baby?" She took the wet bunny from his mouth and studied it in astonishment. "He actually likes this?"

Slade frowned. "What's the matter? He's allowed toys, right?"

"No, that's not the problem. I've tried to give him stuffed toys all the time and he hated them. Almost as if they were beneath him. He only enjoyed the occasional bone or ball."

Denying her statement, Robert reached out, grabbed the toy, and began working the hidden squeaker. Chirpy sounds emitted from the bunny, and each time his ears pricked.

Slade laughed. "Guess he thinks it's manly enough now. Maybe I had to give it to him so he knew it was all right. Probably didn't want to embarrass his mom by acting like a puppy."

Pleasure bloomed as she watched him play. When she finally broke her gaze, she smiled and looked up.

Fire.

Kate caught her breath as the connection caught and buzzed between them. Hunger gleamed in his green eyes, and he seemed to hold himself in a muscle lock, as if afraid to even move for fear of grabbing her. She fisted her hands and prayed for strength. Jumping into his arms and pulling off his clothes was a bad idea. She was tired, worn out, and emotionally vulnerable. If she stood strong, she'd get past this hurdle and leave him behind.

"Kate—"

"I better get going, it's really late. Thanks for doing this for me, I really appreciate it."

"Did you eat?"

"Yes, just came from dinner."

"You look exhausted. Look, let me make you a cup of coffee before you go. It'll perk you up a bit for the drive. Sit down."

"I don't think—"

"Please."

Her feet throbbed and her eyes itched. Coffee would probably be good. A few more minutes wouldn't hurt. She nodded. "Thanks."

He disappeared into the kitchen. "Why don't you try out the recliner?" he called out. "The remote's on the table."

A merry squeak of agreement cut through the air.

She shook her head and eased onto the chair. The supple leather cradled her rear, and it was already warm. She cranked up the heat a digit more, reclined the seat back, and swallowed a moan. Best. Chair. Ever. With her feet up, the blood flowed back into her toes. "This thing should be illegal." His laugh echoed. The scent of freshly ground beans drifted from the kitchen. "Is this where you make the magic happen for your clients?"

"Nah, that's where I recover."

"What made you decide to go into divorce law? Were your parents divorced?"

He materialized beside her with a mug. She went to get up, but he stopped her. "No, stay and relax." She took the cup and sipped the strong, hearty brew. Heaven. "My parents died in a car crash, so no, I can't claim a set of emotionally abusive parents. I just kept seeing the effects of what broken relationships did, even before marriage. Too many times one person gets screwed. I wanted to fight and be the voice for him. Or her."

Fascinated, she probed his gaze. Behind that charming, seductive exterior beat the heart of a complicated man. She'd gotten glimpses of it the night they spent together, but Kate bet there was a world more to discover. A pang hit her when she realized she wouldn't be the woman to complete the treasure hunt. "I'm sorry about your parents," she said softly. "My dad died a few years back and there's still a hole inside. Jane is lucky to have you looking out for her."

"She's not letting me do much anymore. But I still feel responsible."

"Why?" she asked curiously. "What happened that has you so afraid Jane will get hurt?"

He shifted his feet and she prepared herself for the expert dodge of her question. Instead, he dragged in a breath and answered. "Jane was very emotionally sensitive. She was bullied in school and had some bad relationships with men who used her. After our parents died, I tried to look out for her. She got involved with this guy who was a musician. I knew it was a disaster from the beginning, but she refused to listen. He ended up taking all her savings and leaving town."

"What happened?" she asked.

"I came home one night, walked in the bathroom, and found her lying on the floor. She had overdosed on pills and was unconscious. Got her to the hospital in time, they pumped her stomach, but it was a while before she mentally came back. That son of a bitch had broken her. She'd believed in him, and he'd broken her heart."

She didn't answer for a while. The air between them heightened with awareness, and Kate sensed he rarely told anyone about that part of his life. "Love is a funny thing," Kate said softly. "If we don't love ourselves first, the emotion can be redirected in harmful ways. I've seen Jane these past few weeks. She's grown, she's confident, and she's ready for this journey. I don't think she would've made it this far without you. Personally, I think the woman you give your heart to is lucky. She gets it for life."

Emotion clogged her throat and she fought the urge to scurry out of his house like a rat escaping an exterminator. It was just too much. His green eyes darkened as if he sensed her need to run. "I'm sorry about that morning, Kate." His simple apology blasted the room like cannon fire. "I was an asshole."

She fought a half laugh. God, the man even knew how to apologize correctly. "Accepted. We were both a bit off-kilter."

"I panicked."

"Yeah, I seem to do that to men."

He chuckled. "I'm kind of nuts about you. And the night we spent together was one of the best in my life."

"And here comes the *but*."

"But I don't think I can give you what you need."

The grief surprised her, but Kate had a new respect for this man willing to face the truth. "I know."

He jerked back. "You do?"

She gave a sad smile. "I want marriage. Children. A man to say he loves me and means it with his whole heart. I want a guy to love Robert like his own and be willing to involve himself in the chaotic mess that's life with no guarantees. I need someone with a lot of courage. Because that's what it takes to even have a fighting chance with someone."

He looked stung by her words, but Kate was tired of pretending. Better to clear the air now, accept their insane connection, but move onward logically. It was the only way.

"Ouch."

"Sorry."

He fell back on the other chair and pondered his cup. "Perhaps you're right. Day after day of watching people pick up the broken pieces doesn't give me much hope. I'll pull out of Kinnections."

"You're not afraid we'll take all of Jane's money and match her with a con artist?"

Slade shook his head. "Nah, I still think you're misguided by mistaken beliefs, but you'll take care of Jane."

She thought of him alone, in his beautiful apartment, working night and day to counsel heartbroken couples, reaffirming that there is no hope or happily ever after. No. He deserved more, dammit, even though she wasn't meant to be his. "I think you should stay on as a client."

He frowned. "Why?"

"Because I don't only match couples who want the big ending, you know. There are plenty of women out there who hold the same belief as you do, and they're wary of getting involved again. You said you wanted a companion. A friend. Maybe a family down the line. What if there's a match for you with a woman with the same ideals? I'll have Kennedy go back to the beginning and we'll give it another shot."

Slade studied her in the dim light. "I can't keep up with you."

"Good, don't try. Just give us one more shot."

"No more hot yoga or makeovers?"

Kate laughed. "No, you completed the process. We'll

just refit the puzzle pieces and see if we can match you with someone more your kind. Less . . ."

"Pollyanna?"

She scowled. "Expectant. Deal?"

He put his feet up on the matching ottoman and leaned back. "Can I skip the mixers?"

"Maybe. I'll leave it in Ken's hands."

"Okay. I'll try again."

A comfortable silence settled between them. The connection still sizzled, but there was a deeper softness to it, almost as if by acknowledging the desire and accepting it, they were able to move forward. Kate sipped her brew, and the flicker of the movie on the massive screen pulled her attention.

"Oh, my God, one of my faves. *The Hangover*! The original!"

"Me, too. Turn it up."

She pumped up the volume and watched the city of Vegas sprawled before her. "Classic."

"Not as much as *Office Space*, though."

She gasped. "You love that too? I watch it all the time. Have every line memorized."

"Women hate that movie."

She stuck out her tongue and pulled the fleece blanket over her weary legs. "Don't be chauvinistic. I'm a comedy addict."

"All-time champion?"

She crinkled her nose and thought hard. "Still *Wedding Crashers*. Vaughn was pure genius."

"Agreed."

The heat from the seat warmed and softened her muscles, and Kate relaxed into the leather, the coffee hot on her tongue, the blanket soft on her body. She didn't remember when she lay the mug down and decided it was almost time to go. Didn't remember much of the conversation back and forth as they discussed the best comedies of all time and argued their fine points. Her last thought before the room went fuzzy was how much she liked Slade Montgomery, and how sad it was he didn't believe in love.

SLADE WATCHED HER SLEEP. Sometime during their feisty dialogue, he realized she was fading, but he didn't want to push her out the door. Robert had already stopped squeaking and dozed in his special bed, a doggy grin on his face from the day's events. He waited till her head lolled to the side and golden strands of hair slid over her cheek.

Warmth radiated inside his chest. Who would've thought she shared his wicked sense of humor, love of banter, and obsession with raunchy comedies? He wished she were a divorcée, jaded and looking for a life of companionship rather than magical emotions. They'd be perfect together.

He held back a wimpy sigh and got up. Cleaned the

mugs, turned out the lights, and flicked off the TV. She grunted softly and adjusted. His hands itched to carry her into his bed, strip her naked, and thrust between her thighs. Her scent still haunted him, and Slade swore he'd never be able to go to a carnival again without remembering her heady sugary scent, like spun cotton candy in his mouth when he tasted her. Instead, he did the right thing. Tucked the blanket carefully around her legs, smoothed back her tumbled hair, and pressed a kiss to her forehead. She smiled in her sleep, and if he had a heart left to give, it would've broken right there.

Slade trudged into his room alone and left her asleep.

When he woke up in the morning, he headed out toward the living room, prepared to make her a killer breakfast, take care of Robert, and spend a little more time with her.

But she was gone.

The blanket was neatly folded and lay upon the table. Robert's bowls were placed in the sink. His chest tightened with a strange feeling, and emptiness pulsed in his gut. She hadn't even left a note. Just a vacant space that still smelled of her sweet scent, and a silence that cut through him with an agony he never experienced.

thirteen

"OU WANT ME to set him up with another woman."

Kennedy shared a glance with Arilyn. They had gathered at Kate's house after work to go over the expo and play catch-up. They lounged around her living room — Arilyn cross-legged on the throw rug, Kennedy stretched out on the sofa, and Kate holding her throne in her recliner. They wore comfy sweats and T-shirts, and had already blown through most of the large cheese pie. A bottle of Chardonnay held only a few dregs left. The television droned the last credits of a weepy chick flick. Kate had lost the bet and Arilyn had won. *Steel Daisies* or something ridiculous like that. Robert snoozed contentedly in his doggy bed next to his bunny, still sated on the remains of the pizza crust Arilyn and Ken sneaked to him.

Kate had to give them credit; they'd left her alone most of the week and refused to pose questions regarding her night with Slade. She'd avoided telling her Kinnections crew in order to buy a bit more time to settle her emotions. She knew it cost Ken the most. Her friend actually had an eye twitch, bursting at the seams for all the details, so she'd finally broken down and invited them over for pizza night.

"Yes," Kate finally answered. "I want you to set him up with another woman."

Kennedy tapped her fuchsia nails against her lip and waited a few beats. "You did sleep with him, right?"

Kate gave up and gave in. "Yeah, I did."

Ken arched a brow. "Well? Details, please. All of it."

She sighed and briefly went over their encounter. Silence beat in the room for a while as her friends processed the information.

"God, Kate, you had a frickin' orgasm your first time?" Ken groaned. "You are so lucky. It took me forever to even discover why women liked sex in the first place."

Kate tilted her head. "No way. You didn't climax your first time?"

Ken snorted. "Not even close. Until I met bad boy Caleb Street. He was three years older and drove a motorcycle. I snuck out one night from my window and he took me for a ride." She gave a lusty sigh. "What a ride it was. After that I swore off nice men forever, they're too disappointing. How about you, Arilyn?"

Arilyn shifted her strawberry hair to the other shoulder. "Nope. He didn't even know what a clit was, let alone how to find it."

Kate smothered a laugh at her friend's crass statement. "Wow, I had no idea it was that hard. Actually, he gave me three."

They stared at her as if she'd sprouted two heads. "Three?" Ken choked out. "He's a master."

Heat bloomed on her cheeks, but she felt a weird type of pride in her lover's expertise. "Yeah, too bad my being a virgin totally freaked him out. I mean, really, what's the big deal?"

Arilyn shook her head. "He was probably feeling too close to you. When men bond, the first thing they do is try to cut the ties. Sort of like a wolf caught in a trap. They'll chew their own paw off just to get free."

Ken laughed. "Nice visual. Hell, it's not like you told him you loved him and wanted to get married. You were super cool about it. Okay, so let's go over the summary one more time. You had amazing sex, he acted like a dick, you kind of broke up, and now you want me to keep him in Kinnections and find him other dates?"

"Correct."

Arilyn leaned forward and rested her thumbs on her knees. "Sweetie, do you think that's healthy? Maybe we should just cut him loose."

"No. We need a crop of new women. I made a tactical error thinking I could force Slade to believe in love, but we'll never win that battle. We need to match him with a woman with the same philosophies. He'll feel safe with her, and perhaps be able to open up to a long-term relationship."

Arilyn nodded in agreement, but Kate knew she was already reaching for her counseling tools. "Okay, if that's what you truly want. You're ready to release him to another?"

"Yes."

"Bullshit." Kennedy glared and stabbed a finger through the air. "You're into him. We tried this before, and he ended up at your front door and took you to bed. What makes you think it won't happen again?"

Kate crossed her arms in front of her chest. "We understand each other now. Realized we want different things. Besides, we needed to get the sex out of our system."

"Did it bring back the touch?"

Kate snagged her wineglass and drained it dry. "No," she muttered.

Her friends let out deep sighs. "Aww, shit," Ken said. "I really thought the sex would do it. What did your mother say?"

"One visit was enough, thank you. She almost got me arrested by sneaking a joint into my purse. I refuse to bother her with this. We'll just move forward and see if it comes back. Besides, we're set up for success with or without my extra benefit. Let's not lose sight of the goal."

Arilyn nodded with enthusiasm. "Kate's right. This is happening for a reason to lead her in the next step of a journey. We'll be patient and open. Let the universe guide us."

"Me and the universe do not have the same understanding. I find success happens when you kick the universe's ass and do what you want," Ken said.

Arilyn gave her a pointed look. "Maybe you need a session of hot yoga."

"Maybe I need a session of something else hot but much more pleasant."

Kate fought a grin. "Are we in agreement? Ken will take over Slade's matchmaking and we'll move on."

Ken blew out a disgusted breath. "Fine. I think this plan sucks, but I'll do it for you. At least he was nice enough to watch Robert so you could go to the expo."

The image of waking up in Slade's house flashed before her. Tucked in the blanket with Robert at her feet, she felt safe. Taken care of. He hadn't tried to drag her into bed or leverage their sexual attraction.

She pictured them having a cozy breakfast together and completely lost it. There was no way she could continue fighting her instinct to surrender to him. So, in the middle of the night, she'd packed Robert up and sneaked out like a bad one-night stand.

She wondered if he missed her when he woke up. She wondered if he even cared or thought twice, or was just relieved he wouldn't have to deal with her company.

Yeah, she was officially nuts and nuts about him. She had to set him up with another woman before it was too late.

"Oh, look, *9 to 5* is on!" Ken shrieked.

Kate swiveled her head. The classic female buddy movie always made her laugh. Arilyn jumped up and down with excitement. "I love this movie! We need more wine."

"I'll get it." Kate trudged to the kitchen to snag another bottle. "My favorite is when they all get high and imagine creative ways to kill their boss."

"I love when they wheel the dead body out of the hospital and get caught with it in the trunk!"

"Wait!" Kennedy called out. "I have an idea."

Kate and Arilyn looked at each other. "That's never a good thing, Ken. Your ideas usually involve breaking the law or cute boys."

Her friend practically preened. "It's girls' night. We need to let loose. And I bet Kate still has that joint Madeline gave her. Don't you, chickie?"

"You want to get high?" Kate shrilled.

"Hell, yeah. Go get it."

Kate paused only a moment. Arilyn looked intrigued by the idea. And for a little while, she didn't want to worry about Slade or rules or anything. She wanted to hang with her best friends and let loose. "Okay, I'll get it."

She scooped it out of the zippered pocket of her purse, searched her junk drawer for matches, and brought it into the living room. They all sat close together around the battered coffee table as Dolly Parton strutted her stuff in the boss's office.

"I can't believe we're doing this," Arilyn muttered. But she took the joint, sucked in a deep breath, and held it. Kate and Kennedy giggled like teenagers and passed it around.

"You should've seen Slade's face when it rolled out of my purse!" Kate said, inhaling hard.

"What did you say?" Arilyn asked.

Kate snorted. "I denied the whole thing! Said it wasn't mine!"

That collapsed them into more laughter. "Why do men have to make life so complicated?" Kennedy grumbled, expertly plucking the joint between her fingers and placing it against her lips.

Arilyn let out a dreamy sigh. "Because they're the other half of us. It's supposed to be complicated."

"Is your new yoga teacher complicating things for you, Arilyn?" Ken asked slyly.

Kate studied her friend's blooming cheeks. "Are you having an affair with your instructor?" she asked in surprise. Arilyn was hard-core when it came to not dating her instructors or students. She held herself to a higher standard than others.

Arilyn frowned and gracefully stole back the joint. "I had a relapse. Once. Twice. Okay, maybe a few times."

Ken leaned in. "How fun. Are you hiding it from everyone? Do you do it in his office or after hours?"

"Maybe." Kate laughed. Arilyn was always able to surprise her by challenging Ken's gutsy questions. "Let's just say Downward Facing Dog will never be the same for me."

Ken sucked in a breath. "You go, girl."

"It's nothing long-term. He doesn't believe in monogamy, so I won't be staying with him for long."

Kate let out a long breath. "Slade doesn't either. He believes in oxytocin. A hormone that's emitted after sex and disguised as love."

Arilyn pushed the joint into her hands. "Here, sweetie. Have another hit."

"Thanks."

"I say we don't need any men. I say screw them."

Kate nodded at Kennedy's booming statement. Funny, her head was floating a bit off the top of her shoulders, but she looked good that way. Almost like a fairy. "Yeah, you're right. We don't need men at all. All we need is each other."

"And good movies," Arilyn chimed in.

"And wine," Ken declared. "Forever and ever!"

"Girl power!" they all shouted.

She didn't remember what happened afterward. The room drifted, warm and cozy, and her friends voices were like music in her ears. She floated to a happy place, where she didn't care about Slade Montgomery or his next date or his stupid oxytocin. From now on, she'd concentrate on her own journey and have fun and maybe eventually find someone who loved her back.

Someday.

"YOUR PLACE LOOKS GREAT, Jane. So do you."

Slade took in his little sister with a bit of a pang. She was different. Yes, still sweet underneath, a bit shy, but she walked with a feminine confidence he'd never seen before.

He was definitely screwed up. All he'd wanted was for her to stand strong on her own, but now he felt as if she didn't need him anymore.

Jane smiled and pushed over the chips and dip, his weakness. The place was small but happily cluttered, with various books, papers, and magazines scattered among antique tables, a deep sectional, and a tiny breakfast nook that held French doors opening onto a patio. Spring tinged the air with a teasing freshness, and he pictured her outside planting a garden. She always had a green thumb but couldn't really experiment with their place in the city. From the eclectic pottery and watercolors, he finally caught a sense of Jane's true taste.

"Thanks, big brother. I told you I would be okay. Verily is the perfect fit for me. I'm even taking a pottery class on the weekend, and Brian is teaching a creative poetry workshop I plan on attending."

Her work always drowned out most of her social activities, and she'd been afraid to push outside her social barriers. Now, she seemed relaxed in her well-fit jeans, Coach sneakers, and sequined black T-shirt. Her hair had been tamed and pulled back to accentuate the strong lines of her face, and her trendy new glasses brought out a confident edge she'd never exhibited before.

Slade grabbed a handful of chips. "So, tell me about this Brian."

Her gaze narrowed, probably from past experience. "Don't start."

He laughed and threw his hands up. "I'm not, I promise. I really just want to know about him. I have no intentions of sticking my nose in your personal life anymore."

Jane wrinkled her nose. "Why?"

"Because you seem happy and healthy." His voice caught with emotion. "That's all I ever wanted."

Her face softened, and she snagged his hand to give it a quick squeeze. "Thank you for that. Brian is great. Kate said we were moving a bit fast, but she seemed to trust my judgment. We get along well, have similar interests, and decided to be monogamous."

"Hmm, it's only been two weeks, though, right?"

"Slade."

"I know, sorry. Hard habit to break. Just listen to your gut. If you feel like he's going too fast, slow it down. You're in control."

"Got it. Right now I'm going with the flow and enjoying every moment."

Worry nagged at him. Kate was definitely keeping an eye on his sister, especially if she made that comment. Maybe he should talk to her briefly about Brian. Not to cause any trouble, but to make sure Kate realized the implications if this guy wasn't being careful. How many times did men throw themselves into a relationship only to get spooked when they realized it was the real stuff? It was a weakness in his gender he knew quite well. Slade glanced at his watch. Maybe he'd drop by her house, check on Robert, and ask some innocent questions.

He spent the next hour catching up and snacking before he made his way out. Should he call first? What if she told him not to come by? Ever since that morning, it seemed they had an agreement to stay away from each other. Kennedy already had a date lined up for him this Friday night, and there was no real reason to contact Kate.

Still, he was in the area and he really was a bit concerned about Jane.

Slade maneuvered his way through the town. Crowds spilled over the sidewalks, walking dogs, lingering with coffee at outside cafés. The river flowed, the frost and ice finally broken up, and the bridge gleamed in the partially cloudy sky. Funny, he was actually growing to enjoy the little town. A bit eclectic, with artists sporting purple hair, piercings, and tattoos galore, but at the same time there was a level of acceptance and positive energy flowing through the crooked streets. He passed a sign advertising hot yoga and winced.

Her Fusion was parked in the driveway when he pulled up. He fought the urge to swipe his palms down his pants and wondered what the hell was wrong with him. Nothing to be nervous about, just a quick stopover to chat about his sister.

He rang the bell and waited.

When she opened the door, he knew why he'd been wary.

She took his breath away.

Hair caught up in a ponytail, face bare of makeup, she wore black yoga pants, Reebok sneakers, and a baggy yellow T-shirt. Her blue eyes widened when she caught sight of him. Her presence jacked his body to life, and he tamped down the urge to step through the door, haul her into his arms, and kiss her senseless. She was so frickin' beautiful and real.

"What are you doing here?"

"Came from visiting Jane. Wanted to check on Robert."

Of course, it was almost two weeks that had passed, and he knew the infection was completely cleared up. Her brow hiked as if she suspected his lame excuse, but she opened the door anyway. "Come on in. Robert, Slade's here!"

The scurry of paws echoed through the air. The dog raced over to him and crashed into his open arms. Slade laughed, petting him, then leaned over to press his forehead to his. "Hey, buddy. I missed you. Feeling good?"

He barked once.

"I'll take that as a yes. Do you still have Bunny?"

Robert turned, vanished into the living room, and charged back with the tattered, sopping-wet bunny in his mouth. A fierce pleasure pounded through Slade, knowing the dog still loved the gift.

Kate shook her head and grinned. "It's his favorite thing in the world. I insisted on washing it the other day, and he waited in front of the dryer for half an hour."

His throat tightened. "I'm glad." He straightened up and hungrily took her in. Her cheeks were flushed, but he figured she'd been exercising. Thinking it was over him would hurt too much. "Am I interrupting?"

She shifted her feet. "I was going to take Robert to the dog park. Let him run a bit."

"Oh." He stared at her like a teenage chump. "Maybe I can come with you? I want to talk to you about something."

Kate hesitated and pulled her lower lip between her teeth. His gaze focused on those lush, pale pink lips and he wished to hell she was sucking on something else. "I guess so."

Her reluctance made him grin. Always trying to get rid of him, even from the first. "Great. Let's go."

He reached for the cart, called for Robert, and deftly hooked up the straps. She grabbed two water bottles, a NY Mets ball cap, and headed out the door. Their long strides ate up the pavement as they walked into town, and the wheels of Robert's cart steadily whirled. "Baseball fan?" He pointed to the cap perched on her head. Damn, she looked adorable with her ponytail bouncing.

Kate laughed. "Nah, Gen's sister Alexa is a huge Mets fan. She gives out gear for birthdays and Christmas."

"Hope her husband isn't a Yankees fan."

"Uh, yeah, better not go there. How about you? Sports guy?"

"No time. But I watch the Olympics."

"Hard-core."

The dog park was half filled with a variety of breeds. Kate opened the gate, which housed a large lawn, various toys, and huge water bowls. Exchanging greetings with the other owners, they leaned against the gate and watched Robert take off in his cart, whizzing round and round with his ears pinned back and his tongue lolling in ecstasy. Slade relaxed, chuckling at the simple pleasures of taking a walk on a beautiful early spring afternoon. Usually he was at the office catching up on work, at the gym, or trying to do something halfway productive.

"What did you want to talk to me about?"

Oh. Right. Back to the real goal of his visit. "Jane. I just came from her house."

Kate let out a sigh. "You know I can't discuss her situation, right?"

"No, this is different. She told me she's dating this guy Brian, a poetry teacher, and things are getting a bit intense. Said you advised she was going too fast. What did you mean by that comment?"

She watched Robert run and seemed to mull over her answer. "I can't give you much without breaking confidentiality. I always counsel my clients on diving in too fast, just in case. I always advocate slow and steady because it seems to work better for the percentages of successful relationships."

He strummed the gate with his fingers. "Do you think she's in any trouble?"

Kate shook her head. "Jane seems fully capable of handling the situation. That's all I can say for now, which was probably too much."

He nodded. "Good enough."

"That's it?" she teased. "You trust me now? Don't think I'll raise my prices and make Jane mortgage her apartment?"

He studied her face, her soft smile, and shining eyes and wondered if he'd ever get over her. "I trust you, Kate."

The words drifted softly in the breeze. She stiffened, recognizing the hidden meaning in his statement, and she stepped closer. Time stopped. Sexual energy swarmed and pulled them together. Helpless to resist the spell as luring and sweet as spring, he bent over and touched his lips to hers.

The kiss was gentle. Undemanding. A slight brush of the lightest touch, whisper soft and as heady as a shot of adrenaline on a bungee jump. Her eyes darkened to a stormy navy blue. He scented her arousal from here, and his nostrils flared with the need to take, claim, possess.

Instead, he swallowed a curse and drew back. He didn't apologize, and she didn't demand one. They stared at each other for a while, until Robert's barking broke through their bubble and dragged them back to reality.

"Want to visit the doggie bakery?" Kate asked.

Robert barked twice.

"Somehow, I don't think that was a no," Slade said. "Let's go, buddy."

They strolled into town. Stopped in the bakery for Robert and got him a frosted, organic peanut butter donut and a pepperoni twist for later. The Swan Pastry shop was next door, and Slade dragged her inside and bought a bag of biscotti, honey almond, double chocolate, and lemon divine. They munched and weaved their way through the crowds, admiring art in the windows, and spent almost an hour in the secondhand bookshop. The smell of leather and paper hung heavily in the air, and he breathed it in like a drug. He purchased a biography of FDR and got her *The History of the Pit Bull*, which featured a glossy photo that looked exactly like Robert.

After a satisfying lunch at the hot dog truck, they sipped chocolate mochas and then headed back. The wind grew crisp and the sun disappeared, signaling an end to the idyllic day. When he stopped in front of her house, regret pierced him. He wanted to come inside, cuddle up on her worn-out recliner, and watch the sunset. He wanted . . .

He cut off the thought and forced the words out. "I have a date tonight."

She stiffened. Then nodded. "That's good. Who with?"

"Tammy. I spoke with her on the phone a few times.

Seems nice. Different from the others—a bit older and seems to hold similar philosophies."

Slade ached for her to meet his gaze, but she ducked her head and concentrated on finding her keys. "Ken knows what she's doing. I hope it works out. Thanks for keeping me company today."

"Thanks for telling me about Jane."

"Welcome." The key slid in the lock and she opened the door. "See ya."

He petted Robert good-bye and watched them disappear. The light went on in the living room, and soon the sounds of the TV drifted through the half-open window. He stood on the pavement for a while, looking in before finally turning away.

This time, he didn't look back.

TAMMY.

She hated her already.

Kate stabbed her spoon into the small carton of Chunky Monkey and shoved it into her mouth. Why did he have to appear on her doorstep today of all days? Before his date with another woman who was probably perfectly matched? She'd been fine these past two weeks. Better than fine. She was almost cured of Slade Montgomery, and that wicked one night, and decided she may even want to date. Soon. Very soon.

But now he screwed up her head again, with those gorgeous jungle eyes, and sinful mouth, and tousled golden hair. His scent was a delicious mixture of ginger and spice that made her want to howl like a bitch in heat. She wished she had never introduced him to the idea of jeans, because those Levi's molded his ass and showed off his other assets. Assets she had personally explored and enjoyed. Assets that weren't hers anymore.

Assets that Tammy better keep her hands off of.

Kate fumed and ate. She glared at the TV where *The 40-Year-Old Virgin* played and didn't even gain a chuckle. If Steve Carell failed, she was doomed. Even the extra fudge chunks weren't helping.

Groaning in defeat, she wondered if she should climb out of her sweats and go out. Mugs was still open, and a call to Kennedy would give her a date. She could have a few beers and socialize instead of sinking into a black depression alone, regarding a man who was not meant for her.

Life kind of sucked.

The idea of putting her feet into boots instead of her fuzzy slippers confirmed her choice. She finished the carton, tipped back two glasses of wine, and let her mind fade into television numbness. Somewhere she read that every hour spent sitting and watching TV cut off her life by two minutes. Oh, goody. Maybe she'd be done with this hell sooner rather than later.

Forget it. She'd go to bed early, switch off her brain, and

be better in the morning. And she'd be much more careful about letting Slade into her house or even engaging in a conversation. He was too dangerous, and she was an addict.

Kate shut off the TV, turned out the lights, and stomped to bed.

"I'M SO GLAD WE finally set this up."

"Me, too." Slade gazed at the woman across the table. Her black hair was fashionably short and her smile real. She liked the gym, worked as an attorney in property law, and was divorced. So far, the date had gone perfectly, and he honestly liked her.

"I'm surprised you're open to a matchmaking firm," she commented, cutting into her steak. Her appetite was so much better than those of the other women he took out. Not as good as Kate's, of course, but still worthy of his need for consistent gourmet food. "I interned for a divorce firm in my younger days and it's a real bitch. Kind of ruins your idea of a happy ending."

Surprised at her astuteness, he grinned. "Yeah, I got slightly singed along the way."

"More like roasted, I bet."

He chuckled and took a sip of wine. "Let's just say I'm open to the idea of a companion. Someone without high ideals but willing to date and explore a relationship on rational terms."

She nodded with approval. "Me, too. Freaks me out when a guy starts talking about his biological clock or settling down. I love my work, my life, and have plenty of hobbies. But sharing it would be nice. Seeing what happens."

"Exactly."

Ken had hit the jackpot. Not only did he like Tammy, she was attractive and matched his sense of humor. The pieces he'd been searching for clicked into place. They finished dessert—the woman actually had cake without an apology—and made their way out of the restaurant. She chattered a bit as he walked her to the car, and Slade hesitated. Should he invite her back? No, better off waiting for the next time. And there'd definitely be a next time.

"I had a great time. Do you want to go out again?" she asked.

"Definitely. I'll give you a call this week. I'm glad we met."

"Me, too." She lifted herself up on tiptoe and gave him a peck on the lips. "Good night."

"'Night."

He watched her pull away. He was back on track. This was the type of woman he needed in his life, one who understood him, knew how life worked, and was eager to meet him halfway. He got into his Jag and started home.

Cranking up the radio, he listened to Daughtry croon about the start of something good, and pictured his future. Partner at his law firm. A beautiful, intelligent woman sharing some good moments. Jane happy. His designer apartment. Life was indeed good.

The words of the song hit his ears and his gut at the same time. This was what he wanted, right? What he had always wanted? This was the best it was going to get.

He thought about his afternoon with Kate. About Robert. About the empty ache in his gut that never seemed to get full, no matter what food he ate or alcohol he drank or work he did. He remembered when he touched Tammy, and the pleasantness of her company, and how on every rational level she seemed the perfect fit.

But she wasn't Kate.

He was in love with Kate.

The knowledge sank in and tore at his flesh like talons. No. Not possible. He didn't believe in love, or at least not in love that lasted. She'd wreck him to pieces and make his existence a mess. She'd turn him upside down and inside out and never stay in the carefully drawn lines of his life.

Tonight, he didn't care.

Tonight, he needed her. Craved her. His blood roared in his veins, and he stomped on the accelerator, making his way toward Verily. Time passed in a blur, and Slade felt drunk as he finally reached her house and stumbled out of the car. Vision blurred, he pounded on the door, and waited.

She stood on the threshold, her arms clutched around a short, silky robe thing. Pink fuzzy slippers. Her hair tumbled over her shoulders and her eyes were sleep blurred as she stared at him. Her mouth formed a little *O* of surprise, and she shifted from one foot to the other as if trying to decide to invite him in or slam the door in his face.

"The date was perfect. Tammy was perfect," he said.

"Then go to her. I can't do this, Slade. I can't."

Her voice broke and he was lost. He stretched out his hands in surrender. "I don't want her, Kate. I only want you. I'm . . . empty without you."

She blinked. A sheen of tears threatened, and he waited for her to push him away and retreat for safety.

Instead, she reached over and pulled him into her arms.

Her body was on fire. Soft flesh hit his chest, surrounded him. He groaned deep in his chest and took her mouth, drowning in her taste, plunging his tongue deep to drink and drink, wondering if he'd ever be sated.

He kicked the door closed with his foot, lifted her up, and took her into the bedroom. Ripped his clothes off, tugging at her robe until her breasts were bared to his sight. Her nipples peaked hard and tight, and he sucked them into his mouth, licking, biting until she arched and cried out in pleasure. Her scent soaked his nostrils and the connection between them seethed with electricity. She opened her thighs to him and his fingers dove into the sweet honey, coating her clit and teasing her to that first climax. She shuddered and dug her nails deep into his shoulders. Slade watched her come apart with a fierce satisfaction, but he was nowhere near done, barely skimming the surface of what he wanted to rack from her body. He kissed his way down her stomach, parted her swollen lips, and rubbed his mouth over her pussy, scraping his jaw on her quivering inner thighs, licking and sucking her clit until she pulled at his hair and writhed beneath him, surrendering to her second climax. He gave her the suction needed to keep the orgasm going, pinning her thighs down to the mattress and licking her slit, his fingers still working in and out of her channel, trying to drag him in. His dick throbbed, but he refused to be done yet, wanting to immerse himself in every part of this woman who had crashed through each barrier he'd carefully built. Slade fumbled for the condom in his pants, rolling it over his erection, and pushing her wide apart, slid home.

She clenched him in a silky vise, and he groaned, the sensation of being held so tightly inside her sheer heaven. He kept still, enjoying her wet heat that tried to burn him alive. Slowly, he eased back all the way, thrusting back in to the hilt and keeping the ride easy and slow. She fought him like a wildcat, arching up and trying to take him faster and deeper, but it was too good, too sweet to be over. He added a bit of friction to her swollen clit, and she dug her heels into his back, twisting madly from side to side. Slade laughed low and sucked on her nipple, scraping his teeth against the hard tip as he picked up the pace. Faster and faster, his hips pistoned and moved until he hit the sweet spot and she screamed out, bucking under him. His fingers twisted hard within hers as he held her down and slammed into her again and again, the piercing pleasure so erotic it bordered on pain, taking him to the edge and over until he exploded.

He spilled his seed and ripped her name from his lips. Skin damp with sweat, he rode out the last of the after-shocks before slipping out. Kate collapsed into the sheets, arms and legs flung wide as her breath came in and out in choppy waves. He got rid of the condom, climbed back into bed, and pulled her close. Laying her head against his chest, she wrapped her arms around him.

"Don't leave me tonight."

Her whisper made him pull her closer. "Don't want to. I'm staying."

She snuggled closer and they slept.

KATE MOVED HER LEG and bumped against something hard. Inching her hand down the mattress, her fingers wrapped around a very proud erection. She murmured with pleasure as she surfaced from sleep, and stroked him from root to tip. Like steel sheathed in smooth satin, she enjoyed the texture and strength of his arousal. Groans rose from his chest and he thrust into her palm for more.

With a wicked grin, she ducked her head under the

blankets and found him with her mouth. His breath hissed through his teeth, but Kate was far gone, lost in his musky taste. She licked and sucked him, swirling her tongue around the tip, while her hands pumped up and down his length.

His fingers worked its way into her hair and held her, giving himself up to her ministrations. Power surged through her, and she opened wider, until he slid to the back of her throat and his balls tightened.

"Kate!" Her name was ripped from his lips, amid hard pants. "Condom, now."

"Where?" she teased, swirling her tongue around his leaking tip.

"Ah, God, pants pocket. There!"

She reached down, grabbed one, and sheathed him, never breaking contact or the rhythm of her swirling fingers. Already wet and aching for him, she climbed on top, spread her legs, and sank down onto his length.

Kate threw her head back as the delicious sensations skittered over her skin and teased her clit. So good. The heat between them only added to the edge, pumping up the tension. She looked up his body and got trapped within the seething burn of his green eyes.

"Ride me, baby. Ride me hard."

She shuddered and obeyed. He cupped her breasts and rubbed her nipples as she ground herself against him, closing in toward her orgasm, pumping her hips as her gut clenched and her skin prickled and her nipples tightened to hard, achy points.

Slade grasped her hips, moved her forward, and slammed her back down. Once. Twice. Then—

"Slade!" She came hard, and he kept guiding her up and down, extending the orgasm into mini convulsions. He shuddered beneath her and followed, and she ached for the feel of his skin against hers, ached to get rid of the condom and take his seed deep inside her body. She slumped over him, completely boneless, and he stroked her back with soothing strokes.

"Best morning wake-up ever."

She laughed and bit his shoulder. "Hmm, better than my coffee." Two sharp barks made her crane her neck. Robert looked up with endless patience and wide eyes that took in her bare ass. "Oops, sorry, baby. I'll take you out."

"Want me to get him?"

She pressed a kiss on his lips. "Nope, I got him. Be right back." She donned her robe, ignoring his hungry gaze and keeping her distance before she jumped back in bed and Robert had an accident. She took him out, ground the coffee beans, and got the pot started.

"Kibble or wet food this morning?"

Two barks.

"Kibble it is." Kate filled up the bowl, humming under her breath, and turned to a spectacular sight framed in her kitchen doorway.

Slade Montgomery. Buck naked. Thighs braced apart, hands on hips, his impressive erection confirming round five was about to come up. She drank in all that raw male beauty, with his flat stomach, defined pecs, and toasty brown skin. His lazy gaze probed under her robe and stroked her body.

"Thought I was better than your coffee."

She pursed her lips with interest. "I did say that, didn't I?"

He cocked a hip and that's not all that got cocked. "Maybe I need to prove my worth again."

She licked her lips and dropped her gaze. "I think your worth is pretty damn big."

"Flatterer."

She loosened her robe and began to pull it open. "Counselor. I think—"

"Honey, I'm here! Whose car is in the driveway? Oh!"

Her mother stood before them, open-mouthed, staring at Slade with, first, astonishment and then pure appreciation. She closed her mouth and broke into a wide grin. "Oh, honey! You're finally getting some—I'm so happy."

Kate yanked her robe closed and jumped in front of Slade. "Mom, what are you doing here?" She grabbed for the blanket over the couch and thrust it into Slade's hands. He wrapped it around his hips, but the broad, loopy holes in the afghan didn't hide much.

"I haven't seen you since I got back from my sex conference and thought we'd have breakfast together. But I see you've already taken care of breakfast. I must say, it's even better than Wheaties!"

Color flooded her face. Slade studied her mother with a fascination she was used to, as if an exotic, otherworldly creature had just burst through their universe. Madeline wore a canary-yellow top, a cream lace skirt that flirted with her knees, and lace-up sandals. Her floral headband held back her white blond hair, and bangles jingled on her wrists. Robert ran over to say hello, and Kate took the pause to push Slade behind the counter so at least his bottom half wasn't exposed. Madeline watched his retreat with a twinge of disappointment.

"Sex conference?" Slade drawled, glancing back and forth. "How interesting. Forgive Kate for not introducing us. I'm Slade Montgomery."

Madeline marched over and stuck out her hand. "A pleasure to meet you, Slade. I'm Madeline. I do apologize for interrupting, my daughter rarely allows herself to enjoy these opportunities."

Kate groaned. "Thanks, Mom. Umm, maybe you want to call me later?"

Slade steepled his fingers together as if he were in a business meeting. "Nonsense, stay and have coffee with us. We're in no rush."

"I'd love to. Is it those organic beans I bought you, dear?"

This was so not happening. Kate glared at Slade, but his delighted grin told her he was having too much fun. "Yes, I'll get it for you." She stomped over and poured her mother a mug, then slid it over the granite countertop.

"May I ask how the conference was?" Slade asked.

"It was truly wonderful. I'm a sex therapists, so it's important for me to keep up with the new techniques. I learned many ways to unblock a man toward orgasm. Have you ever had problems with impotence, Slade?"

Kate gave him credit. He didn't even choke on his coffee. "Happy to report that's a negative."

"Hmm, I'm not surprised from what I caught. Still, many men suffer from the condition and it's usually some mental block. They taught us certain moves to go about breaking down barriers."

"What a fascinating job. Kate never told me."

"I'm not surprised. Kate's been blocked for years."

"Mom!"

"So, tell me how you two met."

"I'm a client at Kinnections," he said.

Madeline sucked in her breath. "You're not the divorce lawyer, are you?" she whispered.

Slade hiked a brow. "You know about me? Kate, how sweet. I had no idea you told your mom about us."

Kate squirmed with sheer frustration and shot him a glare. "Look, Mom, let's not talk about this here, okay? I'd like to keep this whole thing private."

"But darling, this is the one you experienced the touch with! You've found a way to make it work, I'm so happy. We'll need to clear a bit of that negative karma, but if you're sleeping together, I'm confident in the outcome."

"Touch?" Slade frowned. "What touch?"

"Nothing."

"Kate didn't tell you?" Madeline chirped. "She has a gift that's run in our family for generations. A sixth sense for matching people. She experiences a jolt of recognition when she meets a couple meant to be together."

Slade stilled. Kate barely breathed, hoping she'd become the guy from *The Time Traveler's Wife* and disappear through space. "Has she ever experienced the touch for herself? Or is this just for other people?" he asked.

The disaster loomed before her, like a volcano ready to erupt, and she was just as helpless to stop her mother as she was to stop the forces of nature. Madeline laughed as she played with her bangles. "Silly man. It's you, dear. She connected with you—you're her soul mate. I wasn't too thrilled regarding the divorce lawyer thing, but the universe is more powerful than humans, and we must bend to its will. At least you overcame your initial protests. Denying the touch is dangerous. Who would've known what could happen? Your cousin Rose died alone and miserable."

Kate swung her head around. "You said you didn't remember what happened to my cousin! You said it was a family secret never spoken about."

Madeline sighed. "I lied. I didn't want to tell you she died an old cranky spinster, destined for unhappiness since she refused to believe in her gift. I think she owned about fifty cats and no one came to her funeral except the local pet shelter representative."

Kate buried her face in her hands and gave up. The morning had started out so rich with promise. Sex. No pesky virginity trouble. Denial galore regarding their future relationship. Now, big, bad reality was here to stay. And Slade looked like he'd swallowed a sharp object and was just about to dial 911. Kate wondered which caused more horror—her virginity or her touch. Definitely a tie.

Slade cleared his throat. "Funny, I didn't hear about this before."

"Kate didn't tell you? Maybe she was easing you into it. Some men have trouble believing in the concept of soul mates and love forever till you die."

This time he choked. Kate pounded him on the back until he seemed back in the land of humanity. "Mom, I think Slade and I need to talk."

"Of course, I really am sorry I interrupted." She blew an air kiss to them and headed out. Her bangles clinked and Robert gave her a quick lick good-bye. "Why don't you two come for dinner one night? I promise not to smoke any pot if it makes you uncomfortable, and you can meet my new lover, Richard. You'll adore him."

"Sounds great. 'Bye, Mom."

"'Bye, darling."

The door slammed. She waited in the dead silence, wondering if he'd just leave now or stick around to ask a few questions. "She gave you the joint, huh?"

"Told you it wasn't mine."

He nodded. Took a big sip of his coffee and straightened to full height. She remembered another requirement in his perfect companion. No embarrassing family members. Yep, she had officially blown every item on his list to smithereens. "Is that the reason I get an electrical shock when we touch? Because of this gift?"

She gave him the space he seemed to need, though her chest hurt. She'd been crazy to think an extra night of mind-blowing sex would solve their issues. Already, she tried frantically to shore up the gaping hole in her chest, but she needed bricks because the big bad wolf had already blown down her first two attempts at shelter. "Supposedly."

"Didn't want to mention it before, huh?"

A flare of anger pushed away the grief. "Actually I did, at your first mixer."

"A few more details would've been nice."

"Oh, sure, let's see how that dialogue would go. 'By the way, Slade, I have a witchlike gene that senses when a couple is meant to be together. And guess what? You're the one for me! Sorry about the shock, but isn't that great, when's the wedding?'"

He narrowed his gaze. "You could have tweaked the speech a bit, but yeah, maybe that."

A humorless laugh escaped her lips. "I wanted to pretend it never happened. I begged you to stay away from me, remember? You're the one who knocked on my door last night! I was ready to try and move on, forget this—this thing between us ever occurred. We've been mismatched from the beginning."

"Do you believe in it, Kate? Believe you can match the right couple just by touching them? Is this what you built your company on?"

Ice trickled down her spine. His tone flicked with disbelief and already she sensed his distance. How could he believe in something that was almost as magical as love? Something undefined but full of hope? The question tore through the last of her defenses, and suddenly, Kate realized she had nothing left to fight. She could tell him the gift was gone and she had no idea if it was coming back. She could deny the whole thing, laugh it off as some crazy joke her mom played, and save her pride. Instead, Kate gave him the truth.

"Yes. I've used my gift to guide many people together. I've sensed if it's a true and proper love match. I never experienced it with myself, though. Until you."

He jerked back and coffee sloshed over the rim of his mug. He shook slightly as he mopped it up with a towel. "I can't deny what's between us," he finally said. "But do I believe in this type of love-spell witchery? No. How can I? Do I believe we were meant to have a happy ending just because we got a shock when we touched? Do you know how that sounds?"

She huddled into her robe, desperately longing for warmth. Her skin chilled and goose bumps broke out on her arms. Yes. It sounded juvenile and silly. But it was the truth, a truth he'd never believe or believe in. She opened her mouth to defend herself and end the conversation. Retreat to her isolation and lick her wounds one final time. Then finally get over Slade Montgomery. For good.

The phone interrupted them and beat out the seventies version of the pop song "We Are Family." He cursed. "My sister. I better get it."

She nodded and turned away. The murmur of conversation drifted to her ears. Kate wiped up the counter and refilled Robert's water bowl, numb to the rapidly rising conversation. She had no time to transition before Slade stood in front of her, male fury vibrating from his figure in raw waves.

Her heart skipped. "What's the matter?"

"I have to go. Jane was very upset on the phone. Seems this guy you set her up with—the one who was pushing her for more—broke up with her this morning."

Her hand flew to her throat. "Oh, no. What happened? Is she okay?"

His face tightened. Green eyes held an accusing light

that churned her gut. "He explained he's just not that into her, not for a long-term relationship, and took off after spending the night. Is this the type of operation you run? Did you use your magical power to set Jane up with this asshole and tell yourself it would all work out?"

Pain sliced deep. She leaned slightly forward to catch her breath. "No! We set her up with two dates and she preferred Brian, but there's no guarantee each date or relationship will work out. Let me come with you, I'll talk to her, maybe set her up with a session with Arilyn if she's upset."

"No, you've done enough." His voice flicked like a whiplash. "You still don't understand, do you, Kate? She's not made for this. I almost lost her once because I didn't take care of her. I wanted to trust you, even though my instincts told me she could get hurt again."

"Slade—"

"She's all I have left!"

His words shattered around her. Her throat tightened, and she caught a glimpse of a raw vulnerability and fear swirling in those green eyes. He'd lost most of the women in his life. Kate realized his responsibility toward his sister was so much deeper than she imagined. When he loved, he gave everything. Unfortunately, he didn't believe he was enough for any of them. As much as she wanted to make him stay, to beg him to talk to her and open up, she knew it had to be on his terms. Perhaps he'd never be ready for more.

He disappeared into the bedroom and came back out dressed, hair mussed, jaw full of stubble. He remained cool and distant, as if she were someone he didn't recognize any longer. "I need you to leave her alone, Kate. Please."

He walked out without a glance back.

Robert whimpered and slid over, pressing his warm body firm against her leg in full support. She sank down to the floor and put her arms around him, laying her cheek against his flat head, and soaked in his presence.

SLADE WATCHED HIS SISTER and tried not to panic. Her eyes were red and puffy, and the box of Kleenex on the side was getting a workout. Crumpled balls littered the floor. Her bare feet peeked out from her long terry cloth robe, an old favorite she used to wear around the house when she needed comfort. He flexed his fingers and tried to remain calm. He'd stay all day and all night if possible. Hell, she could move back into his apartment, get her old job back, and leave Verily behind. He'd do anything in his power to make her feel better.

Her lower lip trembled when she finally looked at him. "I feel so stupid," she sniffed. "He kept pushing us to spend more time together. Asked me to spend the night. Invited me to his class to speak. I knew Kate was right when she mentioned we were moving too fast, but I was so happy I just wanted to believe it would work."

Helplessness rattled his core. "It's not your fault; the guy led you on and dumped you without a hitch. Kate should've seen this coming. Why was he a client there anyway? And why the hell would she have set you up with him?"

"Not Kate's fault. I could've picked Tim, who also seemed super nice, but Brian had a bit more edge, which I thought was exciting. Arilyn warned me in counseling not to leap too soon. She said I tended to do that in my past as a way of ignoring some of my blocks and hang-ups."

He growled under his breath. "You're fine the way you are. That asshole is the one with a problem."

A watery smile curved her lips. "Thanks, big brother. I'm so sorry I dragged you out of bed this early. I got too used to calling you when I'm in trouble. Hard habit to break, I guess."

"That's what I'm here for, Jane. To take care of you. Listen, I've got this whole thing figured out. You can move back in with me and get back on your feet. I'll get your money back from Kinnections and you start with a clean slate. Hell, I bet your old job will beg you to come back."

Jane frowned. "What are you talking about? I'm not moving back with you."

He leaned forward and rested his hands on his knees. "Just for a bit, not permanently. Hell, I've got a better idea. Why don't we go away for a mini vacation? Clear your head a bit. I'll have the movers take care of your apartment, and we'll pretend the whole thing never happened."

Her eyes widened like she was staring at a troll rather than at her brother. "Are you crazy? I love my job, and I love Verily. I don't need a vacation."

He tried to speak gently. "You shouldn't be alone right now. Not after what he did to you."

She shook her head hard. "No, Slade, I think you misunderstood. Yeah, I'm pissed and upset that Brian ended up being a jerk. I didn't see it coming. But I'll be fine. That's what women do. Bitch, cry, eat ice cream, get drunk. The girls at Kinnections showed me I can be normal, let my emotions run free, and still be okay. I'm not having a breakdown, and I'm sure I'll get right back in the dating scene once I get over this."

He gritted his teeth and tried not to lose his temper. What were they selling over there at Kinnections? Didn't they realize she was fragile? When her relationships ended, she plunged into a black hole of blame, thinking she'd never be enough. He'd learned to avoid the minefields by protecting her, but after the suicide attempt, he never allowed her to stray too far. Yes, she'd finished years of therapy and declared her independence, but what if she was at the tipping point and he failed her? "I'm glad you're being reasonable about this, I really am. But I think it would be better if you stay with me for a little while."

Her tears dried and her chin lifted. Uh-oh. That tone

snapped into place and suddenly she didn't seem fragile at all. "I'm not going anywhere. God, this is my fault. I should've never called you."

Slade flinched. "No, I'm glad you called me. I want to be there for you."

"Listen, love sucks sometimes. Doesn't mean I don't believe it won't eventually work in the end. I'll always regret putting you through an emotional roller coaster, and I know you want to protect me. But I don't need your help anymore. I can handle this on my own now."

He studied her for a long while. He'd taught himself she was like delicate china, yet . . . she didn't seem that breakable. Not like before. Was it possible her strength was greater than he realized? That somehow, along the way, she'd blossomed into a full woman who could handle life's curveballs on her own? "I don't want to let you down again," he whispered.

Jane blinked back tears. "God, Slade, are you kidding me? You're the only one who *never* let me down. The reason I can believe in love, that I believe in myself, is because of you. You taught me that. I watched you through your divorce, through Mom's and Dad's deaths, through years of counseling brokenhearted couples in your career. You never lost your heart. You're a caretaker, and now I'm ready to take the reins. Do you understand? You're the one who saved me."

Her words reached deep and broke open a mass of

emotions he'd pushed down for years. The truth stunned him, the idea she could actually believe in him, that somehow along the way, he'd done something right and good. His throat tightened and it was a while before he could speak. "Thank you."

She smiled at him, her face open and lit and beautiful. "You're welcome. Now, as the best-friend cliché you've now become, would you run out and get us bacon, egg, and cheese sandwiches? They have this great deli right down the block. Oh, and hash browns!"

Slade chuckled. "Done. I'll scoop up a few of those awesome doughnuts while I'm there, too."

"Great, you probably haven't eaten. Hey, how did you get here so quickly? It took you under ten minutes. Where were you?"

The image of Kate naked and sprawled on top of him, taking him deep within her body, flashed before him. "Umm, stopped by to see Kate about something."

A tiny frown creased her brow. "This early?"

"Yep. I'll get going."

"Stop right there, buddy." Jane crossed her arms and studied him with the scary teacher look that made him shake. "Holy crap. You're sleeping with her!"

He clenched his jaw. "Was. Not anymore."

"Oh my God, I didn't see this coming. But in a weird way, you're perfect for one another."

Slade gave a bitter laugh. "Hardly. I don't think they

can create two people who are so completely different. Can I ask you a question?"

"Sure."

"Did Kate say anything about having a special gift? When she set you up with Brian, did she, uh, touch you or say she felt a spark between you two?"

Jane shook her head. "Nope. I never heard anything like that. They use a pretty scientific approach. On paper and from a few conversations, Brian seemed perfect. But they warned me ahead of time that it's a journey that could take some time. And I'm okay with that."

"Good. I'll be back with the sandwiches."

He headed out the door and wondered if he had made a huge mistake. Blaming Kate for his sister hadn't been right. They were both right: there were no guarantees. Kinnections did nothing wrong except believe in something his sister did, and he had no right to blame Kate or hold her responsible for what happened.

His head throbbed when he thought of the way he'd left. Two for two in the dickhead department. But it had just been too much for him to handle. First, her mother, then a magical power, then Jane. And where did that leave them?

Slade didn't know. And for the first time in his life, he didn't know what to do about it.

fourteen

"LET ME GET this straight. You sleep with him. Break it off in the morning. Decide to go your separate ways and set him up with another date. Then he shows up at your doorstep right after said date, and you sleep together for the second time. Then break up in the morning. Again. Do I have it right?"

Kate lowered her forehead to the cool granite and groaned. Sunday morning and twenty-four hours since the episode. She hadn't slept or changed out of her ratty pjs. And a shower was definitely on the agenda. "Yep, that about covers it."

Gen shoved the last of the crumb cake in her mouth and chewed. "It's official. You've lost your mind along with your virginity."

"I know. He freaked out when he found out about the touch/curse. Didn't believe me, which I can't blame him for, but still. Now he thinks I screwed up Jane's life and I'm a criminal. I've been afraid to call her because he was so upset."

Gen tapped her finger against her mug of coffee. "Let him calm down—seems he's the overprotective sort. Give it a few days to settle, then call Jane if she hasn't reached out."

"I don't understand, she was doing so well. He acted like she was going off the deep end. I knew they should've slowed down. Why didn't I make them listen?"

"Can only lead the couples to the water, girlfriend. Can't make 'em drink."

"I guess. I'm sorry, I'm always babbling about my problems and you're newly engaged. I frickin' adore the ring! Are you excited?"

The three-carat, princess-cut diamond sparkled in the morning light, but Gen's smile didn't reach her eyes. Maybe they were too tired. "Sure. I've been working nonstop and fielding questions about the wedding. It's a bit overwhelming."

"I can imagine." Gen avoided her gaze, concentrating on her cake, and once again Kate felt that twinge of foreboding slither down her spine. "He's good to you, right? I mean, you do want to marry him, right? Because if he's rushing you or it's too soon, you need to stand your ground."

"No, this is the right thing. He's perfect for me, and so sweet. Loves to spoil me rotten yet pushes me to be better. I'll never find another guy like him."

All the right words, yet . . . Kate still felt she was missing something. There were shadows lurking in her best friend's eyes she'd never glimpsed before. Gen grabbed the napkin, slugged a last sip of coffee, and slid off the chair. "Sorry, I gotta run back to the hospital. Listen, Kate, I know this whole thing is confusing, but I'm going to tell you one thing: I've never seen you look so happy before."

"This is happy?"

Her friend laughed. "You glow when you speak his name. You gave him your virginity and actually experienced the touch for the first time. He's special. I know there seem to be obstacles, and he says he doesn't believe in love, but have you given him a real chance? A fighting chance?"

Kate frowned. "I'm not sure what you mean."

Gen's beeper went off like a fire alarm and she stiffened. "That's David. I'm being paged. We'll talk later, hang in. Thanks for the coffee."

She shot out the door. Robert barely moved his head, used to the quick comings and goings of her friend. Kate thought about her words and cleaned up the kitchen. Odd. Slade already knew she had deep feelings for him, though she kept trying to fight them back and bury them deep. No sense in sharing when there would be no reciprocation or interest in moving forward. Maybe she'd curl up on the recliner and spend the afternoon doing nothing but watching movies and reading books. Paperwork could wait. Gym could be delayed. Nothing seemed that important.

The door slammed open. Kate looked up, startled, and frowned when her mother shot through. "Are you okay?"

she asked, moving forward. "You've never come to see me twice in one weekend."

Madeline crossed the room and clasped Kate's upper arms. Her blue eyes were wide and full of fear. "I had a dream."

Kate fought a smile. "Did you watch the planet get swallowed up by plastic bags and diapers again? People are recycling more, Mom, don't worry."

"No, silly girl, about you. I dreamt you denied the touch with Slade and your entire life was ruined. One bad choice and you never recovered. What happened after I left?"

Unease shot through her. Great, she'd be the cat lady and she'd always been more of a dog person. Kate sighed. "I don't want you to worry. Slade isn't meant for me. Simply put, he doesn't believe in love, marriage, or forever. He believes in oxytocin."

Her mother shook her slightly with impatience. "I don't care what he says he believes. I want to know about you and your actions. Have you told him you love him? That you want to fight for him? That you believe enough for the both of you?"

Panic flared. She broke the grip and stepped back, needing the distance. "Don't be ridiculous, of course not. Women don't do those things today. Besides, I'm sure it's for the best."

Her heart shattered and screamed her a liar. Her body

ached and punished her. And her mother let out a shriek of frustration Kate had never heard before. Madeline was a river, she flowed and melted, becoming one with every challenge in life and rarely fought against the tide. The woman before her quaked, her aura vibrating so wildly Kate would've shoved a joint in her hands if she had one. "Mom, what's wrong?"

"What's happened to you?" Madeline whispered. "When did you stop believing in yourself? In your gift? In what you deserve?"

Emotion choked her. She couldn't handle this; it was too close to home. "I tried. He knows I care about him, and he's been honest about what he can and can't handle. He thinks I've screwed up his sister and that I'm a liar. And as for my gift? I didn't want to tell you, but it's gone. And I don't think it's coming back. I need you to drop this."

"No. You're going to listen to me, darling, and don't interrupt. Now, sit." Her mother pointed to the chair. Kate trudged over, sat down, and waited. She'd learned long ago not to argue when her mother wanted to have an open discussion. "It's time to stop running, Kate. You say you lost your gift. When did this happen?"

"After I discovered Slade and I connected. That was the last time I felt anything. I've been numb, even around couples who are married and have a connection, I get nothing."

"But you still feel the touch with Slade?"

She nodded. "I thought I was blocking myself by denying our attraction. So I slept with him. I figured I'd get it back, but that didn't help either. My gift is gone."

Madeline pursed her lips. "Your gift is being denied, my darling girl. You are the first one in generations to feel this with other people. Most of the women who own the touch can only sense it with her true mate. You have been blessed to spread your knowledge to the world. But when confronted by your own truth, you chose to run and hide. Wrapping it up in sex, having rational conversations about how things can't work between you. You've lost your way."

Kate rubbed her temples. God, when her mother waxed poetic it got hairy. Like a bad acid trip, she supposed. "I don't get it. I didn't hide. I told Slade I believed in love and wanted forever. He said he can't give that to me. We went our separate ways. Over and out."

"Did you tell him you're in love with him?"

Kate froze. "N-n-no. There's no point."

Her mother squinted with intensity. "No point in confessing the truth to the man you love? Have I raised a coward?"

Kate flinched. "Why? So he could say thanks very much, but it's not going to work out? So he can take the last shred of my pride and leave me broken and bleeding? No thanks."

"There is no halfway, no safe place to hide when it comes to love. You are luckier than most to be guided to the man meant for you. By denying the truth, or making light of the connection, you deny the gift, yourself, and are no longer worthy of it."

The words hit her hard, like brutal jabs in the ring, and Kate felt something inside begin to break. Hadn't she been clear enough about how she felt? Hadn't she fought enough? Or was her mother right? She'd rationalized and pushed him away and only allowed him into her bed, not her heart. She'd never stood her ground and challenged his ridiculous beliefs.

"I don't know what to do, Mom," she choked out. "He can break my heart and I'm scared."

"How does he make you feel?"

She dragged in a breath. "Like my better self. He lights up my body, and satisfies my soul. He makes me laugh. He loves Robert and wants to take care of him. He's everything I've ever wanted and I've never been so terrified."

Madeline moved over, took her hand, and squeezed it tight. "You must be fierce and admit to love, my dear girl. It is the only way to win. And if you do lose, well, at least you lose fairly, with your head high and with no regrets. How could you possibly feel shame for leading with your heart? It is simply the bravest thing anyone can do in this world. It is what you based your business on, and your livelihood."

The truth took root, shook her to the core, and grew. In that moment, she realized every step in her journey had been halfhearted. But no longer. She was worthy of more.

Kate reached up and hugged her mother tight. "I love you, Mom. Thank you."

"Welcome. Now go get your man."

"WE'VE GOT A PROBLEM."

Slade studied his boss, who perched behind the sprawling teak desk with a look of concern on his face. Shit. First, his personal life, now his career. Was he upset he'd left early those few days? No, Bob usually let his employees run their own schedules, confident they'd get the job done. Had he realized his relationship with Kate was a big fat lie? Had Melody gotten nailed for the speeding ticket? Slade adjusted his cuffs. "What is it, Bob?" he asked calmly.

His boss pointed toward his computer. "Billing hours came in for approval. Yours doesn't add up. Want to tell me what's going on?"

Relief loosened his chest. That he could handle. "I had a client who wants to pay on the back end once I win the case. Forgot to tell you. I'll send you the details as soon as I get back in my office."

Bob shook his head. "Can't do it. I told the associates you bill up front now. Too many pro bono and cases lost in the firm."

Annoyance surged through him. "Have I ever cost you money on a case? I need some leeway on this one. Guy's wife froze the accounts and he's in a hell of a fix. Needs custody rights. I'll win."

"I don't doubt it. But no more bleeding hearts. His story is no different than a million others coming through those doors. Look, I understand you want to do good by him, but he's got to pay the bill. If I didn't want to make money, I'd be working for the district attorney's office or be a not-for-profit lawyer."

Slade swallowed his frustration and tried to look at the big picture. But God, he was so tired of it. He wanted to do one thing for a person who needed it, and his hands were always tied. "Fine. I'll pay for this one out of my salary. Dock my pay."

Bob lifted a brow. "A bit extreme for someone you don't know. What's going on with you lately? I'm deciding on partner soon, and I need a closer. This is a brutal business — eats you up and spits you out. If you can't handle it, I think Samuel may have the edge."

His boss's gaze was razor sharp and Slade knew it was a test. Did he have what it took? The goal of partnership had been his sole focus for the last five years, but suddenly his future flashed before him and it was all more of the same. More work, more stress, and less satisfaction. The challenge was on the table for him to pick up. Cut the client loose and gain Bob's respect. He sensed he had an edge over Samuel. One tiny agreement and it was all over.

"I lied, Bob."

His boss stared at him hard. "About?"

"Kate. We never had a relationship. I hired her from a matchmaking agency to pose as my girlfriend because I knew you favored executives who are settled. She's not an accountant, her father's no court judge, and she owns a company called Kinnections."

Bob frowned and shook his head. "Wasn't that the name of her accounting firm?"

"No, she's the owner of a matchmaking agency. I set the whole thing up because I wanted to beat Samuel. I've wanted that damn partnership for years, and I wasn't about to let not having a relationship stop me from getting it."

Silence fell. A lightness filled his chest, and he waited for the fallout. Would Bob fire him? Maybe. Throw him out as a contender? Probably. At least he didn't have to pretend to be someone he wasn't.

Bob threw back his head and laughed. "I've seen creative moves before to climb to the top, but this is a first. We had no idea. In fact, my wife was so crazy about Kate, we were going to invite her to dinner this week. You got us good. And though I'm pissed you lied, I have to give you credit for ambition. That's the type of man we want, Slade. You saw the problem, thought of a solution, and went for it. Too bad, though. Melody's gonna get nailed for that ticket."

Slade managed to catch his surprised gasp and turn it

into a badass grin. "I'm glad you're not upset. And I'm sorry if I put you in an awkward position."

Bob cut his hand through the air. "Nothing I can't handle. Appreciate you coming clean before I made my decision."

"I'm not giving up this case, Bob. It won't affect my caseload or billing hours, but I want it."

His boss let out a breath. "Fine, take it. You've always been a stubborn son a bitch. Just make sure you win."

"I will. Thanks." He got up and headed toward the door when he heard his name. "Yeah?"

Bob's eyes twinkled. "Let's just say I think you'll be happy with my final decision on partnership by the end of the week."

The meaning was clear. As Slade left the office, his head spun. Damn. He'd snagged the position. But as he strode down the hallway, a giant emptiness pulsed in his gut, a need for a woman he'd pushed away, and a question if he'd ever feel satisfied again.

KATE WAITED ON HIS front steps. She glanced at her watch again and hoped he wasn't working too late. She'd already been sitting for an hour, and with every minute that ticked by, she'd been tempted to dump the plan and hurry back home. Nothing like a big love confession to freak a woman out.

"Kate?"

She turned her head to the right and her heart leaped. He was so beautiful. His towering length and lean muscles filled out the navy blue Prada suit, his snowy white shirt and red tie cutting a sharp image. He'd probably gone to court. Lines bracketed his mouth and his eyes, hinting at his fatigue. The gold-rimmed glasses gave him the scholarly look that only made him sexier. She stood up and drank him in with her gaze, her body already alight with the need to touch him, push back his hair, caress his hard cheek. She swallowed. "I need to talk to you."

He nodded. "Come inside."

They climbed the steps and entered his apartment. The silence of the empty rooms pulsed with a hunger for noise and laughter and mess. Why hadn't she seen this before? The way he controlled his life and kept people at a safe distance so he'd never be tempted to fail? Just like her.

"Can I get you something to drink? Eat?"

"No."

"Do you want to sit down? I'm sorry I'm late, I had a court date."

"I love you."

He stiffened. Ah, crap, leave it to her to blurt something out with no finesse. She completely sucked at good love confessions so she'd better backtrack. Was that horror, shock, or pleasure on his face? He looked as if he'd gotten hit over the head with a brick.

His voice broke. "Kate, I—"

"No, please listen to me first." She wiped her palms on her jeans and closed the distance between them. His delicious scent swamped her senses, spice and a hint of citrus. She curled her hands into tight fists to keep from reaching out. "I accused you of being a coward, but I'm the one who's been holding back. From the moment we touched, I sensed you were the man for me. But it's so much more than physical. I hid behind your conceptions of relationships and your refusal to believe we could work long-term. But I believe enough for both of us, Slade."

She surrendered to impulse and touched him. Her fingers closed over his shoulders. The heat pulsed and danced between them, confirming her heart's choice. "I want you to give us a chance. I've seen the man you are. How you protect and take care of your sister. Your gentleness with Robert. How you fight for your clients and try to make them hurt a little less. And the way you look at me when we make love." She stood on tiptoes and cupped his cheeks, staring into his beloved face. His green eyes swirled with desire, confusion, fear. "I love every damn part of you, your body and heart and soul. I love your mind and your stubbornness and your humor. Give us a chance to be more. Give me a chance to love you in the way you deserve."

She didn't hesitate, just pulled his head down to hers and kissed him with all her pent-up longing and emotion. He groaned and opened his lips, his tongue sweeping inside and drinking deeply. He kissed her for a long time, conquering every part of her mouth until there was nothing left to give. When he ripped his mouth from hers, a mad light gleamed in his eyes.

A joyous laugh broke from her chest. She had won. He was hers.

Kate reached up for more, but he staggered back. Stark regret carved out the lines of his face, even as she noted his full erection and the hot need in his gaze. "I can't, Kate. Dear God, I can't do this to you, won't hurt you and break your heart. I love you too, I do, but I can't follow this road. Eventually, we'll hurt each other, and I'd rather die."

Red-hot anger misted her vision. She trembled with a rage of emotion. "You'll deny both of us our happiness for a future we know nothing about? What about the relationships that do work? Don't you want to take the chance on us? The chance to be a family and wake up in each other's arms every morning? Or are you afraid to settle with me in case there's a better option later?"

He snapped his jaw closed. "Don't. That has nothing to do with it. I'm crazy about you. Since the moment we met I've been trying to catch up and I've never felt like this before."

"Then why are you doing this?"

"Because you want everything!"

She sucked in her breath. He jerked back, pushing his hand through his hair. The silence squeezed with merciless tension, and Kate finally realized she had come here to win, but he had already made his choice. Raw pain rose from her gut and choked, but she managed to wrestle out her last words.

"You're right. I do want everything. I'm sorry that's too much to ask, but I believe we're both worth it. I'm sorry you don't."

"Kate."

Her name was a good-bye, a plea, a prayer. Her eyes were bone dry as she stared at him. "Good-bye, Slade."

This time he didn't stop her. She walked out of his apartment for the last time and knew he had chosen.

fifteen

"YOU OKAY?"

Kate forced a smile and looked up as Kennedy strolled into her office. "Sure. Is Jane coming in today?"

"Should be here in a minute. She's ready to go back out there, so I wanted to sit down with her for a one-on-one. Too bad Brian ended up being a jerk."

"Yeah, occupational hazard, I guess. Still, I'm proud of her. She seems much stronger in who she is and didn't let this affect her inner core."

"I had good teachers."

Kate laughed as Jane appeared behind Ken and gave her a hug. Jane had definitely blossomed. She accepted the breakup and her emotions, and healed. Now she was excited about the possibility of a new journey, and this time Ken would probably screen even more carefully.

"How are you, Kate?" Jane asked.

"Fine."

The two women shared a look. Kate fought a sigh. She'd been asked that question every day for the past two weeks and her answer never changed. Still, her friends knew it was a big, fat lie. Since that day she lost Slade, she walked around empty, caught between massive pain and a strange numbness. She buried herself in work, stayed home with Robert, and tried to believe it would get better. Someday.

Jane had become a close friend of the group and now joined them for Friday nights at Mugs. Kate was glad she never mentioned her brother or asked any questions. "Anyone want to catch a drink after work today?" Jane asked. "I finished my research paper and would love to celebrate."

Ken gave a whoop. "You go, girl. Of course we'll go. But first come into my chamber so we can go over a few things. I think I have a great guy for you to meet."

Their heels clicked down the hallway, and Kate stared at the stack of folders on her desk. Funny, the last few months her client list had almost doubled. The expo probably helped, and everyone had adjusted well to double their efforts now that she had lost her gift. Not that she tried it out anymore; most of her time was spent with Robert and the television.

She wondered if Slade missed her. Wondered if he got the partnership. Wondered if he ever thought of calling her or had already moved on.

The bell tinkled and there was a knock on her door. She smiled as Tim peeked in. "Hey, Kate, do you have a minute for me?"

"Of course." She waved him in. "How did Friday night's date go?"

Tim sat in the chair and shrugged. He was one of her favorite clients and really wished she'd be able to match him correctly. Slightly overweight, he had gorgeous golden eyes and thick brown hair, and his wicked sense of humor always made her laugh. He wasn't flashy, or broody, or a bad boy. He was just literally nice, with a great personality. Time to work harder.

"She was sweet, but I don't think we were a good fit. She's a gym rat, and though we had a great conversation, I kind of caught her looking at the hot waiter."

Kate shook her head, remembering her own date from hell that she'd hooked up with the busboy. "Sometimes this sucks, huh? But don't quit on me, Tim. I think I have a better idea of who to match you with."

"I'm no quitter. Hey, at least I get to date a bunch of cool women and eat out. My television remote was getting too much of a workout before I came to Kinnections."

Point taken.

The door flung open. "Kate, I'm headed out. I'll see you at Mugs—oh, I'm sorry to interrupt." Jane smiled at Tim. "Hi, Tim, good to see you again."

Tim grinned. "You too. Getting hooked up again?"

Jane laughed. "I guess we're two peas in a pod, huh?"

Kate rose from the chair and her friend walked into the room. "Did Ken take care of you?"

"Yep. We may try a mixer. I may be ready."

"Sounds good."

Tim stood and paused in front of her. "I'm sorry the last guy didn't work out for you," he said. He stared at her hard, a smile curving his lips. "He must've been stupid."

"Aww, thanks. Same with you, not sure why you'd be in here again."

Kate turned to give them some space to continue the conversation, and her hands brushed against the both of them.

Snap.

Crackle.

Pop.

Her skin burned and an electrical shock cut through her system, causing her to jerk back. Holding her breath, Kate stared at them, her heart pounding so hard she swore they'd hear it. But they didn't. They were looking at each other and the energy simmered like a live wire around them.

Oh. My. God.

The touch was back.

Kate tried to remain cool, though she felt like sticking her hands in a bucket of ice water. She'd forgotten what a jolt it could be when she sensed a connection, but she wanted to throw her head back and laugh with joy.

"Hey, Tim. Jane and I are heading to Mugs after work around five o'clock. We'd love for you to join us."

"Oh, I don't want to intrude on ladies' night out."

Jane shook her head and touched his arm. "No, come. It'll be fun."

"Cool. I'd love to."

Kate tamped down on a giggle as she watched them make moony eyes at each other. "I better get back to work. I'll walk you out."

"See you later."

She watched them chatter easily and the door shut behind them.

Tears pricked her lids as she sank into the chair. Somehow, she'd been lucky enough to receive her gift back, and she'd never take it for granted again. The image of Slade flashed before her. God, she missed him. She wondered what he was doing right now.

Kate rubbed her eyes, tried to refocus, and got back to work.

HE WAS IN HELL.

Slade stared out the window, trapped another day in his office. Two weeks. The days were endless, but the nights were worse. He kept waiting to feel a sense of satisfaction that he'd done the right thing and released her. Tried to convince himself he was strong for being honest about his limitations and not wanting to wound her. But the inner Ted voice was back, cackling with glee and mockery.

She confessed her love and you threw it back in her face. You're a pussy and a coward. And alone.

Shut up. Better to hurt her now than later.

What did you really think could happen?

Anything. Probably not cheating. Probably not betrayal. And Kate didn't lie. But they could grow apart. Maybe careers could take a toll. Fighting. Of course, fighting with Kate was fun, and making up was even better. No, things happened in good relationships all the time, especially if one embraced the idea of love and forever.

Like I said, you're a pussy and a coward.

He shut the box on his crazy mental companion and tried not to think about her. He wondered how she was doing. He tried not to pump Jane for information, knowing that if he heard she was dating, he might lose his sanity. His sister seemed happy and didn't need him any longer. She went back to Kinnections and was still hopeful of finding someone. How was it his sister believed in the happy ending and he didn't? She'd been hurt time and time again, driven to emotional extremes, yet she kept trying. He just didn't get it. But her last words haunted him, consistently pushing him to the edge.

You were the one who helped me believe in love.

The intercom buzzed. "Mr. Montgomery, your three o'clock is here."

"Send her in. Thank you."

He straightened his jacket and eased back to lawyer mode. The woman who entered his office was easily in her seventies, with short gray hair, glasses, and dressed in a polyester pantsuit with old lady shoes. Her smile was kind and generous, and she greeted him in a soothing voice and a firm handshake. Slade prepped himself, sensing this would be a bad one. Maybe her husband going for the younger woman? Blowing through their retirement? Sleeping with the maid?

"Mrs. White, it's a pleasure to meet you. I know you said you were filing for a legal separation, and I'm very sorry for your troubles. Would you share some of the details with me?"

She eased back into the chair with a serene air that puzzled him. "Of course, thank you for seeing me on such short notice, Mr. Montgomery. You've helped some friends I know and they spoke very highly of your reputation. I've been married to my husband for forty years. We have four children. I'm seeking a legal separation for now so he can be free for a while to explore."

He fought a frown and flipped through the folder where he'd made previous notes. "I see this is uncontested. What brought about the separation? If he's threatening you or been unfaithful, I can make sure you're protected."

Her laugh tinkled in the air with merriment. "Oh, goodness no, he's never cheated. We've had a wonderful life together, but he longs to travel and see the world. You see, we married young and with the children and the difficulty in saving money, we didn't have much time to do anything. Charles always dreamed of traveling and having adventures. I preferred the home life, so he compromised throughout our entire marriage. We raised our kids, paid off our house, and saved for college, then retirement. But now he doesn't want to leave me. We've fought about it, but he refuses to listen. I want him to go and have his adventures, even if it's without me. It's his turn, you see, so the only way is to get a legal separation."

Slade had heard some crazy stories, but this one caused his mind to blank. He tried to make sense of her words. "I apologize, Mrs. White, I'm trying to understand. Your husband did nothing wrong, yet you want to file papers separating with him. How will this help?"

"It will cut the ties he believes he has to me and our marriage. Oh, he loves me, I've no doubt. But I want him to be happy. He's given me joy for the past forty years, compromising to be what I needed. Now it's his turn. The only way is to set him free. If he wants to get back together after his journey, we shall."

He cleared his throat and tapped his pen against the desk. "This is an odd request. I've never counseled anyone on legal matters when they're happy and satisfied with their spouse."

"It must seem strange to some. You see, love is a funny thing. There are no guarantees, just the day-to-day and the moment. You make vows, hope for the best, and do your damnedest to love the person you're with. We struggled through childhood cancer with my son, two miscarriages, and my daughter's divorce. But it always came back to us. Do you understand?"

Slade struggled with the pieces of her story. "No. You

went through all that and now you want to separate? How was that possibly worth it? He may leave, and not want you back when he returns. This whole thing would've been for nothing." Anger cut through him, raw and angry. "If he gave you so much, why won't you go with him? What about your sacrifice? Isn't he worth it?"

She leaned over the desk and clasped his hand within hers. Slade flinched, startled by her touch and the strength in her slightly gnarled hands. Her brown eyes were filled with peace and knowledge. "I'm dying, Mr. Montgomery. I would do anything to go with him, be by his side while he finally sees the world. But I can't, and if I tell him, he'll never leave. I can't live with that knowledge. So, I will let him go, and when he returns, I'll give him the truth. But not before he gets what he needs."

Shock held him immobile. His heart beat faster. She continued speaking, her voice warm. "The possibility of love is worth everything, Mr. Montgomery. Pain, heartbreak, grief. It is the only thing worthwhile to fight for in this life. And though there are never any promises, if one is true and brave enough to give, there will never be regret. If I lost my husband tomorrow, I would be heartbroken, yes, but I'd never regret or change any of my decisions. And I've experienced the type of love that transcends death. A love worth sacrifice and someone else's happiness. My goodness, what are the alternatives? To be safe but alone? That's not a life; that's an existence."

His hand trembled. The realization crashed over him, dragged him through the rocky, watery sand, and threw him into the icy waves.

So stupid. He'd fallen in love for the first time in his life and thrown it away because it didn't come with a signed contract of success. He set himself up for a life alone when he could have Kate in his bed, her laughter in his ears, and her body under his. He held himself above all others like God and pitied the world for being beneath him.

Yet, he was the one to be pitied. And it might be too late.

"Mrs. White, I have to go. Right now."

She blinked, pulled her hand away, and nodded. "I understand. Good luck, Mr. Montgomery. Will you file the papers?"

"Yes. I'm sorry. I'll be in touch."

He raced out of his office, knowing what he needed to do.

KATE DROVE HOME FROM Mugs, the full moon in the sky ripe and glistening with an orange light that shimmered like magic. Jane and Tim had hooked up at Mugs and barely said a word to anyone else in the place. Their heads close together, silly smiles on their faces, Kate sensed the relationship would proceed rapidly, but this time it would be okay. They were simply meant to be together.

Her heart ached, but she'd gotten used to it, pushing her way through the days and nights on automatic pilot. She pulled up to her house, grabbed her purse, and walked toward the door. Let Robert out, a quick snack, and time to order the new Wilson-Vaughn movie. Probably not as good as *Crashers*, but if it gave her a chuckle she'd call it a success.

She entered the living room and stopped cold.

Her bag fell from her grip.

"Hi."

Slade stood before her. Robert sat by his side, not moving to greet her, his body shaking with enthusiasm but refusing to break rank. Kate fought confusion and wondered if she was hallucinating. "W-w-what are you doing here? W-w-where's your Jag?"

"I parked it up the street. I was afraid you wouldn't come inside if you saw it."

"How did you g-g-get in?"

"Arilyn took pity on me. Said she keeps your key in case you need help with Robert."

Robert panted as if waiting for the big reveal. Kate shook her head, her emotions too raw and bloody to fight. "P-p-please don't do this to me," she whispered. "I c-c-c—" Frustrated, her stutter took over and shut down her brain and her calm. The words got stuck in her throat, refusing to emerge, and her body shook for control. He waited her out, not interrupting, not trying to finish her sentence, and finally the inner music and calm broke through the block. "I can't do this anymore."

"I know. I won't. I'll never do anything to hurt you again, Kate. I just want you to listen to me, though I don't deserve shit from you. Not after what I pulled."

Robert wiggled his chest, then settled.

"I wasn't prepared for you, for what I felt. My entire life and career all I've known is not to get stuck in the endless cycle of broken relationships I see day in and day out. I thought I was smart and honest and real by denying them. But I was stupid and scared instead. I love you. I love you with everything I've got, and I'm not going away. This time, I'm going to fight for you, beg for your forgiveness, prove my worth. I'm not going anywhere ever again, until one day you can look into my face and trust me completely. Know that I'm not running and that I want to spend the rest of my life with you."

The words were too much, and hope shimmered in the distance like a mirage. "What changed your mind now? Why? Are we going to have sex, and then in the morning you decide again you need to protect me and yourself? How can I trust you?"

He tightened his jaw. "Because I'll prove it. Starting tonight. I got you a present."

She covered her eyes with her hands and let out a humorless laugh. "I don't think flowers and candy can fix this, Slade."

"I know. But maybe this can show what I see for us. Robert?"

Robert barked twice and turned. Dragging his legs, she watched him run into the living room and scramble up a ramp, plopping his body on a full recliner. Her mouth dropped open as she gazed at the object. Lower to the ground, the ramp led up to plush cushions that reclined back and supported his rear legs. The bunny lay beside him in tattered remains, his face filled with doggy joy.

"It's a specialized recliner just for him," Slade explained. "It's orthopedic, and has a heat control and his own remote. And this one's yours." He pointed to the brand-new leather chair beside Robert's. Dark chocolate, soft to the touch, Kate stroked her hand over the backrest while her heart thundered. "Fully equipped with all the buttons you need."

"You bought me a recliner." Kate stared at the chair, a symbol of something bigger and deeper than any ring could ever promise. Afraid to break the spell, she noticed the second chair edged up close to the first. "There's another one."

"That's mine." Her head rotated. Jungle-green eyes filled with love and determination gazed back into hers. "Because I'm not going anywhere ever again, Kate. I want to sit next to you and watch movies with Robert. I want to sink between your thighs every day, make you coffee every morning, and cuddle up with you every night, under that ratty afghan with a stocked DVR. I want a life with you, a real life, with the day-to-day shit and a partner to share it all with. I love you, Kate Seymour. I think I loved you the moment you electrocuted me and told me to go away. The only question left is, will you give me a chance?"

Joy broke through and flooded the doubts. She looked at the matching recliners, at Robert's happy face, and knew she was ready to take her own chance.

"Yes. I love you, Slade. I'm not letting you go again."

He pulled her in tight and kissed her. Hungry, deep thrusts claimed her as his. The familiar fire hit and heated their blood, softened their muscles, and they melted into one another, surrendering as soul mates.

"No more trying to match me with other women?" he murmured, kissing her cheeks and burying his fingers in her hair.

"You finally met your match, counselor."

"That I did. Now let's seal the deal."

Kate laughed as he scooped her up and walked to the bedroom.

"YOU LOOK WAY TOO happy. In fact, it's a bit sappy, even for you. And what's up with all the recliners? I feel like I dropped into a man cave."

Kate grinned, stretched out, and turned her head to the left. "You're just jealous David got you a ring and no household furniture. Pop a squat and see why it's worth everything."

"Fine. But my ring is damn gorgeous and—holy hell, this thing should be illegal. Can I adjust the heat?" Kate laughed and tossed her the remote. Gen sighed and stretched luxuriously. "Slade won't get upset I'm in his chair, right?"

Kate snorted. "His hours have been insane since partnership, but I think he's beginning to get a handle on it. He's working a difficult case with a single father and putting in extra hours to make it up to the firm."

"Why?"

Kate beamed. "Because he's not charging him. And I learned not to piss my man off in court. He's a shark and a bear rolled into one."

"I can't believe he gave up his Tribeca apartment. I thought he hated Verily."

Kate snorted. "Are you kidding? I wanted to keep two residences for a while and see how it worked out, but the man never wanted to leave. He knows everyone in town. Gets his fresh bagels from Martha at the bakery, brings his laptop to the café and hangs with Jim, and opened up an account with Hector at the bookstore. Verily worked its magic, so we decided to keep this place until we get something a little bigger."

"I'm so happy for you, Kate." Gen blinked furiously. "You deserve this."

"Please, no tears. We'll never get through two weddings. Dual maids of honor, right? You first, of course. I'd never steal your August date."

"David was stuck on August, but I couldn't care less." A shadow crossed over her face and she eased her way out of the chair. "Back to the hospital. Can I borrow that book on stuttering? One of my patients is having trouble and it would be good to get some solid information and tips. Hard to build a good relationship when she's always nervous about opening her mouth."

"Sure. Over there on the shelf."

Gen walked over, scanned the titles, and plucked it from the shelf. "Got it. Hey, what's this?" She pulled out a small purple book and studied it with curiosity. "A book of love spells? You holding out on me, Kate?"

Kate slid off her chair and crossed the room. "I forgot about that. I got it at the secondhand store, thinking maybe it would be fun for one of my clients."

Gen stroked her hand over the violet fabric. "You didn't do the spell, did you?"

Kate winced. "No. Yes. Well, after Slade and I split for the first time, or second, I can't remember, I was lonely and thought, what the hell?"

Gen shook her head. "You are too cool. You own a magical gift and have the guts to create a spell. Guess it worked, huh?"

Kate paused. How odd. Of course, it was a complete coincidence that the casting of the spell led to love and an engagement. Right?

The list.

"Wait a minute, let me check something." She raced to her bedroom, stuck her hand under the mattress, and pulled out the crinkled paper. Unfolding it, she read through the qualities she requested in a soul mate.

1. A sense of humor
2. Intelligence
3. Loyalty
4. Trustworthiness
5. Protective of family
6. Character
7. Fights for what he believes in
8. Loves dogs (Robert)
9. Loves TV and movies (comedies)
10. A man I experience the touch with
11. Great lover
12. A man willing to believe in love

Kate gasped. The list encompassed all the qualities her future husband exhibited. She shoved the paper back under the mattress and walked back to Gen.

"What's the matter? You look like you've seen a ghost."

"Think I did. Let's just say I think the spell worked, which is impossible because I don't believe in Earth Mother or burning lists in fires or coincidence."

Gen stared, then looked down at the book. "Can I have it?"

Kate laughed. "You already found Mr. Right."

"I know. But maybe Izzy would get a kick out of it. She's been so difficult to talk to lately, I thought we'd get a laugh. Maybe talk about the old days. Boys usually help the bonding experience."

Kate hurt for her friend, who missed her twin deeply. "Of course, take it."

"Thanks."

A strange premonition misted her vision as Gen's fingers closed around the book. Almost as if she sensed something big was going to happen, and the path would not be easy. A shiver worked down her spine. Gen was happily ignorant of her worry, patting Robert's head and drifting out the door with a hearty good-bye.

Kate prayed David would give Gen everything beautiful. Her friend deserved a lifetime of happiness.

She stared down at her own ring, the gorgeous round stone simply and beautifully cut, sparkling on her finger like a million rays of joy. Finally. It had been so worth the journey to get here. With a light heart, Kate settled back into her recliner, with her dog and her remote, and waited for the man she loved to walk through the door.

epilogue

THE SUN STREAMED through the open windows and over my fur, warming my body like a heated blankie. I snuggled deeper into my bed and gave a big sigh. Bunny Squeak lay close to my paw, and the delicious scents of meat drifted in the air. Hmm, dinner. Mommy and Daddy were talking behind me. Laughing. Then the sound of slurping. Kissing they called it. I closed my eyes halfway and dozed for a bit.

I remember when I was able to run, really really fast. I had all my legs then, but I wasn't happy. The bad people hurt me, and I tried to keep being better, but I was never good enough. The first time I saw Kate, I thought she was an angel. She picked me up from that hill and saved me. Her eyes were very big and very kind.

I didn't think she'd want me. My legs were broken, and I knew I couldn't run and play anymore. But she didn't care. She got me a cool cart and taught me to run as fast as the wind, and she spent hours talking to me about important things. I always listened. I loved watching silly movies with her, and cuddling in bed, and staying with her when she cried. I hated when she cried, but then she'd hug me and laugh and things would be okay again.

I always wanted a daddy, for her and me, and now I have one. He gave me Bunny Squeak and walks me at the park and loves Mommy. He got me the best chair and now my butt feels so much better when I lie down. I finally have a real family, just like the other dogs at the park.

I'd rather have no legs and be with Mommy and Daddy. I never thought love existed or if it was really meant for me, but I was wrong.

I guess if you never give up and keep fighting, eventually you find the one meant for you. Or the ones.

"Robert?"

I picked up my head. Daddy's arms linked around Mommy's waist. He held up two bags of treats. "Peanut butter or bacon?"

I barked once.

"Bacon it is."

Daddy walked over, patted me on the head, and gave me my treat. I munched on the crunchy treat, pulled Bunny Squeak closer, and felt happy. I guess sometimes you can't give up hope, even if you are broken.

I hope other dogs and other humans realize it and take their shot.

With a big sigh, I dropped my head back on the mat and slept.

acknowledgments

THANKS TO MY editor, Lauren McKenna, for getting me to the finish line and making this story shine. Also to the team at Gallery for all your support and expertise.

Thanks to my agent, Kevan Lyon, for all her support.

Finally, everyone who knows me realizes I dream of happy ever afters for ALL my characters—both human and canine. Thankfully, the story of Robert is based on truth.

My local shelter, Pets Alive, posted a picture of Robert, who was slated to be euthanized. His legs had been crushed when he'd been thrown from a car. He was a paraplegic and needed critical surgery. He was on death row.

But something in his face spoke to the shelter volunteer. A look that haunted all of us, captured in a photo and posted on the Internet. This dog hoped. He believed. And though he'd been beaten, abused, and neglected, something within him longed for something better.

This was the look that saved him. Pets Alive took him, gave him surgery, fit him with a cart to walk again, and now Robert is adopted and living happily ever after. He even has his own Facebook page, Rockin' Robert. I like to check in on him, see his happy, lolling grin, posing outside with his cart, and know one angelic soul was saved.

Robert taught me the most important lesson in life: Disabled doesn't mean disposable. Everyone should be given a second or third chance. And no one should ever give up.

Thank you, Robert and Pets Alive, for reminding me of what's important. Here's the link if you'd like to visit Robert and see what he's up to:

https://www.facebook.com/RobertPetsAlive